Praise for these other thrillers from *New York Times* bestselling authors
Iris Johansen and **Roy Johansen**

Look Behind You

"Spectacular." —*Suspense Magazine*

"The authors tick off all the thriller boxes and then some." —*Kirkus Reviews*

"Winning . . . One of the more complex and satisfying entries in this bestselling romantic suspense series."
—*Publishers Weekly*

"Truly chilling and tragic—a book whose spell is guaranteed to linger long after turning the final page!"
—*RT Book Reviews*

Night Watch

"Another high-stakes, high-powered thriller in the popular Kendra Michaels series." —*Booklist*

"The plot builds to a stunning conclusion."
—*Publishers Weekly*

The Naked Eye

"The Johansens power up the emotional stakes in this page-turning thriller that cements Michaels's reputation as a force to be reckoned with." —*Booklist*

"This read goes from good to great to spectacular as the hunt between predator and prey never stops. As always behind the name 'Johansen' in reviews, this is a definite 5-Star."
—*Suspense Magazine*

Sight Unseen

"The stellar team of Johansen and Johansen is back with the next installment of this clever and terrifying suspense series . . . Filled with frightening twists and terrifying turns, the book ends on a cliffhanger. The reader's heart will be racing the entire time, so waiting for the next book is going to be difficult!"
—*RT Book Reviews* (4½ stars)

"The Johansens do a page-turning job of tying up all the loose ends in this complex cat-and-mouse game, but they always manage to leave one thread dangling: just the kind of ploy designed to keep loyal series fans eagerly anticipating the next installment."
—*Booklist*

Close Your Eyes

"Gripping . . . The authors combine idiosyncratic yet fully realized characters with dry wit and well-controlled suspense that builds to a satisfying conclusion."
—*Publishers Weekly*

"Mind-blowing . . . The scenes with Adam and Kendra ooze sexual tension, making this thriller a titillating delight."
—*Booklist*

"Intrigue at its best."
—*Reader to Reader*

Shadow Zone

"A sexy thriller peppered with enough science and mysticism to make any beach seem a little more exotic."

—*Kirkus Reviews*

"In this adrenaline-accelerating tale of a high-stakes, high-seas conspiracy, the Johansens adeptly juggle multiple points of intrigue, smoothly balancing the prerequisite whirlwind pacing with plausible, even restrained, personal relationships." —*Booklist*

Storm Cycle

"A fast-paced romantic thriller . . . action fans should be satisfied." —*Publishers Weekly*

"A pulse-pounding adventure intricate enough to satisfy tech-savvy geeks and hard-core adrenaline junkies alike." —*Booklist*

"Enormously exciting . . . escapist thrills of the highest order." —*RT Book Reviews*

Silent Thunder

"Gripping." —*Booklist*

"A roller-coaster ride." —*Rocky Mountain News*

"Talent obviously runs in the Johansen family . . . The duo has no difficulty weaving in fascinating technical details with the explosive action of this nonstop stunner."

—*RT Book Reviews*

ALSO BY IRIS JOHANSEN AND ROY JOHANSEN

Look Behind You
Night Watch
The Naked Eye
Sight Unseen
Close Your Eyes
Shadow Zone
Storm Cycle
Silent Thunder

ALSO BY IRIS JOHANSEN

Shattered Mirror
Mind Game
No Easy Target
Night and Day
Hide Away
Shadow Play
Your Next Breath
The Perfect Witness
Live to See Tomorrow
Silencing Eve
Hunting Eve
Taking Eve
Sleep No More
What Doesn't Kill You
Bonnie
Quinn
Eve
Chasing the Night
Eight Days to Live
Deadlock
Dark Summer
Quicksand
Pandora's Daughter
Stalemate
An Unexpected Song
Killer Dreams
On the Run
Countdown
Blind Alley

ALSO BY ROY JOHANSEN

Deadly Visions
Beyond Belief
The Answer Man

DOUBLE BLIND

IRIS JOHANSEN

and

ROY JOHANSEN

St. Martin's Paperbacks

This is a work of fiction. All of the characters, organizations, and events portrayed in this novel are either products of the author's imagination or are used fictitiously.

DOUBLE BLIND

For information address St. Martin's Press, 175 Fifth Avenue, New York, NY 10010.

Library of Congress Catalog Card Number: 2018010684

ISBN: 978-1-250-07602-1

Our books may be purchased in bulk for promotional, educational, or business use. Please contact your local bookseller or the Macmillan Corporate and Premium Sales Department at 1-800-221-7945, ext. 5442, or by e-mail at MacmillanSpecialMarkets@macmillan.com.

Printed in the United States of America

St. Martin's Press hardcover edition / July 2018
St. Martin's Paperbacks edition / March 2019

St. Martin's Paperbacks are published by St. Martin's Press, 175 Fifth Avenue, New York, NY 10010.

10 9 8 7 6 5 4 3 2 1

For Jennifer Enderlin

Editor extraordinaire, you believed in Kendra and believed in us. You'll always have our love and gratitude.

PROLOGUE

SHE HAD TO STAY ALIVE just a few minutes longer.

Elena Meyer crouched in the alleyway, fighting the dizziness. Keep it together, girl. *Breathe.*

She felt her side. Warm and sticky where blood was still oozing from the gunshot wound.

Fight the darkness. Fight the fog creeping over her forehead and descending over her eyes.

Gotta keep moving. Gotta make it count.

Elena stood and steadied herself against the brick building. Her legs wobbled. As she tried to walk, her feet suddenly felt as if they were encased in concrete.

One foot forward, then the other.

And again.

And again.

A sound. What was that?

She turned. A bottle rolled across the paved alleyway, the high, hollow sound echoing off brick buildings. Someone was behind her.

He was there, somewhere in the dark.

How in the hell had he found her? She'd been so careful. But ever since she'd known him, he was always one step ahead.

"Always remember something," he'd said. "I know you better than you know yourself. You *do* know that, don't you?"

Only now, at the very end, did she truly believe him.

Her vision fogged and consciousness started slipping away.

No . . .

She still had a job to do. She patted her jacket pocket, making sure her precious cargo was still there.

She turned and threw herself forward, toward the lights and traffic of Fifth Street. If she could just make it there before . . .

Click-clack.

Click-clack.

Footsteps hit the pavement behind her, echoing off those buildings. She imagined he was wearing those expensive Berluti leather shoes he was always so damned proud of.

Click-clack.

Click-clack.

The steps moved faster.

Click-clack-click-clack-click-clack.

She couldn't let him catch her. Not now, not after all she'd been through.

Click-clack-click-clack.

Tough luck, you son of a bitch.

Summoning the last bit of strength she would ever have, Elena threw herself into Fifth Street's second lane of traffic.

Wham!

She felt herself flying before she even saw the car. She didn't feel the impact as she collapsed in a heap on the cool pavement.

Squealing brakes. Excited screams. A crowd, which included two police officers, surrounded her. Seconds after that, at least half a dozen cell phones were pointed in her direction, ensuring that her death would soon be online fodder.

She wanted to reach into her pocket and show them all what had led her to them, but she couldn't move.

The sights and sounds grew dimmer by the second, but she could still make out those Berluti leather shoes in the crowd.

He wouldn't dare show himself. Not in front of the police, not in front of all those camera phones.

She wanted to smile, but none of her muscles worked anymore.

I beat you, you son of a bitch.

The shoes backed into the alley, retreating into the darkness.

I beat you . . .

CHAPTER 1

"I WANT TO BREAK BOTH WRISTS," Kendra Michaels said. "Can you teach me that?"

Adam Lynch smiled. "Yours or mine?"

"Yours, of course. Show me how."

They stood on mats spread out over a grassy patch of Sunset Cliffs Park, overlooking a particularly stunning view of the Pacific Ocean. It was always windy there, but the breeze had kicked up considerably in the past few minutes.

Kendra tugged at her worn T-shirt as she crouched into a defensive stance. "I'm serious. I saw it on YouTube. An Israeli military guy demonstrated how to disarm an attacker and break both of his wrists."

Lynch laughed. "YouTube, huh? What do you need me for?"

"I'm beginning to ask myself just that question. You've shown me a few things, but now it's time to get serious. You said you'd teach me how to defend myself."

"Defend yourself, yes. I didn't promise to turn you into a killing machine."

Kendra half smiled. "Then what good are you?"

"I've been attempting to demonstrate that to you for a long time." He flashed that movie-star smile. "Oh, you mean in the more deadly arts that aren't nearly as much fun. Here's the best advice I can give: Once you disarm your attacker, your best defense is to just get the hell away."

"It'll be easier to get away if my attacker is howling in pain and nursing a pair of broken wrists."

"I can't argue with that. But you need to walk before you can run, okay?" Lynch raised a small piece of wood. "Pretend this is a knife, and—"

"Pretty sorry excuse for a knife."

"Pretend, okay? The first thing you need to do is—?"

In a lightning-fast motion, Kendra gripped his wrists, ducked, and spun around. She bent forward, using Lynch's weight against him.

"Oww!" Lynch yelled.

"See?" She still gripped his wrists over her shoulders. "If I had just thrown myself a little more forward, your wrists would now be toast."

From behind, he gently rested his chin on her right

shoulder. "And that might have worked on some people."

"You're saying it wouldn't have worked on you?"

"Afraid not."

He quickly closed his right arm, snapping it across her throat. "I could have broken your neck before you even finished turning around. Or, if I wanted, I could now be cutting off your oxygen in a nasty choke hold." He leaned close and whispered into her ear. "Today's lesson—don't trust your life to YouTube."

She fought to free herself, but he held firm.

He chuckled. "Don't get discouraged. Your move probably would have worked on a common street thug."

"You're a pretty common thug yourself."

He laughed, his breath feeling warm in her ear.

"Are you quite finished?" she asked.

"Not in the slightest." He slid his other arm across her torso. "You're the one who put us into this rather pleasurable position."

"And now I'm trying to get out of it."

"You're not trying very hard."

"Don't flatter yourself."

"I've missed you, Kendra. I'm glad you called."

She found herself relaxing against him. Not a good idea. She could feel his hardness, his warmth, could breathe in the scent of him. She forced herself to stiffen again. "Yeah?"

"How very noncommittal of you."

"I called because you've been promising to show me a few things."

"Oh, I will." He pulled her even closer. "If only you'll let me."

She snorted. "I walked right into that one."

He released his hold and gently turned her around. "You don't think it would be amazing?"

She was about to make another crack, but she stopped herself. It *would* be amazing. She'd known Adam Lynch for over two years, and they'd faced scores of life-and-death situations together, seen each other at their best and worst. But in the past few months, she found herself thinking about him more and more in *that* way. There had been moments that had verged on explosive when she had wanted only one thing from him. She had been so close . . . What was stopping her?

"What's holding you back?" he whispered, as if reading her mind.

She looked away. "You're . . . complicated."

"In some ways. And so are you. But there's nothing complicated about the way I feel about you. That's extremely simple."

"Ha. There's nothing simple about you."

"Stop pretending that's a minus and not a plus."

She moistened her lips. "Look, you promised to show me some self-defense techniques and I just took you up on it."

"Liar. Metcalf or any of your other FBI buddies would have been happy to teach you whatever you wanted to know. And yet you called me."

"I thought I'd feel more comfortable with you. I'm now starting to seriously doubt my judgment on that count."

"I think you were bored. Maybe you thought that it was time to forget about comfort." He chuckled as he strolled over to her backpack and got them each a bottle of water. "Because you knew exactly what you were going to get from me, Kendra. I've been more patient than you've ever known me to be. Both of us had some healing to do after that last case we worked together. But I regard this summons as very promising. You must have missed me." He took a swallow of water. "Think about it."

"I'm thinking that I haven't missed either your arrogance or your ego," she said dryly.

He threw back his head and laughed. "Okay, maybe it wasn't an excuse. So why the sudden interest in breaking men's bones?" His smile faded. "Has something made you particularly afraid?"

Lord, now he was getting protective. "No. And for the record, it's not just men's bones. I'm entirely open to breaking women's bones if the occasion demands it."

"I stand corrected. Why?"

Kendra took a swallow from her bottle and turned toward the ocean where whitecaps collided with the rocky coastline. "By my best estimate, I've come close to being murdered twenty-six times in the last few years."

"Hmm. Interesting. Twenty-six times."

"Yes. That may be a typical Tuesday for you, but I'm a music therapist. I didn't sign up for this."

"You *are* having a bad day, aren't you? You're more than a music therapist. You catch killers on a fairly routine basis. That puts you in a special category."

She grimaced. "Lunatic?"

He shook his head. "No, someone who can't just stand by and watch while people are being hurt. And you have as much a gift for it as you do for music therapy. Maybe more. So suck it up and accept it."

"Your sympathy is incredibly touching."

He grinned. "You don't want my sympathy. You'd punish me if you thought I was offering it. But we've known each other long enough for you to admit that I do understand you." He shrugged. "Look, you were born blind and spent the first twenty years of your life in the dark before you got your sight. That's amazing. But you know what? If you'd never gotten that surgical procedure, you'd still be an amazing person. You made the best of what you had. You adapted. You used your other senses—your hearing, touch, sense of smell, all of them—to pick up things the rest of us ignore."

"All blind people do that."

"True. But now that you have your sight, you also

apply that same level of concentration on things you see."

"Like I've told you, after being in the dark for so long, I can't take things I see for granted. I don't see how anyone can."

"Well, all these things combine to make you an incredible investigator. You walk onto a crime scene and detect things no other cop could dream of picking up. It's no wonder the police and FBI are always fighting over you."

"You're exaggerating."

"Not really. And as much as you claim to be bothered by these cases, the intrusion on your life and your practice, you could always say no."

"I have, many times."

"But there have also been many times when you've said yes."

"Hence the twenty-six attempts on my life."

Lynch shrugged. "You do it because innocent people will die if you don't. That makes you a very special person."

"*You* do it."

"I used to do it. These days I'm well paid to do a variety of things, and a scant few of my activities involve saving lives."

Kendra turned to look at him. "Probably because those variety of things fall into an entirely different and lethal category." Lynch had been an FBI agent, but he now worked freelance for whatever government agency was willing to pay for his services. He rarely talked specifics about his assignments, and she knew better than to try and press him for details.

Lynch flashed his high-wattage smile at her again. "This is a long way of saying that I'm glad you're thinking more about defending yourself. For one thing, I want you to be safe. But it also means that you've reached some measure of peace about helping in these investigations. You're obviously thinking about doing more in the future?"

"Not necessarily. Maybe. But when I do, I want to be better prepared for whatever comes my way."

"Have you thought about carrying a gun?" he asked quietly. "I have an excellent supplier who—"

"I'm sure you do, but I don't want a gun."

"You just want to crunch bones."

"For now."

His blue eyes were suddenly glinting with mischief. "Okay, I can help you with that. Crunching bones is one of my specialties."

She had no intention of asking about any of his other "specialties." "Thanks."

Lynch nodded. "Have you ever thought about a more formal arrangement with the FBI?"

She smiled. "Like being on retainer?"

"Not exactly."

Her eyes narrowed on him. "Surely you don't mean actually joining up?"

"They'd love to have you."

She couldn't believe it. "Quantico, a cubicle at the regional office, the whole bit?"

"Yep." His lips were turning up at the corners. "FBI Special Agent Kendra Michaels. It has a certain ring to it, doesn't it? I knew you'd particularly like the idea of the cubicle. Griffin asked if I'd float it out to you. I told him he was crazy."

"He should have listened. Why didn't he talk to me about this himself?"

He said, deadpan, "For some reason, he thought I might want to flex my considerable powers of persuasion over you."

She burst out laughing.

Lynch nodded. "Exactly the reaction I thought you'd have. First of all, despite my reputation for bending people to my will—"

"They don't call you The Puppetmaster for nothing."

"I still hate that nickname."

"Too bad. Please continue."

"Griffin should know you're fairly unpersuadable by me or anyone else. And even if I could talk you into such a thing, why would I, when I couldn't wait to get free of the FBI's clutches myself?"

"I already have a career."

"I told him that. He thought maybe you could continue doing it on the side."

"Like a hobby?" Kendra cursed under her breath. "Music therapy may not seem like a real job to some people, but I'm a scientist. Research studies, control groups, double-blind experiments . . . I get results and I can prove it."

"I know that, Kendra. And so does Griffin."

"And I *help* people."

"Again, you're preaching to the converted. I've seen what you're able to do for your clients."

She took a few deep breaths. She was attacking the wrong person. She knew she had Lynch's respect. But her anger had just overflowed. Just relax. "If this subject comes up again, tell Griffin I said to go to hell."

"Not necessary." Lynch was gazing beyond her shoulder and he nodded behind her. "Tell him yourself."

Kendra turned to see FBI Agent in Charge Michael Griffin walking toward them on the path from Ladera Street. He was with another agent, Roland Metcalf.

She turned back to Lynch. "You've got to be kidding. You told him we were coming up here?"

"No." Lynch looked totally mystified. "*You* didn't tell him?"

Kendra turned back to watch the two FBI agents, dressed in their dark suits. They looked ridiculously out of place at this oceanside recreation spot.

She called out as soon as they were within earshot.

"Not interested in your job, Griffin. May as well go home."

Michael Griffin wrinkled his brow. He was a slender man with hair that was now almost entirely silver. He headed the FBI San Diego regional office and he seemed to earn the respect of his colleagues even as he annoyed the hell out of Kendra.

Griffin glanced at Lynch, then back to her. "Oh. Guess you won't be getting fitted for that windbreaker."

"Afraid not. Pity."

"But that's not why I'm here. There's something else I need to talk to you about."

"A case?" She stiffened. "No way. I'm extremely busy right now. I have a heavy client list, I have to present a paper in Denmark next month, and—"

"This isn't just any case, Kendra," Roland Metcalf said. He was a tall, attractive agent in his late twenties. Lynch insisted he had a crush on Kendra, and she'd only recently admitted it was probably true. "You'll want to see this."

She shook her head. "I seriously doubt that."

Lynch broke in. "Before you say one more word, I'd like to know how you knew you'd find her here. You didn't, by any chance, pull a warrantless trace on her mobile phone, did you?"

Griffin glared at him. "No. But interesting that was your immediate go-to. Maybe because it's what you would have done?"

Lynch didn't reply.

Kendra glanced impatiently from one to the other. "Never mind Lynch. We all know what intrusive and appalling things he's capable of."

"Thanks for the support," Lynch said dryly.

"So out with it," Kendra said. She didn't like the possibility Lynch had brought up. "How did you know?"

"We tried to call first," Metcalf said. "I guess that's your phone over there by the mat?"

"The one that's powered off? Yeah, that's mine."

"Then we went to your condo and you weren't there. But I just happen to know that your best friend lives one floor down from you, so I paid her a visit."

Kendra mock-slapped her forehead. "Olivia . . . I told her I was coming here."

"And she told me." Metcalf grinned. "None of that fancy electronic snoop stuff for me. Hey, I'm a Federal agent. I know how to do things."

"Yeah, I guess you do," Kendra said absently. She was looking Metcalf and Griffin up and down. "So who was she?"

"Who?" Griffin said.

"Well, I'm not talking about Olivia. The murder victim in the case you're investigating. It *was* a woman, wasn't it?"

The two men nodded.

"Then let's get this over with, Griffin. You got a call in the middle of the night, probably from San Diego PD.

Fortunately, your wife wasn't disturbed because she wasn't with you. Not having trouble again at home, I hope?"

Griffin's forehead creased in annoyance. "Were you this big a pain in the ass when you were blind?"

"Oh, you have no idea."

"Wrong. I have a very good idea. For the record, there's no trouble at home," Griffin said. "My wife has been up in Portland for the past couple of weeks caring for her mother. Okay?"

"Okay."

"Let her continue." Lynch was smiling slyly at both Kendra's demonstration and Griffin's unease. "I love this part."

"I'm not here to entertain you, Lynch." She continued to study Griffin and Metcalf. "After you got the call, Griffin, you could have tasked it out to Metcalf or dozens of other agents at your disposal. But something about this case made you get out of bed and go to the scene yourself. You don't generally subject yourself to that kind of punishment. One of the perks of being boss."

"Sometimes being boss isn't all it's cracked up to be."

"This was obviously one of those times," Kendra replied. "The murder was in the city. The body was outdoors on the street. The police left her out there for quite a while longer than usual. Maybe waiting for you? But not only for you. You decided to call Metcalf to join you.

He arrived not long after you did and spent even more time inspecting the corpse than you did."

Metcalf smiled. He was obviously enjoying her riff, but Griffin still seemed mildly annoyed.

Kendra studied Metcalf for a moment longer. "So you had to get up in the middle of the night, too. But you weren't alone. Overnight female companionship obviously isn't a problem for you, is it, Metcalf?"

"Shit." He grimaced. "Now *I'm* in for it?"

"I don't see why not. I hope you know her well, 'cause it's kind of awkward to leave a stranger alone in your house."

Metcalf smiled sheepishly. "I know her . . . pretty well."

"I think you're safe. I'd say she makes more than you do."

"Right again. She's a software engineer."

Lynch patted him on the shoulder. "As long as it's not another FBI agent. That didn't work out too well for you last time, did it?"

The smile instantly disappeared from Metcalf's face. "Uh, can we move on? Please?"

Kendra smiled. "Sure, Metcalf. But there's one thing I can't figure out . . . Why are you coming to me with this case? You usually wait days or even weeks before you decide you want my help. It's only been hours."

"It wasn't our idea," Griffin said sourly.

Kendra frowned. “Then whose idea was it?”

“The corpse’s.”

Kendra stared at Griffin. “Is this some kind of sick joke?”

Metcalf spoke gently. “Do you know someone named Elena Meyer of Fairfield, Connecticut?”

Kendra thought for a moment. “No.”

Griffin pulled out his camera phone and held it up. “Are you sure? She knew you.”

Kendra swallowed hard as she stared at the image on the phone. It was the face of a dead young woman, maybe thirty, lying on the street. Her cheeks were pale, her lipstick smeared, and brown curly hair fell over her forehead. She looked so young, with her whole life to live . . .

“No,” Kendra said quietly. “I’ve never seen her.”

“This woman bolted out onto Fifth Street and was struck by a car,” Griffin said.

Lynch looked at the photo. “Hit and run?”

“No. It wasn’t the car that killed her. She ran out of an alley with a gunshot wound in her torso.”

“Any leads?” Lynch asked.

“Not so far. Her family didn’t even know she was out here.”

Kendra was still staring at the photo. “What did you mean by . . . it was her idea to bring me into this?”

Griffin swiped his finger across the phone screen as

he spoke. "She was carrying an envelope in her jacket pocket. There was a name and address printed on it." He angled the phone back toward Kendra.

"Mine," she said.

"It looks like she was trying to get to you when she was killed," Metcalf said. "She was on Fifth Street, just a few blocks from your condo. You're positive you don't even recognize the name . . . Elena Meyer?"

Kendra shook her head. "Not at all. Do you know her occupation?"

"She worked for a law firm in Connecticut. She was a paralegal."

Again, Kendra shook her head. "What was in the envelope?"

"A flash drive," Griffin said. "Nothing else. And there was only one file on it, a video."

"Have you watched it?"

"We both have. Pretty much everyone at the office has seen it by now. We . . . don't know what to make of it."

Kendra tried to read their expressions and all she saw was puzzlement. "Show me."

"We have a copy plugged into the A/V system of our van." Griffin gestured toward the street. "We can show it to you there."

"Good." She picked up her phone and keys while Lynch rolled up the two mats they had spread out. As they walked down toward Ladera Street, Metcalf turned toward Kendra. "How did you know?"

"Know what?"

"All that stuff about us. You can't leave us hanging."

"Would I do that to you, Metcalf?"

"You've done it before," Griffin growled. "I think you just like to show us how vulnerable we are to you."

"Maybe sometimes. It depends on how vulnerable *I'm* feeling at a given moment. Most of the time it just saves time and prevents lies."

"And sticks your nose where it doesn't belong. How in the hell did you know my wife wasn't with me?"

"Because you don't seem to know how to take your shirts to the dry cleaner. The only times your shirts haven't been pressed and starched in the years I've known you is the two times you and your wife were separated. Instead, you launder them yourself with an overabundance of scented Bounce dryer sheets."

Griffin gripped his collar between his thumb and forefinger and sniffed it. "Too much?"

"Too much. One is really all you need."

"You could have told me that years ago."

"Oh, but that wouldn't have been nearly as much fun for me."

"Nice. So how did you know about me being rousted in the middle of the night?"

"That's an easy one. You're wearing glasses. The only time you wear those instead of your contact lenses is when you're called to a scene in the middle of the night. Those particular glasses have an antireflective coating that's starting to break down, giving the lenses some annoying streaks you probably wouldn't tolerate if you wore them more often."

Griffin took off the glasses and looked at the lenses. "Is that what that is? They've been driving me nuts all morning. I keep wiping them, but it doesn't help."

"Could be time for new specs."

"Could be." He put the glasses back on. "Tell us how you know about Metcalf's lady friend."

"Actually, his shirt tipped me off. He obviously left in a hurry, and I'm guessing it's the same shirt he wore yesterday."

Metcalf glanced down at his blue, button-down collar shirt. "I thought it looked pretty good."

"It does. Most people would never guess that an attractive young woman was prancing around your home in it just a few hours ago."

"I don't know if she was *prancing* . . ." Metcalf slipped his fingers between the top two buttons and made a show of airing the shirt out. "Am I radiating a womanly smell? Perfume?"

"Body wash. And the smell is very faint. The cops at the crime scene probably weren't making fun of you behind your back. At least not because of the way you smell."

"Good to know."

"But tell me something, what's the special appeal of seeing a half-naked woman wearing your shirt?"

"Depends on the woman."

Lynch nodded. "Depends on the shirt."

"Unbelievable."

Metcalf thought of something. "How do you know she makes more money than I do? Other than your awareness of my pathetic government salary."

"Her body wash is Frederic Malle Carnal Flower. That implies a level of income you and I can only aspire to."

"Hmm. Guess I should let her pay for dinner next time. So how did you know I was examining the corpse on a city street?"

"Whenever you put on evidence gloves, you roll up your sleeves and take off your watch. I noticed that you're not wearing your watch and your sleeves are unbuttoned. The knees of your pants show a bit of street grime and that polyester blend is surprisingly good for picking up fine impressions. The imprint on your knees was surely made by a rock, sand, and asphalt slurry seal, which coats most San Diego streets."

Griffin looked at her skeptically. "Slurry seal and not perpetual pavement?"

"No. Two very different impressions. Metcalf was clearly on his knees on a city street, not a parking lot, evidence gloves on, inspecting a corpse." She looked up at the two men. "And before you ask how I knew it was a corpse, you've never asked me to consult on an investigation where a dead body wasn't involved."

Metcalf gave her a rueful nod. "If you want us to stop bothering you, you should try being wrong a little more often."

"Is that what it would take?" She sighed. "I'll see what I can do."

They reached the path's end on Ladera Street and Griffin led them to a white-paneled van parked near the park entrance. He slid open the side door and ushered Kendra and Lynch inside. "Climb in. The next show starts in two minutes."

Kendra and Lynch slid into the second row of seats while Griffin and Metcalf took their places up front. Griffin turned a knob on the console and a ceiling-mounted monitor flickered on.

Kendra nodded toward it. "Looks like the same setup my friends use to babysit their kids on road trips."

"Not this particular one unless they want to give their kids nightmares," Griffin said. "We've reviewed some of the goriest crime scenes imaginable on that screen."

"What exactly are you about to show me?" Kendra said.

"We're trying to figure that out ourselves. It's what Elena Meyer died trying to deliver to you. I hope to hell you can give us some idea why."

Griffin pushed a button on the front console and the video started playing on the screen.

Kendra didn't know what she was expecting, but it

wasn't Kool and the Gang's "Celebration." The song played over a video of tables of well-dressed, happy people eating, drinking, laughing, and snapping pictures.

The video appeared to be the work of an amateur, perhaps shot with a mobile phone. The continuous shot swept through the large room, which was decorated with helium balloons and multicolored streamers. A DJ lorded over the small dance floor, where half a dozen rhythmically challenged couples moved to the beat.

"It's a wedding reception," Kendra murmured. "What the hell?"

"Kind of the reaction of everyone who's seen it," Metcalf said.

The shot moved past the dance floor to a long table where the wedding party was seated. The bride and groom greeted well-wishers at the center.

The video continued for almost twenty minutes, ticking off the boxes for a typical wedding. The cake-cutting. The teary-eyed toasts. The bouquet toss.

Then it was over.

Kendra stared at the blank screen for a long moment. "Show it to me again."

Metcalf punched a button on the console, and the wedding video restarted.

Kendra watched the video again, this time concentrating on the faces, the voices, the clothing, the fine details she may have missed the first time. Very little had escaped her, she realized.

"Well?" Griffin said after it ended. "Do you recognize any of those people?"

"No. Not one."

"Any idea why our victim would have wanted you to see it?"

Kendra leaned back. "No idea at all. And I don't believe the victim was even at this reception. I didn't see her anywhere."

"We didn't either," Griffin said. "We're thinking maybe she's the one who took the video."

"She wasn't."

Lynch turned toward her. "What makes you so sure?"

"Assuming the videographer was holding the lens at about eye level, it was a tall man, probably around six-foot-two. Crime scene markers in the photos Griffin showed us indicate that the victim was about five-foot-four. For a second, you can see a shoulders-down reflection in a decorative brass wall ornament. Whoever took the video was wearing a tux."

Metcalf jotted this down into a worn leather notebook. "We're checking with the major hotel chains to see if they recognize the venue, but it could also be a reception hall or events facility. Since the victim lived in Connecticut, we're starting there."

"Don't. Start here in southern California. And this is in a large country club, one with a golf course."

Metcalf looked up from his notebook. "Are you sure?"

"Yes. Next time you watch the video, look at the pillars. They're mahogany. It's dark, but you can still see that the top of each one is carved with golf symbols: tees, clubs, flags."

"We missed that," Griffin said. "How do you know it's here in California?"

"Dialects. The groom and his family are from the northeast, but the bride, her parents, and most of her friends are from here. The bride's father was definitely playing host, talking to the DJ, bartender, and servers at various times during the video. I'd say he was a member of the country club, wherever it is."

"Anything else?"

Kendra shook her head. "No. It looks like every boring wedding video ever made. Why would a woman die trying to get this to me?"

"We were hoping you'd tell us," Metcalf said.

"I can't. At least not yet." She glanced at Lynch, and he reached out and gave her hand an encouraging squeeze. He could see this was already getting under her skin. She turned back to Griffin and Metcalf. "I want a copy of this video."

Griffin ejected the flash drive and offered it to her. "This one's yours. We'd appreciate anything else you can tell us."

She stared at the stick. She'd wanted to tell Griffin to go to hell, and now here she was up to her eyeballs in this case.

But this poor woman, for some reason, had spent her

last moments on Earth trying to get this video to *her*. It gave Kendra a strange sense of bonding.

Okay, this one's for you, Elena Meyer of Fairfield, Connecticut.

Kendra grabbed the flash drive and climbed out of the van.

SHE WAS ALMOST TO HER CAR when Lynch caught up to her. "Wait up."

She turned. "You had no idea they were coming for me today?"

"Of course not."

She gave him a doubtful look. "Really?"

"Yes. You think I was here on a recruiting mission? I left the FBI a long time ago. *You* called *me*, remember?"

He was right. She was being paranoid. But she was aware of what machinations Lynch was capable. Governments and companies paid him enormous amounts of money to go into seemingly impossible situations and change the outcome to suit themselves. It was difficult to trust a man with those kinds of abilities. Yet she did trust him . . . most of the time. "I know. I'm sorry. I'm sure it happened just like Metcalf said. Olivia would have no reason not to tell them where to find me." She looked at the flash drive in her hand. "Anyway . . . this one is personal. This is one I need to do."

"I know you do."

"I just wish I knew why she chose me."

Lynch put his hands on her forearms. "I'll contact some of my NSA sources. I'll see if there's any common ground between you and her as far as work or educational background, associates, whatever. She may have just read about one of your cases sometime. Your energy is best spent figuring out what she was trying to tell you with that video."

"I'm already working on it. It'll be hard for me to work on anything else."

"I know," he said lightly. "It's that obsessive streak I find so endearing. I'm always plotting how to get you to focus it on me." His smile faded. "But you can't let it take over your life. Let me take you to lunch at Mister A's. I guarantee their Maine lobster strudel will take your mind off everything else."

"Can't. It's a work day. I have three clients this afternoon."

"Then dinner."

She held up the flash drive. "I'll be eating leftover pasta while I watch this ridiculous wedding video over and over again."

He raised his hands in surrender. "I thought I'd try. If you feel like getting away from it for a while, we can always work on those wrist-breaking techniques." His voice lowered to teasing sensuality as he turned and strolled away. "Or any other holds that interest you. I live to serve . . ."

La Jolla Shores
La Jolla, California

Gil Corkle hated the beach.

Nothing about it was the least bit appealing to him. Not the coarse sand. Not the cold and dirty water. Not the incessant roar of the pounding surf. He wanted to be anyplace but here.

But Vivianne Kerstine had insisted.

Corkle stopped at the edge of the parking lot to take off his shoes. Damned if he was going to ruin a two-thousand-dollar pair of Berluti loafers to accommodate his boss's foolishness.

He carried his shoes as he trudged barefoot through the sand. It was hot. Another thing he hated about the damned beach.

He could see Vivianne in the distance, ankle deep in water.

She didn't face him as he approached. "You told me Elena Meyer wouldn't be a problem."

He stopped just short of the surf. "She was smarter than any of us gave her credit for. It would have been better if you'd realized that from the beginning."

Vivianne turned and glared at him. In almost any other context, she would be considered beautiful, with high cheekbones, full lips, and long dark hair. Now she was absolutely terrifying. "So this is my fault?"

"That's not what I said."

"Sounded like it to me."

Corkle swallowed hard. It wasn't wise to piss off Vivianne, especially since he was already on thin ice with her. Damage control. "I'm just saying . . . she surprised us all."

"But once that happened, it was your job to stop her."

"I know. I know. I'm sorry. She made it to a crowded street before I could get to her."

"Unfortunate."

Corkle didn't like the way she said that. He'd seen what happened to people who disappointed Vivianne. He stepped closer to her, ignoring the water lapping around his trouser cuffs. "That video is meaningless without Elena to explain it to them. The police won't have anything to go on."

"It's not the police that concerns me."

"Then what does?"

"Kendra Michaels."

"I don't see a problem. Surely without Elena to—"

"Don't underestimate Michaels, Corkle. I've researched her, and she produces when no one else is able to do it. That means we're now all at risk. Elena was trying to get to Kendra Michaels for a reason."

Corkle said softly, "I can do something about that."

"Like you did last night? I don't know if we can withstand any more of your ham-fisted problem solving."

He didn't like the coldness of her voice. "I'm better than that," he said quickly. "You know it."

"Just cool your jets, Corkle." Vivianne once again turned to face the ocean breeze. "Before you do something rash that will make everything more of a disaster than it is already. I've been thinking about it. Kendra Michaels may be of some use to us . . ."

CHAPTER 2

"*LIZ, I THOUGHT WE'D never get rid of you.*"

So said the bride's father as he toasted the happy couple, following a rather flat speech by the maid of honor. The rest of his speech was sweet, and it seemed no less heartfelt the tenth time Kendra watched than the first. She leaned back on the living room sofa in her condo studying the wedding guests around him. There was nothing in his words or their reaction that seemed out of place. Time to move on. She was wasting her time with him.

A knock at her door.

Her friend Olivia's knock. And the fact that she was using just one knuckle made it apparent she was already holding the door key in her hand.

"Come in!"

Olivia inserted the key, threw the lock, and opened the door. "You're pissed, aren't you?"

"For practically drawing Metcalf a map to my location and destroying one of my few precious moments of leisure time? Why would you think that?"

"Sorry." Olivia closed the door behind her. Her long brown hair was tied in a bun, which only accentuated her strikingly beautiful face and olive-toned skin. Kendra had known her since they were children at the Woodward Academy in Oceanside. Kendra had spent years overcoming pangs of guilt for leaving her friend behind in the darkness, but Olivia had only expressed happiness for Kendra's good fortune. "I did think about it. But Metcalf can be persuasive. He said he had something you'd want to know about."

"He was right. It's good that you told him."

"My excellent judgment triumphs again." Olivia cocked her head at the sounds coming from Kendra's television. "What are you watching?"

"A video of a wedding reception."

"Whose?"

"I have no earthly idea."

Olivia sat on the couch next to her. "This reality TV craze has gotten out of hand."

"It's not a TV show. It's a video that a dead woman wanted me to see."

Olivia nodded. "Huh. If it was anyone else, I'd swear you were joking."

"Pretty sick joke."

"It's not a joke, just your sick life." She got more comfortable on the couch. "Tell me about it."

Kendra brought her up to speed on what Griffin and Metcalf had told her about the young murder victim and her mysterious video. Then she played the video through for her again.

After she finished, Olivia sat in silence for a long moment. "Just one question. Who at this wedding reception thought this was a bad idea and needed to get the hell out of there?"

"What are you talking about?"

"You didn't hear?"

"Hear what?"

"Rewind the video. Go back to right before the Bonnie Raitt song begins . . . 'Feels Like Home.'"

Kendra eyed her skeptically. "Are you punking me?"

"No. Do it!"

Kendra picked up her TV remote and rewound the video. She stopped a few times before coming to the section Olivia had indicated.

Kendra listened for a few seconds. "I don't know what you're—"

"Shh! Listen!"

Kendra cocked her head. The room was noisy with guests making good-natured fun of each other's dance moves. Then there was a rasping sound, like a harsh whisper. But the whisper was so extremely soft it was totally unidentifiable.

Olivia turned. "Hear that?"

Kendra skipped back a few seconds and turned up the volume full blast.

More rasping, then a slightly more intelligible, *"We need to get the hell out of here."*

"Now do you hear it?" Olivia asked.

Kendra skipped back again and leaned forward. She concentrated and this time she heard it all.

"This is a bad idea. We need to get the hell out of here."

"Then someone else speaks," Olivia said. "They're whispering to each other. Play it over."

The second whisper was even more muffled.

"Why? When it's all here."

Kendra replayed the two segments several times.

"This is a bad idea. We need to get the hell out of here."

And then the answer.

"Why? When it's all here."

The first was spoken with a sense of urgency, Kendra thought. Of danger.

As far as she could tell, the second person was almost lazy, amused.

Olivia smiled. "I can't believe I caught something you didn't. I think relying on your eyesight is starting to make you soft in the hearing department."

"I've always said you had better hearing than I do. I just worked harder training myself to listen. But this one went right by me. Good job, Olivia."

"This is a bad idea. We need to get the hell out of here."

"Why? When it's all here."

Kendra shook her head. "But I can't even tell if either one of them is a man or woman. Can you?"

"No. They're both too low and the noise drowns them. I guess this could be anything," Olivia said. "Someone who has run into an ex they didn't expect to see or an estranged family member . . ."

"This is a bad idea. We need to get the hell out of here."

"Why? When it's all here . . ."

Kendra let the video continue as she thought for a moment. "I don't think it was either of those things. There was an edge to that first voice. Yet I can't be sure of anything because it was too darned soft. But I do know it wasn't one of the speakers in the bridal party or anyone else that I heard on this video. It might have been one of the guests. It was a huge wedding. Maybe if I go through it enough times, I'll catch another voice that sounds familiar."

"How many times?"

Kendra sighed. "Oh, maybe fifty or so . . ."

"Then maybe I should listen," Olivia said slyly.

"Rub it in. But you're welcome to stay. Have you

eaten? I could order in from that Italian restaurant on the corner."

"Thanks, but I have to get back to work."

"Work" for Olivia was her popular web destination, *Outtasite,* which featured news, interviews, and product reviews, all geared to a vision-impaired audience. In the past few years, the site had grown from a hobby to a six-figure annual income for Olivia.

Kendra checked her watch. "It's already almost ten o'clock. And you accuse *me* of being a workaholic."

Olivia stood. "No rest for the weary. I have a conference call with the company in Japan that does my website language translations there."

"Wow. When did you get to be such a media mogul, Olivia?"

"Around the same time you started catching killers. Guess we each have our own way of passing the time. I like mine better." She walked toward the door. "Later."

"Good night, Olivia."

"Yeah, we'll see. Depends on the Japanese." Olivia left the condo and pulled the door closed behind her.

Kendra suddenly felt very tired. Her eyes were stinging, but she couldn't take them from the screen. Maybe just a couple more viewings . . .

"This is a bad idea. We need to get the hell out of here."

"Why? When it's all here."

* * *

BUZZZ. BUZZZ.

Kendra jolted awake.

She checked her watch. 7:50 A.M.

She was still on the couch, and the video file had been playing all night on an endless loop. She had drifted in and out of consciousness, catching snatches of a song or an occasional few words from a toast swirling in her head like some kind of bizarre dream. But she felt no closer to solving the puzzle than she had the night before.

Buzzz. Buzzz. Buzzz.

It was her main door buzzer that had awakened her, she realized. It sounded more persistent now. Impatient.

Lynch. He favored three button presses when two failed to get an immediate response.

Buzzz. Buzzz. Buzzz.

She moved to the intercom and pressed the button. "If you didn't bring coffee, I'm sending you away."

"I brought coffee." Lynch's voice. "Come down and get it."

"Why would I do that?" Kendra ran her hands through her messy hair. "I just woke up."

"We're going on a road trip."

"Like hell I am."

"Get down here, will you? I'm double-parked."

"A road trip to where?"

"The country club where that wedding reception

was held. The FBI tracked it down. If you want them to handle it on their own, it's your choice. I just thought—"

"I'll be down in three minutes."

A change of clothes, a quick hair brushing, and a spritz of mouthwash later, Kendra stepped outside her building and climbed into Lynch's Ferrari. She picked up the large coffee waiting for her in the cup holder.

"I'm surprised you didn't let yourself up," she said. "You still have that spare key, don't you?"

Lynch shifted the car into gear and pulled away. "I do, but I didn't want to abuse the privilege. You're a woman who never likes to be taken for granted. Plus, I was double-parked and this car has a way of attracting the attention of San Diego's finest."

"I wonder why? It couldn't be more ostentatious. Serves you right."

"I tried calling you, but it went straight to voicemail."

"Because my phone's dead. That reminds me." Kendra pulled her phone from her pocket, unplugged Lynch's phone from the lighter socket, and inserted her own phone in its place.

Lynch glanced down at his phone. "I was *charging* that."

"Then you should have two charging cables in here. I'm a guest in your car. Don't be a rude host."

"Hmm. I think there's only one rude person in here."

"Relax. I'll plug yours back in as soon as I get a little juice."

"So you say."

Kendra took a swig of coffee. "So where are we going?"

"Via Pacifica Country Club in San Clemente. Your buddy Metcalf burned the midnight oil to track it down."

"How'd he do it?"

"He took screen grabs of the place in the video and ran them through an online image recognition tool. Probably Google Image. He compared the hits with the reception hall in the video."

"Score another one for social media."

Lynch nodded. "I'm surprised Metcalf didn't call you himself. He rarely misses an opportunity to try and impress you."

"It's not like that. Metcalf is very popular with the ladies."

"Except for *this* lady. The one he really wants. And stop denying it. You know I'm right."

"Maybe."

"Definitely."

She looked out the car window. "I'm surprised he called *you*. I didn't think you and he were so tight."

"We're not. He has no idea I know."

"Then how—?"

"I worked out of that office for years. As hard as it may be for you to believe, some of my old coworkers actually have some affection for me."

"So much affection that they're willing to commit a

felony by handing over confidential details of an in-progress Federal investigation?"

"What's a little jail time in the face of my blinding charisma?"

"I'm feeling a little ill."

"In any case, I keep my sources private. Metcalf is meeting with the country club's operations manager at 9:00 A.M. He won't mind us crashing in. At least he won't mind seeing *you* there."

"So the FBI has no idea we're joining them?"

"None whatsoever." Lynch tightened his grip on the steering wheel as he pulled onto the I-5 freeway. "It's more fun this way, don't you think?"

EVEN WITH THE USUAL morning traffic, they made it to the upscale coastal town of San Clemente in under an hour. A few minutes after that, they pulled onto the sprawling grounds of the Via Pacifica Country Club, whose large logo signs featured the words GOLF-TENNIS-SWIM in bold gold lettering. They made their way to the large clubhouse and parked.

As they walked across the parking lot, Kendra gazed at the spectacular valley view. "Stunning. You can see why this would be a great place for weddings."

"From what I hear, the golf isn't bad either. I know a Secret Service agent who retired nearby after working on Nixon's detail. He gets guest passes as a perk for doing occasional security work for them. They have quite the wealthy clientele here."

He pulled open the tinted-glass door and motioned for Kendra to enter.

The foyer was striking, with Italian tile and two-story floor-to-ceiling windows. A cherrywood reception counter stood vacant in the center of the area and plaques and framed photographs covered the wood-paneled walls.

Kendra walked over and looked at the photographs. "Charity events, celebrity golf tournaments, even a movie wrap party."

Lynch nodded approvingly at their surroundings. "*I'd* host a party here."

"That's what we like to hear!" A chipper voice sounded behind them.

Kendra and Lynch turned to see a small, blond woman entering from a doorway at the foyer's far end. She extended her hand. "Hannah Coltrane, events director. Beautiful here, isn't it?"

Lynch smiled and took her hand into his own. "Extremely."

Kendra couldn't help rolling her eyes at his cheesy flirtation, but the woman obviously enjoyed it.

At that moment, the front door opened and Metcalf stepped in. He looked surprised to see Kendra and Lynch. "Oh, hello . . . Here for a round of golf?"

"Hardly," Kendra said. "Good work on ID'ing this place from the video. You didn't waste time."

Metcalf shot Lynch a sour glance. "Good news travels fast."

Hannah glanced from one to the other. "So . . . you're *not* here to book an event?"

Lynch cocked his head toward her. "Go ahead, Metcalf. Do your thing with the badge."

Metcalf flipped open his wallet and displayed his ID with all the flair and authority of a someone who had watched far too much television as a child. "Roland Metcalf, FBI. Are you Hannah?"

She took a step away from Lynch. "Yes. I was told to expect you, Agent Metcalf."

"Good. I promise this won't take long. Can we see your large event room?"

"Of course. Follow me."

She led them down a short hallway Kendra recognized from a shot in the video of guests signing the guest book. They stepped through a pair of open double doors to find themselves in the large events room, which was filled with large round tables being set by a staff of about a dozen servers.

"We're having a real estate awards luncheon here today," Hannah said. "Sorry things are a bit hectic."

"No problem," Kendra said. She scanned the area, paying special attention to the carved pillars. "This is it, all right. The pillars, the doors, the carpet pattern . . ."

Kendra glanced around. It may have been the video's subtle brainwashing while she slept, but every corner of the room now had a sound, tune, or speech associated with it.

"Liz, I thought we'd never get rid of you."

"Chicken or fish?"

"Do you have vegetarian?"

"This is a bad idea."

"We need to get the hell out of here."

She turned back to Metcalf. "Definitely the place."

Hannah looked quizzically at them. "If you don't mind me asking . . ."

Metcalf raised his iPad and showed her frame grabs he'd made of the video. "There was a wedding reception here, probably sometime in the past couple of years."

"Last fall," Kendra interjected.

Metcalf turned back. "Really?"

"Yes. I checked the women's clothing and shoes against the online catalogues. It was probably no later than last November."

Metcalf nodded and turned his attention back to Hannah. "Okay. A wedding here last fall. Would you be able to tell us which one it was, based on these photos?"

Hannah looked doubtfully at the screen grabs. "We have so many events here. I'm afraid that—" Her eyes narrowed on one picture. "Wait."

Kendra craned her neck to see. It was a photo that

included the bride's parents. "Do you know that man? He seemed familiar with the staff."

Hannah bit her lip. "I wonder if I might take this to the general manager. He may know. That's him over there." She motioned toward a stocky man on the other side of the room. "I'll be right back."

She took Metcalf's iPad across the room to a large oak bar where the general manager now stood looking down at his phone. He looked at the iPad screen, furrowed his brow, and said something to Hannah. He glanced up, curtly waved to the group, then left the room.

Hannah handed the iPad back to Metcalf. "I'm sorry, he didn't recognize him."

"But *you* seemed as if you might have."

"I was mistaken. I've never seen him before."

Lynch smiled. "I find that hard to believe. Just sixty seconds ago you registered a fairly strong reaction when you saw this man. Now you're telling us—?"

"I'm telling you I don't recall seeing him." Hannah suddenly adopted a defensive tone and body language. "If you'd like to leave your information, I'll see about putting together a list of our October and November weddings from last year."

"How about just those paid for by John Hollingsworth?" Kendra said.

Hannah looked up with a start.

"Because we know that's who he is." Kendra lowered

her voice. "And we know you and your manager both know it. Get us the contact information for him and anyone else connected with that wedding. And while you're at it, you can also tell us why you and your boss thought you needed to lie and protect Hollingsworth from an FBI investigation. That's called obstruction of justice."

A flash of panic crossed Hannah's face. "It wasn't my fault. My manager told me to say that. I'm sorry."

Metcalf was clearly caught off guard by Kendra's play, but he quickly jumped aboard. He rubbed his index finger over his lips, and Kendra discreetly nodded. She'd read the lips of Hannah and her boss from across the room. She had been fascinated by the interplay of tongue, lips, and teeth upon gaining her sight and lip reading was an interesting byproduct.

"Hollingsworth is a member?" he asked.

"A founding member. He's on the board. I can't believe he'd do anything wrong, but we always try to protect the privacy of our people."

"Your people?" Lynch shook his head and strode toward the door.

Hannah practically chased after him. "Where are you going?"

"To talk to your GM. If he's not on the horn to Hollingsworth yet, I'm betting he soon will be. Right?"

Lynch threw open the door to see the general manager standing just outside in the hallway. He was talking on his phone.

He eyed Lynch, Kendra, and Metcalf warily as he continued his conversation. After another moment, he extended his phone toward them. "It's for you."

"What?" Kendra asked.

"John Hollingsworth. That's who you were asking about, wasn't it?

Metcalf took the phone. "This is Special Agent Roland Metcalf." He listened for a moment. "Yes. Yes. Fine."

Metcalf cut the connection.

"Well?" Kendra asked.

"Hollingsworth is here now."

"In town?"

"No. *Here* here. Playing golf, believe it or not. He's going to meet us at the bar near the ninth hole." Metcalf handed the phone back to the manager. "Did you know?"

"Not at all. I was merely calling him as a courtesy to let him know you were asking about him."

Lynch looked outside. "How do we get to the ninth hole bar?"

The manager made a sweeping motion toward the outer doors. "There's a golf cart just outside. I'll take you there myself."

"CURB SERVICE. I love it!"

Kendra immediately recognized the bride's father from the video. He now wore a white goatee on his broad face, and he was dressed in white slacks and a green plaid golf shirt. He stood in front of the open-air bar, where several other men were seated at square tables centered by umbrellas. He shook each of their hands. "John Hollingsworth, pleased to meet you." He patted the manager on the back. "Thank you, Patrick."

Patrick was obviously in no hurry to leave, but he took the hint and reluctantly climbed back in the golf cart. He still sat there for a long moment as Hollingsworth motioned for the investigators to join him at one of the outdoor tables several yards away.

"I would ask you to join me for a Bloody Mary, but seeing as you're all on the clock . . ." Hollingsworth took a large swig of his drink. "Lovely day, isn't it? I don't believe I've ever had a visit from the FBI before. Now the SEC is a different matter. I'm certain you'll be much more intriguing."

Kendra couldn't stand any more small talk. "Mr. Hollingsworth, does the name Elena Meyer mean anything to you?"

"No. Should it?"

Metcalf pulled up her photo on his tablet. Probably her driver's license photo, Kendra guessed. "How about now?"

"Sorry." Hollingsworth shrugged. "Pretty girl, though."

"She's dead."

Hollingsworth looked up. "What?"

"She was killed the night before last on a street in downtown San Diego," Kendra said. "Are you sure you don't know her?"

Hollingsworth took a closer look at the photo. "Positive. That's terrible. What makes you think that I—?"

Metcalf was already swiping his fingers across the tablet. "She was carrying a video. It may be what got her killed. Take a look." He once again turned the tablet in Hollingsworth's direction.

The man's eyes widened. "That's my daughter's wedding reception."

"Then is it possible your daughter knew the victim?" Kendra asked.

"I . . . don't know. Even if she did, I'm almost positive this woman wasn't at the wedding."

"We don't think she was either," Kendra said. "But there was something about this video that was very important to her. We're not sure what that could be. Do you think your daughter can help us?"

Hollingsworth seemed baffled. "I'm sure she'll do whatever she can. But I have a feeling she'll be as confused as I am."

Metcalf pulled out his well-worn pocket notebook. "What's your daughter's name?

"Elizabeth. Elizabeth Gelson. She and her husband live in Escondido."

"Where does she work?" Kendra asked.

"She works for a lab. Sennett Laboratories, downtown."

"Is she there now?"

Hollingsworth pulled out his phone. "I can find out." He punched a number and after a moment he spoke. "Elizabeth Gelson, please."

A look of concern crossed his face as he listened. "This is her father. Do you know where I can find her?"

After another long moment he cut the connection.

"What is it?" Kendra asked.

"She hasn't shown up yet. Her assistant said she's actually missed a meeting and they haven't been able to reach her." He checked his watch. "She should have been there an hour and a half ago. I'll try her cell." He punched another number and listened. After a few moments, he put down his phone. "Voicemail. This isn't like her."

"Does she have a home phone?" Kendra asked.

"No. She and her husband just use their cells. I would call him, but he's in China on business." Hollingsworth stood up. He was still frowning. "Shit. Is there something you're not telling me? Some reason I should be worried?"

"Nothing we know about," Kendra said gently.

"You'd probably say that anyway. Why else are you here? For God's sake, you just told me that some woman was murdered who had my daughter's video. That's not supposed to make me feel panicky? Liz is my only child." Hollingsworth wiped perspiration from his upper lip. "I'm going to her house. I need to know she's okay."

Lynch got to his feet. "Mind if we follow you?"

Hollingsworth shrugged. "You'll have to keep up. I plan on breaking every speed limit until I hear from her."

"Not a problem," Lynch said. "Let's go."

HOLLINGSWORTH WAS TRUE to his word as he led them on a thirty-minute ride to the suburb of Escondido that should have taken closer to forty. Lynch and Kendra followed close behind with Metcalf always within sight. Soon they rolled in front of a two-story stucco and clay-tile-roof home in a neighborhood of almost identical houses. They parked and met Hollingsworth in the driveway.

"I called her office three times from the road," he said jerkily. "Still no sign of her. And she's still not answering her cell." He pointed to a white Toyota RAV 4. "That's her car."

"Maybe she just got back," Metcalf offered.

Kendra shook her head. "No. We'd be hearing the clicking of engine parts dilating, like the sounds now coming from all our cars. This vehicle hasn't been driven in a while."

If Hollingsworth was already on edge, this sent him into a definite panic. He ran for the front porch, pounded on the door, and rang the doorbell. "Liz, honey? Liz? Liz!"

No answer.

Hollingsworth tried the knob. It was unlocked. He turned back to the others. "She *always* locks the door. Especially when Jeffrey isn't home."

Lynch and Metcalf both pulled out their handguns. "Stay here and let us clear the house, Mr. Hollingsworth," Lynch said. "After we've checked it out, we'll—"

Hollingsworth bolted inside.

"Or not," Metcalf said dryly. He and Lynch charged in behind him with Kendra bringing up the rear.

The front door opened directly into the living room. Kendra glanced around. Nothing remarkable there. A nice home entertainment system, karaoke microphones, and a shelf loaded with games. The couple obviously liked to entertain. The room opened into a large kitchen. Unread mail on the counter, along with . . .

"Keys, mobile phone, and purse on the island," Metcalf said.

Kendra flipped open a manila folder next to the personal items. "Notes for the morning meeting she didn't attend."

Hollingsworth swore and ran for the stairs, Lynch and Metcalf running after him with firearms still drawn.

Kendra paused on the steps before she followed them. She didn't like this.

But after their quick tour of the garage, exercise

room, master bedroom, and what appeared to be a nursery in the making, it was clear there was no one else in the house.

Hollingsworth was gazing at the colorful animals stenciled on the nursery walls. "I didn't know they were doing this yet. They didn't tell me. Guess they want it to be a surprise." He moistened his lips. "But where the *hell* is she?"

"Is there anyone in the neighborhood who could have seen something?" Metcalf asked.

"I don't know their neighbors. Jeffrey and Liz never talked about them. Maybe . . ." Hollingsworth was becoming more visibly upset by the moment. "I just . . . don't know."

"It's too early to start worrying," Metcalf said soothingly. "There could be any one of a number of explanations. But I'll get some personnel out here to start canvassing the neighbors. Maybe she's just having coffee with one of them."

Hollingsworth nodded. "I have to call her husband . . . He might know something. I'm not sure if his phone even works overseas."

"Let's do that outside," Metcalf said. "I need to get some more information about your daughter."

They walked downstairs and Metcalf and Hollingsworth stepped out the front door. Before Kendra could follow them, Lynch closed the door and then whirled back to face her.

"Okay, you're too quiet," he said curtly. "And I've seen that intent look on your face too many times to mistake it. You know something, don't you? Something you didn't want to say in front of her father."

Lynch would realize that she had been trying to hide the fear and pity she had begun to feel as she'd walked through this house. He knew her so well he could almost read her mind, damn him. Kendra nodded slowly. "I do believe it might be good to question the neighbors. But not to see if she's been over at one of their houses having a coffee klatch. Elizabeth Gelson was attacked and abducted here in her home this morning, sometime in just the past few hours. We need to look for a silver full-size van or SUV."

Lynch stared at her. "A silver full-size— Okay, you're going to have to walk me through this one."

Kendra led Lynch back to the kitchen area. "It happened here. She was about to eat her breakfast when a person—or persons—barged in. There was a scuffle and they subdued her. They dragged her through this door to the garage and put her in the van, then quickly cleaned up in here. They didn't want to arouse suspicion."

Lynch smiled. "Interesting. Go on. You know how much I like watching you do your thing."

"Can we not do this now?"

His smile disappeared as he saw her expression. "Sorry. Hey, I know these are always real people to you.

I'm just a callous bastard who's been at this so long I sometimes forget the human element and get intrigued by the process." He wrinkled his nose. "It might be a form of self-protection. Go ahead. I'll be good."

"Good? That would be too much of a strain for you. But maybe you're not so callous." Kendra walked toward the kitchen dinette table. "There's a sticky patch on the floor. I heard it when Metcalf stepped on it when we were here before."

"I didn't hear anything."

"Yes, you did. You just weren't listening."

"You keep telling me that and I still don't believe you."

"It's true. You made the sound yourself less than thirty seconds ago when your left shoe stepped on the spot." Kendra kneeled on the floor. "Orange juice residue. But there's no dirt visible, so it obviously happened recently."

"She could have just had a spill. No altercation necessary."

"Her breakfast cereal was also all over this floor."

"More sticky sounds?"

"No. A faint odor of sour milk, but not so sour that it's been here for more than a couple hours. I picked it up as soon as we hit the front door. In the garage, there's a damp mop with these very odors on it. And if you look along the baseboard, you'll see broken shards that match the bowls and juice glasses on those shelves. There's no liner in that trash can, leading me to believe that they took the pieces with them. This table was moved. Notice that it's a little cockeyed, totally out of character with every other piece of furniture we've seen in this house."

"Okay. Very good. But why a silver van?"

Kendra motioned for him to follow her out into the garage where she hit a switch that opened the large roll-up door. The bottom of the door stopped about a foot from the top.

"Just what I thought," she said. "Not a problem for a normal-sized car, but it's low enough to clip a van or SUV."

"How do you know it was silver?"

"Look at the bottom of that door. It scraped some paint. Recently. That's fresh. You can see it even with the garage door closed."

"Well, maybe *you* can."

"You saw it too. You just weren't looking."

He sighed. "Damn, I knew you were going to say that."

Lynch walked over to the open garage door and inspected it. "You think they brought her out through the garage because it would be too easy to spot them otherwise?"

"With houses this close together, a weekday morning when people are heading out to work and school . . . The garage seems like the way to go, unless they're willing to risk half a dozen 911 calls from neighbors.

And since they took the time to clean the kitchen, it seems like they were trying to be careful."

"I agree." Lynch gazed at the silver paint. "We should get the forensics lab out here to take some scrapings. They might be able to match this paint to a specific make and model."

Kendra stared at Metcalf and Hollingsworth at the end of the driveway. He was right. It was time to bring out forensics and put the full force of the FBI toward finding Hollingsworth's daughter. She had just wanted to give him a chance to pull himself together before she told Metcalf that he'd have to tell Hollingsworth what she'd observed. Metcalf was a nice guy, he'd be gentle. But how could you tell a father that his life had changed when the FBI had driven up in a golf cart on this sunny day and asked a few questions that caused a darkness to appear on his horizon? "Why? Why did this happen? It's too much of a coincidence. First Elena Meyer and now Elizabeth Gelson?" She shook her head in frustration. "And I'm still no closer to finding out who Elena Meyer was and why she died on that street trying to get to me."

"You *are* closer," Lynch said. "We don't even know if Elizabeth Gelson is dead or not. A kidnapping isn't murder so don't bundle them together. And you're not responsible for either one anyway. Stop being impatient. You're just not seeing the big picture yet."

She grimaced. "It sounds like you're trying to use my words against me."

"It's the truth. You've already gathered a lot of pieces of the puzzle. Pieces no one else could have found. And I know we'll find more."

"We?" She turned toward him in surprise. "The FBI's contracted you to work this case?"

He chuckled. "Oh, no. Griffin can't afford to pay my rate just to work a homicide investigation."

"Then why are you here?"

Lynch shrugged.

"Seriously," she said. "Why are you here? Shouldn't you be smuggling a scientist out of Russia or trying to ferret out a spy at some foreign embassy?"

He smiled. "Why would I want to do anything so boring when I could be here with you?"

She looked away from him. "You think I need a bodyguard?"

"Well, I haven't shown you how to successfully break your attacker's wrists yet."

"I have Metcalf. He has a gun, you know."

"Mine's bigger."

"Oh brother . . ."

"And I'm a much better shot than he is."

"So that's why you're hanging around?"

Lynch smiled. "No."

"Then why?"

"For someone with such remarkable powers of observation, you can be incredibly obtuse sometimes."

"Ah. You want to stick around so you can bust my chops."

"Well, I do thoroughly enjoy that."

"Obviously. Anything else?"

"You called me," he said simply. "It was too promising. Until I find out the real reason, I have to stick around and see if a promise can become reality. I'm betting it can."

She was suddenly having trouble breathing. "Yeah, sure."

He placed a finger under her chin and gently raised her head to face him. "So defensive. Who knows? I might have stayed with the Bureau forever if someone like you had been around to keep me entertained."

"No, you wouldn't have. You have to work for yourself. You need the option of walking away when the higher-ups get too stupid or annoying."

"True." He paused. "But I'd never walk away from you."

She couldn't look away from him. That intensity and charisma was overpowering. He was totally enigmatic and she was never sure whether or not to believe him. But in this moment, she did believe him. Or was it only because she so desperately wanted to believe what he was saying to her? Either way it could be dangerous to her. There had to be a reason why she had walked away from him after that last case and buried herself in her work. She tore her gaze away from him. "Really? You'll have to tell me how many times you've said that to a woman. Seeing that you've had practically a harem, it—"

Lynch's phone buzzed in his pocket.

He grimaced. "I should know better than to mix business with the personal. I'll discuss that nasty charge later." He fished his phone out and read the screen. "Elena Meyer's parents are flying in to claim her body this afternoon. Their flight lands at 4:15."

She drew a deep breath. Of course she was grateful for the distraction. It was only the sudden absence of tension that made her feel this flat. "Who sent you that text?"

"Griffin. But he actually sent the text to Metcalf."

"Then how did you—?" She rolled her eyes. "Oh, no. You hacked Metcalf's phone."

"Of course. It took me all of fifteen seconds as soon as we were within Bluetooth range of each other." He nodded toward Metcalf, who was staring at his phone at the end of the driveway. "Oh, look. He's getting the message now."

"That little trick is going to get you arrested one day."

"It already has. The president of Spain really doesn't have a sense of humor where his privacy is concerned."

"Metcalf should snap on the cuffs right now."

"He'd never do it. Not if he wants your help."

"You're assuming I'd step in on your behalf."

He asked softly, "Wouldn't you?"

She didn't look at him. "Depends on how charitable I was feeling."

Metcalf walked toward them, leaving Hollingsworth at the end of the driveway. "Elena Meyer's parents are flying in and they should—"

"Four-fifteen, we know," Lynch said.

"How in the hell—?" Metcalf looked at the phone in Lynch's hand. "Oh, man. Stop it. Right now."

"Just my way of staying in the loop."

"I'm already keeping you in the loop. Stay out of my phone, Lynch. Or I'll have to—"

Kendra interrupted, "I want to speak to her parents."

"So do we," Metcalf said. "Trust me, it'll happen even if we have to meet them at the medical examiner's office."

She grimaced. "*That* would be a fun place for the interview."

"They just lost their daughter. It won't be fun anyplace we do it."

Kendra nodded as she took one last look around the house. Had she missed anything? "Keep me posted, will you?"

"You got someplace to be?"

"A group session back at my studio." She glanced back at Hollingsworth in the driveway and felt another wave of sympathy as she saw the tension of his back and shoulders. The worst didn't always happen, she told herself. Lynch was right, the fact that Elizabeth had been taken didn't mean murder. But that wasn't going to comfort this father whose daughter had disappeared for no apparent reason. And now it was time to forget about comfort and tell him the truth. She braced herself and turned back to Metcalf. "But before I go, let me tell you why you might want to get forensics out here right away, and definitely question those neighbors to see if they can tell you anything about a silver van or SUV . . ."

CHAPTER 3

LESS THAN AN HOUR LATER, Lynch pulled up to the small medical building that housed Kendra's office. He turned to Kendra. "Can I come inside?"

"The observation booth will already be packed with parents. You don't have to stick around. I'll catch a Lyft back home."

"No. Call me instead. I'll be down the street, drinking coffee and catching up on emails. And while I'm at it, I'll check my sources and see if I can find any connections between Elena Meyer and Elizabeth Gelson."

"Sounds good. Thanks."

Kendra climbed out of the car and hurried into the building, where she knew some of her clients would already be waiting. Sure enough, Serena Davis, Tim Shales, and Haley Sims, aged nine, eleven, and seven, respectively, were waiting outside her office with their mothers.

"Ready to make some music?" Kendra said.

Only Haley responded with a weak "Yeah." As usual, none of the children made eye contact with her. They were autistic, and they were there precisely because of their difficulty connecting with others. Kendra welcomed them into her studio, a large carpeted room with a piano, a drum kit, and several other musical instruments on stands. The children went straight to their preferred instruments—the drums for Serena, a guitar for Tim, and an electronic keyboard for Haley.

Kendra made small talk with the mothers while two more children, David Gray and Vicki Misner, arrived with their parents. David picked up a bass guitar and Vicki grabbed a cowbell. Kendra nodded to the parents and they adjourned to a small observation room with a one-way glass window.

"Have you been practicing?" Kendra asked the children.

"No," Haley said listlessly. The others didn't respond.

Kendra smiled. "Points for honesty. Okay, this is all about learning to play in a band."

Vicki started striking the cowbell.

"Not yet, Vicki. Vicki?"

Vicki stopped.

"Okay," Kendra said. "There's more to being in a band than just playing your parts. You must also pay attention to what everyone else is doing. That's the most important thing. Does anyone remember why you must pay attention to each other?"

"So we can stay together and keep the sound balanced," Tim said.

Kendra knew Tim would be the one to answer, just as she knew he would answer with a word-for-word recitation of what she'd told them at their last session.

"That's right, Tim. Very good. We're going to start with 'Ob-La-Di, Ob-La-Da.' I know you guys really like that one. Let's try to stay together this time." Kendra started the time count by clapping her hands. "Ready . . . Go!"

Vicki started with the cowbell and Haley jumped in with the keyboard a measure later. A few bars after that Serena joined in on the drums and David and Tim started on the guitars.

It was probably one of the worst renditions of the song Kendra had ever heard, despite some good keyboard playing by Haley.

But it was wonderful.

Because the kids were loving it. Their smiles grew broader with each passing note. And most importantly, they were working together, accommodating each other's rhythms and dynamics.

Kendra found herself smiling as broadly as any of the kids. These children had difficulty communicating on any level, but maybe, through music, she'd helped them crack open a door. There were weeks and months of work ahead, but if this could help them connect with the world around them, it would be worth it.

She'd needed this, she realized. At that moment the horror of the murdered and missing women were a million miles away. Here, in this room, there was only joy.

And hope.

ONE HOUR AND SEVEN similarly mangled pop classics later, Kendra said good-bye to the children and their parents. It was a good day and everyone knew it. She watched them through the tall glass windows of her building corridor. They seemed happy as they piled into their minivans.

"That was beautiful." Lynch's voice.

She turned to see him standing in the hall behind her.

"Where did you come from?" she asked. "I thought you were going to get coffee."

"Changed my mind."

"So where have you been?"

He pointed to the outer doorway to her observation room. "Watching you."

"After I told you to go away?"

"I entered from out here. The parents were very accommodating. They made room for me. Nice people."

She clicked her tongue. "Too nice, obviously."

"Sorry, I couldn't help myself." He grinned. "I love watching you work."

"The kids were doing all the work."

"No, the kids were having a blast. And believe me so were their parents. I can understand why you wouldn't want to leave this behind."

She stiffened at the thought. "And I never will."

"You shouldn't. You're breaking new ground here. How often does anyone get to do that?"

She smiled. "When I see it working, there's nothing better."

"I can see that. You're positively . . . luminous."

She instinctively looked away. "Yeah, sure."

He leaned toward her. "And that shouldn't make you uncomfortable."

"It doesn't."

"Yes, it does. With one glance you pick up just about all there is to know about everyone you meet. But you hate it when you give away anything about yourself. Even if it's something kind of wonderful."

She was about to argue, but she stopped herself. "I guess I just like to be in control of what I choose to share. You should identify with that, you're into control in a big way, Lynch."

"Guilty. But sometimes it's good to let go."

"I did that a lot back in my wild days right after I got my sight."

"I wish I'd known you then."

What would it have been like to have encountered Lynch during that period when she had never run across a boundary that she didn't try to break? Exciting? Breathtaking? Challenging?

Dangerous . . .

"Maybe. Maybe not. I had a lot of fun, but I was probably pretty selfish. I wanted to taste everything life had to offer."

"Then I would have shared the cup and filled it for you to the brim again. You'd earned it."

She shrugged. "That's what I told myself."

"Well, if you're worried about that rosy glow of yours making you appear too vulnerable, I've got something that will wipe it right off your face."

"Meeting a dead woman's grieving parents?"

"Yep."

"That would do it."

He raised his phone. "Metcalf sent us both a text about fifteen minutes ago. They're going straight from the airport to the medical examiner's office. We're going to meet them there."

Kendra nodded, imagining that glow he'd mentioned was fading fast. "They're making her parents come to ID the body in person?"

"No, it's their choice. They could have looked at a photo, but they wanted to come see her and bring her home themselves."

"I can see that they would." Kendra was heading for the door. "They're probably hoping there was some mistake. It's the first thing that every parent thinks when it's their child that's been taken. That it couldn't happen to them and their family." She added wearily, "I wish they were right this time."

IT TOOK THEM THIRTY MINUTES to get to the medical examiner's office, and as they pulled into the parking lot, Kendra registered a text from Metcalf:

ID made, now's the time. Conference Room #1.

Kendra grabbed the passenger door handle. "Let's go."

They entered the building and took the stairs up one floor to the administrative offices. Then they made their way to a small conference room at the end of the corridor. Metcalf was already seated at a long table across from the couple. He looked at them in relief as they came into the room. He might be an experienced FBI agent, but dealing with a victim's parents had always been difficult for him. All the training in the world couldn't change the fact that he hadn't been able to develop the calluses needed to keep him from empathizing. What the hell? Neither had Kendra. And one glance was all it took to see that the Meyers were far from stoic.

The man was withdrawn to the point of catatonia and the woman's face was stained by tears. Probably the absolute worst time to pry information from them, Kendra thought. She took a seat next to Metcalf. Lynch stood behind them.

Metcalf quickly made the introductions. "Keith and Cynthia Meyer, this is Kendra Michaels and Adam Lynch."

Kendra leaned toward them. "We're very sorry for your loss. We know you've already been through a lot. We'll try not to keep you any longer than absolutely necessary."

No reaction from the couple. They were probably still seeing their daughter in the morgue downstairs, Kendra thought. Like they'd ever forget it.

Metcalf broke the long moment of silence. "We have reason to believe your daughter was trying to make contact with Kendra shortly before her death. Did she ever mention the name Kendra Michaels to you?"

Keith and Cynthia shook their heads "no."

Kendra wondered if they'd even heard him. They seemed to be totally numb. "I didn't know your daughter, and I don't know how she knew me," she said gently. "But I want to help find out who did this to her. Will you help us do that?"

A single tear streamed down Keith's face as he nodded. "Whatever you need."

"Thank you," Kendra said softly. "Where did your daughter work?"

Cynthia dabbed her eyes with a crumpled tissue. "She was a paralegal. She wanted to be an attorney, but after she graduated from college she decided to get some work experience before she started law school. But the firm kept her so busy that law school never happened for her."

"Which firm?" Metcalf asked.

"Collins, Collins and Levinsky."

"It's a big firm," Keith added.

Metcalf jotted the name into his notebook. "One of the biggest. They have offices all over the world."

Keith looked up and blinked back his tears. "They really liked Elena. She was a hard worker."

"I'm sure she was," Kendra said. "She worked for them in Connecticut?"

"Yes, but she sometimes travelled for them if they were working on a big case," Cynthia said. "She was sometimes gone for weeks."

"Is that why she was here? For work?"

Cynthia shook her head. "That's what's so strange. She'd been out here for the firm a few times in the past few months, but not this time." She had to stop a moment as her voice broke. "We're her emergency contact with them and they called us Monday morning asking us how to get in touch with her. We didn't . . . even know she was gone."

"So her firm didn't know either?" Kendra asked.

"No. Not a clue." She dabbed at her damp cheek. "But they seemed awfully anxious to get in touch with her though."

Lynch took a seat next to Kendra. "Do you have any

idea what could have brought her out here? Maybe a friend she'd made or someone she was dating? Anything at all?"

"No." Keith took his wife's hand and held it tightly as if trying to share his strength with her. "She didn't especially like coming here, did she, Cynthia? She wasn't able to talk about cases she was working on, but I had a feeling she didn't like the ones she was assisting with out here."

"When was the last time you saw her?" Kendra asked.

Cynthia and Keith looked at each other for a long moment before Cynthia replied, "Sunday."

"You're sure?"

She nodded. "Elena took us to lunch."

"Was there anything unusual about her?" Metcalf asked.

"No. Nothing at all."

"Except maybe—" Keith stopped.

Kendra leaned closer. "Except what?"

"It wasn't anything really." He thought for a moment. "She squeezed tighter."

"What do you mean?" Kendra asked.

"When she hugged me goodbye, she squeezed extra tight, you know? Like she didn't want to let go."

"Unusual? She'd never done that before?" Lynch asked.

"Elena was very independent. We knew she loved us, but she wasn't demonstrative. It would take something for her to show us that she needed us. Maybe when she was having a rough time at work or problems with a guy. She never liked to talk to us about that stuff, but her daddy could tell." Keith's eyes welled with tears again. "I could always tell."

Kendra felt tears stinging her own eyes. First Hollingsworth and his missing daughter, now this couple. It had been a hell of a day.

Keith's phone buzzed and he looked at the screen. "Elena's ride is here."

"Elena's *ride*?" Kendra asked.

"Her transport to the airport. We arranged it through the funeral parlor back home." His hand tightened on his wife's. "Ready, honey?"

"You're flying home *now*?" Kendra said.

Metcalf shrugged. "The ME released the body."

"That sounds so . . . cold," Cynthia said unevenly.

"They don't mean it like that," Keith said. "They didn't know her." He looked at Kendra. "I'm sorry we couldn't help you. This has us all confused. It doesn't make any sense. If you think of anything else you need to ask, you can call us."

"I'll do that." She reached out and shook his hand. "But you can never tell what pieces will come together to make a picture. You might have told us something that will be very important. It was very kind of you to take the time."

"It wasn't easy." He swallowed and cleared his

throat. "But there must be a reason why my Elena was reaching out to you. My wife goes to church every Sunday and believes in angels and saints and all that business. I never believed in much of anything." His voice broke. "But this is all *wrong*. There has to be some reason." Keith stood up and helped Cynthia to her feet, slipping his arm around her waist to support her. "We do hope with all our hearts you find whoever did this to her," he said as he turned his wife toward the door. "But right now we just want to take our little girl home."

KENDRA WATCHED AS THE door shut behind them.

"What do you think, Lynch?" Metcalf's gaze had also been following the Meyers. "Is it Saint Kendra or just a minor angel we have in our midst?"

"What I think is that you've just made a huge gaffe," Lynch said, his gaze on Kendra's face. "Not the time, Metcalf."

"You're damn right it's not," Kendra said unsteadily. She jumped to her feet. "I've got to get out of here."

"Right." Lynch was already opening the door. "See you later, Metcalf." He followed Kendra down the steps and out the front door. "He wasn't being insensitive, you know," he said quietly. "He just doesn't have a clue on how to handle situations that emotional."

"Neither do I." Kendra was looking straight ahead as she strode toward his car. "I don't want to talk right now, Lynch."

"No problem."

Fifteen minutes and a traffic jam later, Kendra still felt sick to her stomach, waylaid by the grief and confusion she'd seen in that conference room. She slumped in the passenger seat of Lynch's car, her gaze fixed on the traffic up ahead. "How do you do it?"

"Do what?"

"Sit there talking to people on the worst days of their lives without falling apart yourself? I'm amazed at the way you and Metcalf were able to hold yourselves together."

"So did you."

"Barely."

"But you did it. Because you know you're not helping these people if you can't hold it together. Metcalf and I feel the same way."

"It seems . . . *easier* for you."

"It probably is. I suppose I've built up some emotional calluses in the past few years. That's what happens when you watch enough friends die right in front of you, especially when you feel there was more you could have done to save them."

"That's horrible."

"It was. And still is, no matter how many years go by. But everyone faces grief and loss. It's just life."

There was something deeper, something below the surface of that philosophic statement that aroused her curiosity. Kendra let a moment pass before wading into a territory she knew might be uncomfortable for Lynch. "You've lost someone closer than just a friend haven't you?"

He kept his eyes on the road. "Who told you?"

"No one told me anything. I don't ask questions about you. I would never interfere with your business. I don't know why that question popped out. If you'd rather not talk about it—"

"I'd rather not. At least not right now, okay?"

She studied Lynch. However stoic he may have been with Elena Meyer's parents, this was another matter entirely. She couldn't recall ever seeing him so troubled, so sad.

"Okay. As I said, it's not my business. I'm sorry that I asked."

"I'm not." He smiled. "I like the idea of you delving into all my secrets. But I protect them well and I have to warn you that when you delve too deep, you might run across a trap or two. On the other hand, traps, if properly constructed, can be entertaining."

"That sounds like far too much trouble. I'll just muzzle any curiosity I have," she said wearily. "I wouldn't have asked you anything if I hadn't been a little shaken up about that interview with the Meyers. One thing led to another."

"Yes, it did." He was gazing at her face. "And you still don't look in great shape. I'll take you home. You can probably use the rest."

Home.

We just want to take our little girl home.

"Kendra?"

She slowly shook her head. "Actually . . . I'd rather you drop me somewhere else, if that's okay."

1412 Sundance Place
La Jolla, California

This was probably a mistake, Kendra thought as she pressed the doorbell. She should have called ahead instead of just having Lynch bring her here. It wasn't as if she could expect—

The door was thrown open and her mother stared at her with a frown. "What the hell are you doing here, Kendra? What's wrong?"

"Nothing, Mom." She should definitely have called ahead, Kendra thought ruefully. Her mother was a highly regarded professor at UC San Diego, and she was as busy as Kendra with her classes and extracurricular activities. It was a miracle that she'd even caught her at home. "I was in the neighborhood and I thought I'd take a chance on you being here. Want to give me a cup of tea?" She smiled as she looked her mother up and down. Dr. Deanna Michaels was barefoot and wearing tights and a black exercise tank that made her look vigorous and youthful and more like Kendra's sister than her mother. "No classes today?"

"One at eight this evening." She was still frowning. "You're never in the neighborhood unless you plan to be. And you always call me."

"Does that mean I can't come in?" Kendra asked solemnly. "Did I interrupt something . . . interesting? You don't look as if you're dressed to receive masculine company."

"I was on my Pilates machine." She opened the door wider. "But I guess I can spare the time to give you a cup of tea." She looked over her shoulder with a grin. "And haven't I taught you never to take anything for granted? In this day and age a gymnasium can be as exciting as any bedroom. But as it happens, I prefer to compartmentalize." She padded barefoot to her library, which was the center of her living space. It was also Kendra's favorite space in her mother's house. The stucco bungalow was barely medium sized with a red-tiled roof and appeared vaguely Spanish to blend with the other houses in the neighborhood. Deanna had bought it because the gardens surrounding it were overflowing with fragrant flowers. But she'd made the interior completely different, and it might have been mistaken for an English country house. And this room had always been special to Kendra. She had known every inch of it by heart. Bookshelves filled with leather-bound books, a stone fireplace, French doors that led out to a charming small verandah. Over the years this had been a library filled with students, professors, celebrity guest lecturers, and all of them had been perfectly at home here. Because Deanna's charm and enthusiasm had drawn them to her and made them feel as if this was *their* home. "I like this room."

"I know you do." Her mother was standing at the serving cabinet choosing which tea to put in the beautifully crafted Yixing teapot. "You always did. Even when you were blind, you always liked to feel the leather covers of the books in your hands. Braille can be wonderful, but it lacks the ambience of a well-worn book." She put the chosen tea into the pot. "And then there was the feel of the fire, the scent of smoke and wood, and crackle of the burning logs. All very sensory . . ."

"Yes." And Kendra could remember when she was a little girl sitting cuddled with her mother in that leather chair by the fire while she read to her, surrounded by scents and textures and her mother's soft voice making the stories come alive. Making certain that Kendra didn't miss one bit of the experience because of the darkness. Memories . . . "I'm glad you kept the house after I left home. I thought you might find it more convenient to move closer to the university once I was off your hands."

"Why on Earth would I do that? This is my home.

Convenience doesn't replace what I have here." She was pouring hot water from the electric tea kettle over the tea. "I'll never get rid of it." She slanted Kendra a smile. "I can't tell when you might be in the neighborhood and want to drop in for a cup of tea. One must provide for the needs of one's daughter."

"You always did." Kendra dropped down in the chair beside Deanna's exquisite card table that she'd purchased in an antiques store in London when she'd taken Kendra for her stem cell operation. The top was painted with a landscape of an old castle surrounded by flowers that were blowing in the wind. Her mother had usually been careful to make certain any furniture she chose had carving or raised art work, but she'd deliberately not done it on that trip. She'd told Kendra that wasn't going to be necessary any longer, that she had faith that the operation would work and Kendra would be able to see. But Kendra must also have faith.

And so it had come to be. Kendra's index finger gently outlined the smooth turret of the castle.

"Wake up, Kendra. Help me with this." Her mother was standing beside the table with the tray in her hands. "You take the cups."

"Sorry." Kendra quickly took the cups, saucers, and napkins. "You usually like to do everything yourself."

"Because I do it so well." Deanna poured the tea. "But I wanted to give you your tea so that you wouldn't have an excuse to avoid my questions." She sat down opposite Kendra. "Now tell me why you're here. What's wrong?"

"What a suspicious woman you are." She lifted her cup to her lips. Lychee Black from Ceylon, she identified as the scent swept over her. Her mother knew she'd always loved it. "Why would you think that?"

"You didn't happen to be in the neighborhood. Your car wasn't out front. Who brought you?"

"Lynch dropped me off."

"Lynch?" Deanna went still. "You haven't seen him for a while. Why now?"

"Why not?" She shrugged. "He was teaching me some martial arts moves. No one's better at that than Lynch."

"I'm certain that no one is better at making any kind of moves on you than Lynch," her mother said dryly. "As you know, my attitude toward him is ambivalent. He's a very dangerous man. His only saving grace is that there are times when that's been a plus where you were concerned. Why didn't you invite him in? I wouldn't have bitten him."

"I didn't feel like it." She took a sip of her tea. "Lynch tends to dominate and for once I wanted to relax here with you. I'll take a Lyft back to my condo. Now tell me what you've been doing."

"After you tell me what *you've* been doing," Deanna said. She was gazing at her probingly. "Other than karate moves. A new case? Interesting?"

Kendra nodded slowly. "It's hard to tell. But you might say that it had my name on it. The victim was trying to reach me when she was killed."

Deanna frowned again. "I don't like that."

"Neither do I. That's why I'm involved." She changed the subject. "But let's not talk about that. Let me tell you about the breakthrough with my autistic kids this afternoon . . ."

Yes, talk about triumphs and hope and remember all the joys that she had experienced with her mother through the years. No one could have been a stronger or more loving mother than Deanna. Kendra wanted to reach out, touch her, and relive those years that had bound them together in the darkness and in the light.

As Elena Meyer must have felt when she'd left her parents that last time.

And, like Elena, before Kendra walked out that door today she was going to take her mother in her arms and hold her very, very tight . . .

THE SUN WAS GOING DOWN when Kendra left her mother's house and got into the Lyft car that would take her back to her condo. She tried to settle back and relax but that wasn't going to happen. Olivia was right, she was always on edge when she was on a case. The only respite she'd had was working with her kids today. Being with her mom had been good, but even with her, Kendra had been aware of a constant wariness. Forget it. She was going home. She'd take a hot shower and maybe that would help her unwind. However, she was only halfway home before her phone rang.

Lynch.

"I'm on my way home, Lynch," she said as she accessed the call. "I told you I didn't need you to pick me up. It's not as if I can't take care of myself."

"Don't shoot the messenger. I'd never interfere with your personal space . . . well, almost never. I just received a call from Deanna and she raked me over the coals. Evidently you were too uncommunicative about this case for her taste. By the time she got through with me, she knew everything that you'd been dodging all afternoon."

Kendra muttered a curse. "And you had to spill every detail. You told me once you had to withstand torture on some of your jobs for Justice. And you couldn't hold out against my mom?"

"I could. But that would make my relationship with her harder. I'm already walking on eggshells around her. I have to pick my battles." He paused. "Besides, I took the heat off you. She would have kept digging until she had the entire story. Now she does and she believes she's done as much as she can toward solving the problem."

"Just by putting you through a third degree?" she asked warily.

"No, by giving me orders that I'm to make certain

that nothing of which she would not approve happens to you. I humbly acceded to all demands." He chuckled. "She really is remarkable, isn't she?"

"Of course she is," she said tartly. "She took care of a special child and made every day of my life an adventure. That takes more guts and ingenuity than you can dream."

"And she's still trying to take care of that special child," Lynch said quietly. "I don't mind being appointed deputy, Kendra."

"Well, I do mind. I'm sorry she went after you with guns blazing. I didn't handle it well."

"I'm not sorry. I regard it as an opportunity. By the time we have this case sorted out, Deanna will be considering me not only an asset but totally irreplaceable." He paused. "And we both know that you weren't thinking of anything but what happened at that medical examiner's office today. That's why I didn't ask you any questions when you asked me to drop you off." He added teasingly, "I looked upon it as you going back to the womb."

"Ugh. What a disgusting observation. And Mom would definitely give you a failing grade if she heard it."

"I can take it. Now, get something to eat and go to bed. Deanna said she only gave you tea while you were with her."

"And are you also in charge of nutrition?"

"I believe that may be included under the deputy

bylaws. We'll discuss it when I pick you up in the morning. Goodnight, Kendra." He cut the connection.

She slipped her phone back in her pocket. She should have known that Deanna would make a move as soon as she had left the house. Her mother was too intelligent not to realize that Kendra was upset and did not wish to discuss the reason. So she had spent the hours in casual conversation and let Kendra relax and have that time she needed. She had probably been plotting and planning all afternoon what her next course of action would be.

And she had settled on Lynch.

There was no use confronting her mother directly. It would only cause a brouhaha; Deanna had already made her play and would not back down. Lynch would probably not either since he had made up his mind there would be some benefit to him.

So she would just ignore both of them and go her own way. Let them plot and scheme all they pleased. She was still the "special" individual her mother had loved and nurtured all these years, but she was no longer a child. They would have to learn that a woman could be just as special and also run her own life.

But taking a suggestion or two would do no harm.

Because she suddenly realized she was perfectly ravenous. As soon as she got back to the condo, she would go rummage in the kitchen and see what she could raid in the refrigerator.

* * *

SHE CLIMBED OUT OF THE Lyft car with her house keys in her hand only a short time later. She quickly strode the short distance from the curb to the building's vestibule and front door.

But her path was suddenly crossed by a French bulldog on a leash, cutting her off. An elderly woman was walking the animal and as she moved past, the leash's retractable cord sliced across Kendra's hand.

"Ow!" Kendra stepped back, but the woman continued briskly on her way. Rude, Kendra thought with annoyance. She was all for age having privileges, but the woman should also realize she still had responsibilities. That leash had *stung*. Kendra looked at her wrist. There was a red line, and after a few seconds she realized the skin had been broken.

Dammit! Kendra looked down the street to call after her.

The woman and her dog were gone.

Where in the hell had they—?

Kendra's mouth went dry and her eyes stung.

She couldn't breathe.

What in the hell was happening?

Her legs buckled.

No!

She fell to the sidewalk. Her chest felt like it was exploding.

She lay there for a long moment, trying to get up the strength to stand. It wasn't working. She was only getting weaker.

Her phone. She needed her phone.

She jammed her fingers into her pocket, but she couldn't get the leverage she needed. It was getting harder to breathe.

She looked up next to the door, at her building's directory. She reached up. Could she make it?

It wasn't going to be easy. Hard. So hard.

She forced herself to scoot up the wall.

She was panting as she stretched her fingers toward the intercom buttons.

Her vision blurred slightly.

Just a few more inches . . .

She punched the button next to the first familiar name she saw.

"Olivia . . ."

Had she punched the right one?

Oh, no, she thought in a panic. She was falling again. losing consciousness.

"Olivia . . ."

FLASHES OF LIGHT.

Loud voices.

An antiseptic smell.

That smell . . .

She was in a hospital. A hospital? How had she—?

Olivia was there, she realized, frantically answering questions practically shouted at her by a doctor as they moved down a long hallway. Kendra knew she must be on a gurney, but she felt like she was gliding on air.

Olivia was so scared . . .

Kendra was straining to tell her that she was awake again. That was good, wasn't it?

But she still couldn't speak. Not so good . . .

The voices and sounds around her grew less distinct until they blended together into a low din.

Then they were gone.

CHAPTER 4

"KENDRA?"

She snapped awake. Her head was throbbing, but at least there was none of the fuzziness she'd felt before.

"Kendra?"

She turned in her hospital bed. It was Lynch, standing over her with an odd expression on his face. Fear. But Lynch was never afraid. Perhaps it was the sunlight streaming in through the windows behind him that made it seem that way.

Sunlight.

"It's light outside," she said.

He smiled. "Happens that way pretty much every morning. Strange, I know."

"But it was getting dark . . ." Her throat was so dry

that she could barely get the words out. "Water," she said hoarsely. "Please. I'm dying of thirst."

"Wait for the doctor. I sent the nurse after him as soon as I saw you stirring."

Kendra glanced around the small room. "Olivia. I thought Olivia was with me."

"She was very much with you. Practically joined at the hip. She's getting something to eat. I had to throw her out. She'll be furious that she missed you waking up. She probably saved your life, you know."

"I don't know much of anything. Scared. I remember she was scared. Everything else is kind of a blur." Kendra raised her hand to her throbbing head. "What in the hell happened to me?"

"I thought you could tell us. You absorbed a poison through that wound on your arm."

"Wound?" Kendra looked at her left arm, which was now bandaged.

"Did someone stab or slice you with a knife?"

"No, not at all. I don't see how—" Then she remembered. "Wait, it wasn't a knife. Something else."

"Then what was it?"

"A French bulldog."

"Okay, you have to be delirious. You just accused a French bulldog of poisoning you."

"Not a bulldog . . . A leash." Kendra thought for a moment, trying to pierce the haze. "He was being walked on a leash and crossed in front of me. The leash sliced into my arm. I thought it was strange because they weren't moving that fast. I remember being pissed off because they didn't even stop. I thought it was rude."

Lynch took a moment to process the information. "Maybe it wasn't a normal dog leash."

"Seriously?" She shook her head. "That's a bit cloak and dagger, isn't it?"

"No more than a poison-tipped cane being used to kill a Russian defector on London Bridge. I'm sure you saw the headlines about *that.* Trust me, reality has a way of catching up with the most outrageous fantasies."

"Well, this isn't one of my fantasies. And why me?"

Lynch shrugged. "Why is it *ever* you? Someone obviously perceives you as a threat."

She smiled with an effort. "I guess this now makes *twenty-seven* attempts on my life?"

"Hmm." He reached down and took her hand. "Might be a little difficult learning how to break a French bulldog's wrists. The Humane Society might get involved."

"I don't blame the dog. It looked very sweet. But if I could get my hands on that little old lady . . ."

"Little old lady? You didn't mention that. We'll have to get a description from you. Griffin will probably have footage from every traffic cam, web cam, and ATM in your neighborhood by the end of the day."

"Good. But if she's at the level where she's using devices like that dog leash, she might be clever enough to cover her tracks."

"You never know."

She gazed at him suspiciously. "You don't believe me, do you?"

"Sure I do. Bulldogs. Little old ladies. I'll take anything you throw at me." His hand tightened on her own. "Anything. Whether it's true or just a figment of that poison. I'm just glad you're still around to come up with something this inventive."

"It *is* true, Lynch."

He leaned toward her and said softly, "Then I'll fight and make certain everyone else believes you, too."

Kendra couldn't look away from him. "Thank you," she said awkwardly. Then she forced herself to look down at her bandaged arm. "But why not just pick me off with a rifle? Wouldn't that have been easier?"

"Not nearly as subtle," a voice spoke from the hallway.

Kendra looked over to see a strikingly handsome man in a coat and tie standing in the doorway. Her eyes widened. Tall, powerful, with almost perfect features, he might have been the most stunning man she had ever seen.

"Sorry for interrupting." He entered the room. "I couldn't help but overhear your conversation. Mind if I join in?" He sat down on the foot of her bed, facing both Kendra and Lynch.

She gave him a startled glance and moved her feet. "Make yourself comfortable."

"Thanks, but these hospital beds obviously aren't made for comfort." He looked around. "So when is breakfast served around here?"

This encounter was getting very weird indeed. "No idea," Kendra said. "We may have already missed it."

"Too bad, but the commissary is pretty good here. I might be able to bring you something." He looked between Kendra and Lynch. "Don't mind me. Please continue your conversation."

Enough. Kendra had been so stunned by those extraordinary good looks that she had felt a little bemused. But this was all too bizarre. "Don't take this the wrong way . . . but who in the hell are you?"

"Oops." The man grimaced. "Sorry. I forget that you might not feel as close to me as I do to you. I spent hours in here keeping an eye on you after I told them what they had to do to fix you." He nodded at Lynch. "Over to you."

Lynch shook his head. "I was wondering when you'd get around to behaving normally, Fletcher. You might remember Kendra is already feeling a little dizzy." He made the introductions. "Kendra Michaels, this is Dr. Alan Fletcher."

She looked at him with alarm. "He's my doctor?"

Fletcher winced. "You don't have to say it like *that*."

"Not really your doctor," Lynch said. "Fletcher is an old friend of mine. He works out of the Naval Medical Center. When it became obvious that your affliction was out of the ordinary, I brought him in to consult with the doctors here."

"And they *loved* that," Fletcher said sarcastically. "But you were smart to call me. I'm far better than they are."

Kendra smiled. "With an attitude like that, how could the doctors here *not* love working with you?"

Fletcher shrugged. "Go figure, huh?"

Lynch dropped down in a low chair beside the bed. "We were just discussing why someone would choose this method of attack. Kendra says that slice came from a dog leash of all things. Strange way to try to kill someone."

Fletcher nodded. "Actually, I don't believe anyone wanted her dead."

"How can you say that?" Lynch said. "Two different doctors told me that she almost died."

"Oh, that's correct."

"Then why do you say—"

"It's a chemical called Tribuxin. It's absorbed into the bloodstream very quickly, which is why it affected you immediately. The symptoms are lethargy, extreme nausea, headaches, and can continue for days afterward. But it's almost never fatal. You happened to have an extreme allergic reaction that very few people in the population have."

"Lucky me."

"Well, your allergy did serve a good purpose. We

would've had no idea you'd been attacked, which was probably the plan. But your mysterious illness would have put you out of commission. Is there anyone who would want to do that?"

"The million-dollar question," Lynch said. He turned to Kendra. "Looks like you're back to twenty-six."

Fletcher wrinkled his brow. "Twenty-six what?"

"Twenty-six attempts on my life," Kendra said.

He stared at her, intrigued. "Popular lady."

"It was over a four-year period."

"Oh. Well, then. Nothing to be concerned about." Fletcher thought for moment. "So someone wants you out of commission but doesn't want to make it obvious that's what they're doing. If they had their way, you would think you were waylaid by a stomach flu."

"And not instigating a manhunt for an old lady and a French bulldog," Kendra said.

"Lynch tells me you're investigating a case right now. Assuming this is connected to that one, you're up against someone who is incredibly sophisticated. It's like nothing I've ever seen before."

"I can't say that I regard the bulldog as much in the sophisticate department," Lynch said. "But trust me, Fletcher has seen it all. He's consulted with the CDC on many of their most unusual cases." His voice lowered melodramatically. "Ones that neither of us are allowed to talk about."

Fletcher shrugged. “Unless I’m plied with generous quantities of Don Julio Real Tequila. In which case I’ll tell you whatever you want to know.”

Kendra shook her head wearily. “Unfortunately, you can’t tell me the one thing I want to know.”

“Who did this to you?”

“Yes.”

“No, but I’ll work with the FBI and everyone else to try and figure that out.” He suddenly smiled and those remarkably handsome features lit with warmth. “Trust me, I’m unbelievably good at this stuff.”

She couldn’t help but smile back at him. “There’s that modesty again.”

“You don’t want a modest doctor, Kendra. A modest plumber or a modest landscaper maybe, but not a modest doctor. Was the doctor who gave you your sight a modest man?”

“Actually, no. Charles Waldridge was extraordinary and he knew it.”

“Of course he knew it.” Fletcher patted her blanketed feet. “So I guess I should ask how you’re feeling. But of course I know that already just from talking to you. A lesser doctor might not be able to read all the nuances, but you can see that I just might be as extraordinary as your Charles Waldridge and therefore not subject to the burdens of inadequacy.”

“Ask her anyway, Fletcher,” Lynch said dryly. “She

has a headache and she doesn't need to wade through your ego for solutions."

"Oh, very well. How do you feel, Kendra?"

She thought about it. "Surprisingly good. And my headache is almost gone."

"The headache is a side effect of the medication they gave you."

"But I'm terribly thirsty. Lynch wouldn't let me drink anything until you showed up."

"How cruel of him. I've always thought he was a bit sadistic. I, on the other hand, am your savior. By all means drink." He got to his feet and went to the bedside table and held a straw to her mouth while she drank a cup of water. "Better?"

"Heaven. And my head feels even better now that my throat doesn't feel like a desert."

He gave her a little more water. "It should go away entirely in the next few hours."

"Good." She turned to Lynch. "Because I want to visit the law offices where Elena Meyer worked when she was out here. We need to find out what she was working on. Maybe we can go after lunch."

Fletcher raised his hands. "Whoa whoa whoa."

Kendra turned toward him. "I don't like the sound of that."

"They're going to want to keep you here for observation for at least another night."

"Overnight? No thanks. I'll sign the DAMA form."

Fletcher rolled his eyes. "I know a patient is trouble when they actually know that acronym. Do you know what Discharge Against Medical Advice means? It means you're leaving when a medical professional says it's in your best interest to stay put. Not smart."

"What's your advice?" Lynch said.

"Listen to the doctors here."

"But you've already told us they're not as good as you," Kendra said slyly.

"Very few doctors are. They can't help that. But if they want you to stay, it's for a reason. Make sure there are no more reactions to the poison or the medication. You've already shown one unexpected allergic reaction. If you have another, this is the best place for you."

Lynch turned to Kendra. "The man makes a good point."

"Don't tell me that. If this had happened to you, you would have been out that door already."

"Probably. But I don't always show the best judgment where my health is concerned."

"That's for sure," Fletcher said. "Has he told you about the four days he refused to see a doctor in Qatar?"

"We don't need to talk about that," Lynch said.

Fletcher stood and jerked his thumb at Lynch. "He almost lost a leg. So I can understand if you don't take medical advice from him. But you can take it from me. Go online, make calls, do whatever you want. But don't leave this hospital today."

She turned to Lynch. "We're getting out of here, right?"

"No. Olivia knows you too well. She's already taken your phone, keys, cash, and credit cards. You'll have a tough time going anywhere right now."

She grimaced. "I'm surrounded by traitors."

"No, just by people who care about you," Lynch said quietly.

"Ah, the dispute is settled." Fletcher smiled. "Nice to meet you, Kendra. Now I have to get back and make rounds at my own hospital. It might be best for us both if you didn't share with your doctors how I told you I'm so much better than they are."

"You mean you didn't tell them that yourself?"

"I'm sure they could tell on their own after observing my technique. No need to rub it in." He gave Lynch a salute and walked out of the room.

After Kendra knew he was out of earshot, she turned back to Lynch. "He's extremely good looking. Almost distractingly so."

"You noticed that, huh?"

"Hard to miss."

"I knew that's how you would probably react, but I called him in anyway. He really is the best physician around. I would listen to him when he says you should stay here tonight."

She leaned back in her bed. "Okay, one night. But first thing tomorrow, I want to go to that law firm."

"Deal. I'll take you there myself." He sat down again. "In the meantime, I'll sit here with you until you go to sleep. It won't be long."

"Yes, it will. I just woke up."

He shook his head. "Drugs will sneak up and ambush you. I'll give you another fifteen minutes."

"Then you should leave and go do something else. You've already wasted enough time on me. It must have been excruciatingly boring."

"Excruciating." His lips tightened. "Not boring. I'm looking forward to just sitting here and looking at your face and not wondering if the machines will signal a code blue on you at any moment."

She went still. "It was that close?"

"Close enough." Then he smiled. "Which is why I have to stand here and keep you from leaping out of that bed before Olivia gets in to see you. I only got to be here when you woke because I pulled rank on her. I managed to produce Fletcher, who undoubtedly saved your life, and she owed me."

"Then go get her now. I want to see her."

He shook his head. "She's down in the cafeteria. You might be asleep by the time I got back with her. I'll risk making her wait, as long as she knows I kept you here."

"I feel wide-awake," she said impatiently.

"I know." He paused. "Thank goodness."

Her eyes widened as she looked at him.

Then his expression changed and he reached for her cup of ice again. "Have another drink of water and then you can tell me what you can remember about that little old lady who you pissed off enough for her to want to put you down." He watched her drink and then took the cup away. "Or just think about her and gather your thoughts so you'll remember when you wake up." He put the cup back on the night stand. "Because I believe you're getting woozy again."

She believed she was, too, she thought crossly. Impossible. Only a few minutes ago she had been sure she wouldn't be sleepy for hours. "I hate it when you're right, Lynch."

"I know, it must be a constant torment to you." He took her hand. "Close your eyes."

They were already closing. "Not a *constant* torment. You're not right that often." His hand felt warm and strong and she instinctively tightened her own around it. She whispered, "But thank you for giving me Fletcher . . ."

"You're welcome. But he was only on loan, you're not allowed to keep him."

He had said something like that before and he seldom repeated himself. She found her lips curving with catlike amusement.

"Pity . . ."

* * *

IT WAS PITCH DARK IN THE room when Kendra next opened her eyes.

"It's about time," Olivia said from the seat next to her bed. "You've been restless for the last hour. I was tempted to shake you and wake you up. I was afraid you might be dreaming."

"No, I don't think so. I don't remember. I guess I was just restless. Where's Lynch?"

"I kicked him out," Olivia said. "Which is hard to do. From the minute I called him here, he took over and wouldn't let go." She shrugged. "Not that I didn't want his help. I was feeling pretty helpless and panicky when they told me you could be dying." She paused and then said fiercely, "I really wanted to shake you then. How dare you even get close to that, Kendra? You're my best friend. That's not allowed."

"Sorry." She reached out and took Olivia's hand. "It came as something of a surprise to me, too. But at least I came to you to set it right. Lynch told me that you probably saved my life."

"What else could I do? You were lying there all crumpled up and I thought you might already be dead." Her hand closed on Kendra with a force that was almost painful. "I couldn't think. I was so scared. I'm real cocky about being the blind person who doesn't need her sight to battle anyone toe-to-toe. But I couldn't even remember my first aid training to find out if you still had a pulse. Isn't that funny?"

"No. Not funny at all. But you still managed to do what was needed to get me to the hospital and keep me alive. Thank you, Olivia."

"It was purely self-defense. I couldn't lose you." Her voice was shaking. "I didn't know what I was doing most of the time, and I sure as hell didn't know what was wrong with you. Neither did the doctors at this hospital and that terrified me even more. So I called Lynch. I thought if anyone would know how to keep you alive he would. And he had a vested interest."

"He says you're the one who saved my life."

"He's right, because I knew where to go to make it happen. I went to Lynch and he went to Fletcher. Though I wasn't sure about Fletcher; he's a bit quirky. But Lynch told me that he'd make you well and that was enough for me. I would have let Bugs Bunny treat you if Lynch said it would give you a chance to live."

"Bugs Bunny?" She smiled. "You *were* upset."

"You bet I was. And that's why you can't let this happen again. You were at the condo for heaven's sake. You were home. That attack came out of nowhere. Am I supposed to worry about you whenever you leave there? Stop it!"

"I might be able to do that if I knew what I was doing to warrant an attack. I don't, Olivia. I told you the truth. I have no idea why that woman who was killed had my name." She was silent a moment. "But now I'm beginning to believe that it's more dangerous not to know. I have to have answers. Who the hell knew a little old lady and a cute pooch would try to poison me?"

Olivia didn't speak for an instant. "I think you can rule out the pooch." Her lips were quirking slightly. "He was only an accessory."

Kendra gave a sigh of relief. "You're smiling. Thank goodness. I'm not used to you chewing me out."

"Get used to it. I've been too easy on you. Seeing you in that vestibule croaking was a wake-up call for me. I feel like rigging you up with one those emergency call buttons they advertise."

"Please don't. I'll be very careful." She didn't tell her how handy one of those emergency buttons would have been when she was trying desperately to reach out to push Olivia's doorbell. "It won't happen again. Will you stop yelling at me now? I'd like to just lie here and be with you in the dark. It reminds me of when we were kids and shared everything, even the dark."

"We still share it. You just have to close your eyes." She paused. "I wanted to see so badly last night. Not for myself this time. I wanted to see for *you*. So I wouldn't screw it up. I felt helpless and I never feel helpless." She drew a shaky breath. "But I'd never admit that to anyone but you. I'm Queen of the World, right?"

"Right." Kendra felt as if she were bleeding inside. She had caused this moment of weakness in a friend she had loved since childhood. Strength was important and you had to win it every day, every way, when you had to face the darkness. "And you still reign supreme. You proved it to everyone by getting me through this."

She lifted her chin. "Yes, I did. Those idiots think it was that medical genius, Fletcher, but he was only a tool in my hands. I'm glad you realize that, Kendra." She added, "And, of course, Lynch had a little to do with it. He brought that Brad Pitt look-alike into the mix."

Olivia was back to normal, Kendra realized with relief. "Brad Pitt? I thought he looked more like that guy Chris Hemsworth, who plays Thor, the Avenger."

"Maybe. I had to rely on what I overheard from those silly nurses who were swooning over him. Sometimes I'm glad I'm not affected by appearance. I did like his voice and he seemed intelligent."

"When he wasn't being quirky."

"Some people would say I'm a bit quirky."

"I've noticed. But only when you're not being Queen of the World."

"It's good you made that distinction." She paused. "You're not going to back off from this madness, are you?"

"It's not backing off from me, Olivia. Did Lynch tell you that the bride in that video has disappeared, probably kidnapped?"

"Yes, I made him tell me everything. You said she was very pretty and she seemed so happy."

"Yes, she did. A wedding day is supposed to be one

of the happiest days of a woman's life. Yet something must have happened there that caused all this horror to begin."

"It had already begun," Olivia said. "We *heard* it. And now you're chasing after it." She held up her hand. "Don't say it. I know I can't convince you. But in my august position as the Queen of the World, I'll designate a lowly knight, Lynch, to make certain this foolishness doesn't cost you your life." She added grimly, "And if he doesn't, I'll behead the son of a bitch."

"Poor Lynch."

"Neither of us would ever in a million years feel sorry for Lynch. You must not have come to your senses yet. I think I should let you go back to sleep."

"Or just stay awake and be with my friend Olivia, without talking at all."

"That would work, too. Remembering that wedding video put me distinctly on edge. I don't want to think of bouquets and wedding cakes and a love that should last forever ending like that."

"We don't know it ended. Elizabeth could be alive. I hope she is."

"So do I. But I don't want to think about it now. And I particularly don't want to think about you trying to find out if she's alive or dead. So just lie there and we'll think about Fletcher and how pissed off Lynch must have been to have to bring him in to rescue you instead of doing it himself."

"That seems to be a plan. Though not without faults. Lynch never lacks confidence."

"We can but hope." Olivia leaned back in her chair. "And if you drift off, it will give you pleasant dreams and get you away from that damn wedding video. Right?"

"Absolutely." Yet when Kendra closed her eyes, it was to see that video as if it were there before her. All the gaiety and joy, the lame jokes, the beauty, and the not so beautiful.

The darkness that hovered over the scene that no one had known was there.

And in the center was the radiant bride, Elizabeth, who also had no idea that darkness was closing in on her.

Or did she?

When the darkness finally came, were you expecting it, Elizabeth?

"LIZ, I THOUGHT WE'D never get rid of you!"

Derek sat in the shadows, watching the wedding video for what had to be the thousandth time. Maybe the five thousandth.

All those happy, insipid people.

No one could really be that happy. They were obviously pretending.

Pretending to be happy. Pretending they could actually stand being surrounded by all those other despicable people.

They didn't know what it meant to be truly alive. Not really. But he would show them.

Aah, there was the pretty bride, so stunning in her shimmering white dress. Every hair in place, laughing and crying through Daddy's speech.

So different from the slobbering mess she'd become in her house that morning, begging and pleading for him to spare her miserable life.

Don't worry, dear Elizabeth, the game isn't finished just yet.

CHAPTER 5

"THE CHAIR SUITS YOU," Lynch called out from his car in front of the hospital.

Kendra made a face and stood up from the wheelchair being pushed by the orderly. "Not my choice. Probably more to do with the hospital's liability insurance coverage than anything else." She climbed into Lynch's car and pulled the door shut. "Thanks for picking me up."

"Sure. What took so long?"

"The doctor took his sweet time making his rounds. They wouldn't discharge me until he saw me. I almost made a break for it."

"I'm glad you didn't." Lynch pulled onto Delmar Boulevard. "So where are we headed? Collins, Collins and Levinsky, Attorneys at Law?"

"I just got off the phone with them, and Dale Collins is the only one who can talk to us about Elena Meyer."

"Dale Collins. As in one of the Collins' names on the door?"

"Yes. No one else is authorized to speak about her."

"So let's go talk to him."

"He isn't in the office today. He's at the construction site of their new headquarters downtown. It's going to be in the new Pinnacle Building."

"That chrome and glass monstrosity on C Street?"

"That's the one."

"It's not even finished yet and the neighbors are screaming bloody murder. I've seen it in the news. It's reflecting a nasty glare in offices and storefronts all over downtown."

"Well he's there today and I don't feel like waiting for a spot on his calendar to open up. Let's go to that big, ugly building and ask him some questions."

THE UNDER-CONSTRUCTION Pinnacle Building was visible from all over the greater downtown area, if not the structure itself, then the two massive yellow cranes towering on either side. Mirrored windows covered the lower forty floors, but the upper dozen or so levels were still little more than iron frames open to the elements.

They parked a block south of the building and walked toward the busy construction site. Barriers were plastered with large posters selling the new building as a mixed-use facility featuring high-priced condominiums, offices, and ground-floor retail shops. The sidewalk was closed on all four sides of the structure, but Lynch pulled open one of the barriers and ushered Kendra through.

Kendra looked up at the glass panels. "It's pretty hideous all right."

Lynch pointed to one of the posters. "But it's 'Downtown's Most Exciting New Destination.'"

"We'll see about that." Kendra motioned for Lynch to join her at a construction trailer where there was a small pile of battered hard hats on the ground outside. She picked up two and tossed one to Lynch. "Not sure if it will fit on that big head of yours."

He popped the hat on and smiled. "How does it look?"

Damn it if he didn't look like a ruggedly handsome model out of every cologne ad she'd ever seen. "Disgustingly good. Great even." She put her own hat on. "How about me?"

"Like you have no business ever visiting a construction site."

"Wonderful."

"Consider that a compliment. Do you have any idea where we're heading?"

"The firm's new offices will be on the forty-fifth and forty-sixth floors."

"The firm told you that?"

"No. Google."

He glanced around and adjusted his hard hat. "There's probably a cargo elevator running somewhere. Let's find it before someone throws us out of here."

They quickly found the large open-air construction elevator, which they were forced to share with a half ton of ceramic floor tiles. Lynch grabbed the control box dangling from a yellow cable. He punched a button and the elevator lurched upward. Within seconds they could see the entire downtown and the San Diego Bay.

The sight literally took her breath away. "Beautiful."

"Stunning."

The elevator stopped, and Lynch guided her off. "Floor forty-five."

The unfinished floor appeared to be deserted. Only a few of the rooms had been framed, and the perimeter was still open to the wind, which whistled around them.

Lynch glanced around. "Maybe one floor up?"

Kendra pointed to a footprint in the sawdust in front of them. "That's a dress shoe. Collins has been here recently. Otherwise the wind would have disturbed it by now. And there are no footprints back to the elevator."

"Very good." A man stepped out from behind a pillar. "I take it you're not architects or designers."

Kendra recognized Dale Collins from her online search. He was a round-faced man who actually looked younger than he did in the photos she'd seen, although his hairline had receded a bit. "Mr. Collins, I'm Kendra

Michaels. This is Adam Lynch. We're investigating Elena Meyer's murder."

Collins stepped closer to them. "Elena Meyer. Very sad. But she wasn't based here in San Diego. You'd probably do better to talk to her colleagues in Connecticut."

"She was killed here. And we know she was out here quite a bit for her work."

"Not this trip." Collins turned and stepped toward the gaping hole at the end of what would soon be the corridor. "Whatever brought her out here, it wasn't the job. I talked to the head of her office yesterday. He had no idea she was here."

"Who *would* know?" Lynch said. "Did she have friends in your office she may have been visiting?"

"I don't think so. Every time she was here, she was with her team from Connecticut. She stuck pretty close to them. I don't think I ever heard of her socializing with anyone from my group." He looked behind them as the cargo elevator returned with a group of well-dressed men and women in hard hats. "Speaking of whom, here are some of my colleagues now."

Kendra turned toward them. Four men and two women, all dressed in expensive suits and shoes.

"In less than four months, this will be our new West Coast headquarters. I'm giving some of our partners a first look at their new home." Collins motioned toward Kendra and Lynch. "Ms. Michaels and Mr. Lynch are investigating Elena Meyer's unfortunate death. There's some question as to why she was even in San Diego this week. Do any of you have any idea?"

Collins' colleagues shook their heads.

Kendra studied the group. One of the men and both women were clearly disturbed by the subject of their colleague's death, the others showed no concern. Kendra kept her eyes on them as she spoke. "What case brought her out here?"

Collins shrugged. "We represent a technology company on the East Coast. A major defense contractor. They were being sued by a company here in San Diego. It looked like we were going to trial, but our client eventually settled."

"Any lingering bad blood there?" Lynch asked.

"Like something that could have gotten a young woman killed?" Collins shook his head. "It was a routine case and it's over. And in the end everyone came out of it with a lot of money. Including this firm."

"Which companies were involved?" Lynch asked.

Collins shrugged. "It's in the public record. We represent Maritech Industries. They were being sued by The Philby Group. Ms. Meyer was a paralegal. She had very little direct contact with the principals in this case. She mainly just supported her team when they were out here formulating strategy with us and working through mounds of memos and emails."

Kendra's eyes narrowed on one of the young women she'd targeted for extra attention. She was an attractive redhead whose facial expression had changed from sadness to one of slight annoyance. She was reacting to her boss's words. What was going on here?

Kendra nodded. "Or does anyone know of friendships or possible romantic relationships Elena may have formed during her times here?"

Again, there was no response from the group besides shaking heads and vague shrugs.

The redheaded woman was now typing something in her phone.

"Okay. Thanks for your time," Kendra said. "I'm sure SDPD will be talking to you. Naturally we'll do everything we can to find who did this to Elena."

She and Lynch moved toward the elevator. But as the group of attorneys separated to clear a path, the redhead discreetly flashed her phone screen at Kendra.

The screen was blank except for block letters which read: BROCK LTD.

The woman pressed the phone's side button and wiped the screen clean. She didn't look at Kendra as she moved past her to keep pace with her colleagues.

"BROCK LIMITED?" LYNCH ASKED as they approached his car. "Are you sure?"

"Yes. Brock L-T-D."

"Hmm. Interesting."

"Why? Does that mean anything to you?"

"Brock Limited is a private security company. A lot

of ex-law enforcement and ex-military. They have contracts all over the world."

"Corporate security?"

"Government contracts, too."

"Sounds like your line of work."

"They've tried to hire me several times and I'm sure they've reached out to some of your FBI buddies. They pay extremely well."

"Then why haven't you joined them?"

"They can't afford me. And they have a reputation I really don't want tainting me."

"Surely it can't be worse than the 'taint' you've already acquired over the years. Your own reputation is lethal."

"You'd be surprised. And I used the word very selectively. Just as I choose my jobs and the way I perform them selectively. There's a certain . . . brutality to their methods."

"Isn't that what you want from a security firm?"

"They have the reputation of using a pile driver when a feather duster will do. I've known some of the guys who went to work for them. Kind of a nasty bunch."

"You've yet to convince me that you wouldn't fit in there."

"Trust me."

"It's hard to trust you when no one ever knows what you're doing once you disappear undercover."

He smiled. "You can trust that I'll get the job done. What else is important?"

Kendra shrugged dismissively. "Brock Limited." Kendra remembered the woman's trembling fingers curled around her phone, flashing that message. "What does it mean?"

"You could always ask her."

"I don't even know who she is."

"Don't let that stop you." They approached Lynch's parked car. Lynch crossed around to open the passenger-side door for Kendra then he climbed behind the wheel himself.

He reached under the seat and pulled out his tablet computer. "Collins said she was a partner, didn't he?"

"Yes."

Lynch navigated to the Collins, Collins and Levinsky website. "What do you know? There's a tab here that says 'Our Partners.' Probably bios and photos."

"It's a big firm with offices all over the country. There are probably *hundreds* of partners."

"You're right." Lynch handed her the tablet. "*You* find her."

He started the car and pulled onto the busy street.

Kendra scrolled through the web page scanning the partner photos. "It's amazing how much alike the men in this firm look. Same haircuts, same suits, same ties, even the same square jawlines. At least the women show some individuality."

"Any sign of yours?"

"Not yet. But she has flaming red hair so she shouldn't be too tough to— Wait!" Kendra stopped.

"Success?"

"Yes. Misha Watkins. That's her, I'm sure of it."

"Good. We'll contact her at home tonight."

"Hate to break it to you, but they don't include home addresses on this website."

He smiled. "Don't worry about that. I have other sources for that."

She wasn't surprised. Lynch had contacts everywhere. "Ones that aren't tainted?"

"I didn't say that. I never object to dealing with anyone who hasn't made the choices I have, as long as they're productive. But I don't believe that I'll have to dive too deep in the mire just to get an address."

MISHA WATKINS LIVED in a sleek, modern house in a subdivision in Encinitas.

Lynch found a shady spot under an oak tree down the street from the house and they spent the next two hours waiting for her to appear.

"Stop being so edgy," Lynch said. "You're burning up calories and adrenaline. You don't need that after fighting off that damn allergy."

"I'm fine. I just wish she'd get here. I hate waiting."

"So do I. But sometimes the prize is worth waiting for. You have to make a decision and then just suck it up."

There was something in his tone. Her eyes flew to meet his. "Are we still talking about Misha Watkins?"

He smiled innocently. "What else?" His gaze switched from her face to a BMW roadster driving up the street. "And speak of the devil, I believe I see a redhead at the wheel of that car."

"We don't know that she's a devil. Probably the opposite if she was trying to help us."

But the driver was undoubtedly Misha Watkins, she saw as the woman pulled into the driveway and then jumped out of the car. Kendra watched her go into the house before she turned to Lynch. "I want to go in to see her by myself. Okay?"

"Why?"

"I was the one she contacted. I think I'd have better luck alone. You can be . . . disturbing."

He chuckled. "Only to you. I can be anything I want to be. I'm sure our Misha would find me both soothing and comforting."

Kendra made a rude sound as she opened her door and jumped out of the car. "No way."

"I'm hurt. Didn't you find me comforting last night?"

His hand holding hers in the darkness, just knowing he was there keeping all the terrors of the day at bay.

"Maybe." She started walking down the street toward Misha's house. "But then I was drugged out of my mind. Stay here."

Misha Watkins' eyes widened when she opened the door and saw Kendra. "What are you doing here?"

"Why, weren't you expecting me? Did you think I'd just let it go when you tossed that name at me, Miss Watkins? You must have known I'd regard it as an invitation. May I come in?"

Misha didn't move. "It was an impulse." She made a face. "And I had second thoughts immediately. I should never have done it. I was hoping you'd just accept it as a hint and run with it."

"That's what I'm doing," Kendra said. "But I prefer facts to hints, so I came to the source. I'm sure that as an attorney yourself, you'll understand that philosophy." She repeated, "May I come in?"

"I guess you might as well. You appear very determined." She reluctantly moved aside. "Dr. Michaels, was it?"

"Kendra Michaels." Kendra came into the house. "I won't take much of your time. I just want to ask a few questions. The manner in which your 'hint' was presented was rather odd. And I admit to being curious about those second thoughts."

Misha shrugged. "I was impatient and irritated that no one had mentioned Brock Limited when there was no reason not to tell you about them. I'm not always a team player and I thought I'd throw a wrench into Collins' corporate wheel. Which is probably why I'll end up getting tossed one of these days."

"What did Brock Limited have to do with Elena Meyer?"

"The same as the rest of us on the team. Elena worked on the wrongful death suit involving Brock's private security personnel overseas. We did a stellar job and were successful in defending them. It didn't make sense to not mention Elena was part of the team."

"Did she have a particular role to play in the victory?"

Misha doubtfully shook her head. "Not that I'm aware of. We were a team. Maybe Collins just didn't want you to bother one of the firm's top clients."

"It could be you're right," Kendra said. "But lies usually come back to haunt you, and if it wasn't important, an intelligent man would tell the truth."

"Look, you're not going to go back and tell Collins I told you about Brock, are you? He's my boss and I'm not ready to move on to another job yet. He wouldn't be pleased I didn't go along with his bullshit."

"Have you told me everything you know about Elena Meyer?"

"Of course. I didn't know her that well."

"Then there's no reason to go back to Collins and mention you. I appreciate you taking time to talk to me." She paused. "Providing you take a little more time and watch a video for me. I need to know if you know any of these people, or if this wedding means anything to you. If you'll do that, then I won't bother you again."

"Wedding?" Misha frowned. "What the hell?"

Kendra dialed up the video and handed her phone to her. "Please."

Kendra thought she was going to refuse. Then she shook her head and pressed the button.

Kendra carefully watched her expression but saw only confusion and impatience. However, she stuck it out until the end and then handed the phone back to Kendra. "Total waste of time. I didn't know any of these people. Though the bride's gown was kind of awesome."

"Yes, it was lovely. Thank you for watching it for me." She handed Misha a card. "If you happen to think of anything else that might be of interest, please call."

"I will." Then she grimaced. "Maybe. The more I think about it, the more I'm sure Collins would be pissed off about me opening my mouth to you. He must have had some reason for not mentioning Brock Limited. Remember you promised you wouldn't go back and tell him that I told you."

"I remember." She turned to go. "Mum's the word. Good day, Miss Watkins."

As she closed the door behind her, she saw that Lynch had pulled up to the curb in front of the house. He was leaning against the driver's door with his arms crossed. "How did it go? Were you able to wrest her deepest secrets from her?"

"No, it was a little harder than I thought." She came

toward him. "She'd had second thoughts. And I don't believe she had any deep secrets, but she eventually told me what I needed to know." She amended, "Well, not what I needed, but all she thought she knew." She frowned. "But maybe there is more. Why else would she have made contact with me, unless she had an instinct that something was distinctly rotten in Denmark? And the way she scurried back to hide when she realized what she'd done . . ."

"You're jumping all over the place." Lynch opened her passenger door. "I don't doubt that something could be rotten if it concerned Brock Limited, and I approve of instinct, but I won't be able to judge until you tell me what she told you."

"Not much. Only that Elena was very definitely a member of the team that recently worked on a case that involved defending Brock's personnel team overseas on a wrongful death suit. They won the suit and Elena had no special interaction with Brock as far as Misha knew." She got into the car. "And she got me to promise that I wouldn't squeal on her to Collins in exchange for looking at the video."

"You wouldn't have done it anyway." He ran around the car and jumped into the driver's seat. "But perhaps you're getting less transparent if she believed you."

"I'm not transparent." She leaned back as he started the car. "I was very tough and professional. I just didn't see any sense in being unpleasant when she had tried to help us." She added sourly, "I don't have your insatiable drive to come in first in every race."

"Yeah, sure." He glanced at her with a grin. "Only when it concerns your kids or anyone else you care about. Besides, you knew that you could rely on my competitiveness to fill in the blanks."

She was silent. "You seem to know a good deal about Brock Limited. I think you'll enjoy exploring the situation yourself. It seems your cup of tea. If I'm wrong, then I'll be glad to do it by myself."

"No way." He was no longer grinning. "You don't go anywhere near them without me."

Her brows rose. "You're afraid they'll taint me?"

"You seem to have adopted that word. It's not the one I'd use in this case."

Kendra turned toward him. "You say you know people at Brock Limited?"

"Several."

"Anyone you can reach out to?"

"Would one of the company vice-presidents do?"

She looked at him in surprise. "He's on your speed dial?"

"Practically. His name is Josh Blake. He's head of acquisition and training. He calls me every six months like clockwork, trying to get me to join the company. I have a standing invite to visit their training facility in Jacumba."

"Near the hot springs spa?"

"Yes, it's not far from here. The facility is in the desert, just a couple miles from the Mexican border. I hear they have quite an operation out there."

"Think he would agree to meet with us?"

"I know he would if he thinks I might join their company."

Kendra was thinking quickly. "And would he know about this case that Elena Meyer was working on?"

"I'd bet on it. He's working on moving up in the company and spends half his time at the San Diego office trying to persuade his boss, Vivianne Kerstine, how valuable he'd be if she made him a director."

"Then let's do it. Let's talk to him. How soon can you get us a meeting?"

As if in response, Lynch pulled over and stopped at the curb. He pulled out his phone, browsed his directory, and tapped a name. He raised the phone to his ear and listened. Seconds later, he was speaking.

"Josh, it's Adam Lynch. Good. Very good. I understand we almost ran into each other in Vilnius last spring." He smiled. "Well, you can't win 'em all. Listen, I thought I'd take you up on your offer. I'd like to visit your training facility in Jacumba and maybe get a personal tour. How about tomorrow? Noon? Perfect. See you there."

He cut the connection, winked at Kendra, and pulled back onto the busy street.

"Just like that," Kendra said. "He really *must* want you to work for him."

"What can I say? I'm a rock star. I told you. Every six months like clockwork."

Kendra checked her watch. "I suppose we should check in with Griffin to make sure the FBI is kept in the loop."

"Must we?"

"Yes." She shook her head. "I suspect Mr. Blake wouldn't be so eager to hire you if he knew about your complete aversion to authority."

"It's a two-way street. Authority figures tend to have a strong aversion to *me*."

"Not as long as you keep delivering for them the way you do. But I can see why you're better off as a free agent."

"Infinitely better off."

"Anyway, I'll send Griffin and Metcalf an email after you drop me off at my condo."

"About that . . . I'd prefer it if you stayed with me at my house tonight."

Her brows rose. "I'll bet you would."

"I'm serious."

"I'm sure you are."

He let out an exasperated sigh. "Do I need to remind you that you were attacked in front of your building less than twenty-four hours ago?"

"Believe me, I haven't forgotten. It would have such been a humiliating way to go. Death by dog leash."

"It's not funny."

She shrugged. "It's a little funny. And even your doctor friend doesn't think they were trying to kill me."

"But he did say it was an unusually sophisticated attack. You don't know what you're up against and you shouldn't take chances."

"I'll be careful." She grinned. "But if you want to show me a new martial arts move, I'll accept that."

"You still want to know how to break someone's wrists?"

"Under the circumstances, I'm now more interested in learning to break someone's neck."

"Brutal. The head-grab and twist, like in the movies?"

"Yes."

"It takes an incredible amount of strength plus the element of surprise."

"You sound like you've done it before."

Lynch drove in silence.

Kendra's jaw went slack. "You have?"

Lynch shrugged.

"You've actually grabbed a man's head and—"

"It's nothing I'm proud of. It had to be done."

Kendra couldn't help it. She started to laugh. "Of course! Of course it had to be done! Because sometimes one's only option is to spin a man's head a hundred and eighty degrees."

"It wasn't the only option. Just the best one."

Kendra's smile faded. "Who was he?"

He was silent for a moment. "Well, actually there's been more than one."

"No freakin' way."

"I'm not at liberty to say more, but each of them deserved it," he said quietly. "And they certainly would have killed me if they'd seen me first. I hope you believe me when I tell you that."

She was scrambling to gather her composure. It wasn't often she received a glimpse of the Lynch that agencies and governments fought to acquire. She knew she sometimes deliberately avoided looking at that shadow figure. She had an idea that if she did, she would see an entirely different man than the one who was *her* Adam Lynch. No, that wasn't fair, she thought quickly. He would still be the Lynch who had saved her life, been her friend, and kept drawing her closer with every encounter. There was just so much more about him that she was afraid of learning because it would mean that she'd be pulled into those shadows that surrounded him. But if she didn't take that step, then she would have to trust him or let him go. That was not an option. She couldn't let him go. "I believe you."

The corners of his lips were turning up. "That took you a long time to decide."

"Not really. I'm certain there are all kinds of people who want you dead. I'm sure you were very selective about which ones you decided to separate their heads from their bodies."

"Very selective," he said solemnly.

"Did you tell me all of this so that I'd feel safer staying with you?"

"Or safer having me stay with you."

"That's not going to happen either."

"Too bad. But no, I seldom resort to such tactics. It would devastate my ego. And as you know, my house is fortified against almost any attack. No head-twisting necessary."

Kendra nodded. Lynch was right. His home was a beautiful Tudor located north of the city and most passersby had no idea that it was equipped with motion sensors, steel shutters, and iron-reinforced walls that could withstand a military-style attack. Before she had come to know him well Kendra had often wondered what Lynch had done to necessitate living in such a fortress. He'd only given her the vaguest hints, but the longer she knew him, the more it became clear that there were times that he needed a safe house just to survive.

"No, thanks."

"I was afraid you would say that." He sighed. "Okay. As soon as you find the time, I'll show you some of my favorite fighting techniques."

"But not the head twist?"

"Let's work up to that, shall we?"

She smiled. "If you insist."

In fifteen minutes they were back at her condo. Lynch slowed to a stop in front of the building. "Last chance for a secure and restful night at my place. It could mean the difference between a good night's sleep and keeping one eye open all night."

She opened her door. "I'll sleep just fine, thank you."

"I'm not sure I will."

"What time will you be here to pick me up tomorrow?"

"Eleven."

"Good, I can catch up on some work." She hesitated. She didn't want to leave him, dammit. "Thanks, Lynch. For everything."

"Of course."

She gazed at him for a long moment. She wanted to *touch* him.

Oh, what the hell.

"Bye." She leaned in to give him a quick hug, but at the last moment it became something else.

She kissed him on the mouth, pressing her lips against his, then lingering for a moment after. She kissed him again. Crazy. This was crazy. She tried to pull away, but Lynch was holding her close.

"I'm staying," he whispered.

"No. I don't tease, but this kind of got away from me. But not tonight. Okay?"

"It's not okay."

She leaned her forehead against his. The scent of him, the warmth . . . "It has to be. For now. I'm confused enough about what's going on. I won't be confused about you. Everything has to be clear in my head, dammit."

"Kendra . . ."

She climbed out of the car and closed the door behind her. "No." She strode toward the door before she could change her mind. "I'll see you tomorrow."

"I almost had you," he called softly. "And I didn't even try. Think about it. You're not really confused at all."

"Goodbye, Lynch."

She stopped just inside the door to get her breath.

Close. It had been so close. Her entire body was still hot and shaking from those last minutes. Her heart was beating hard and she wanted to run back out to him. Why not?

Just do it. He was probably right, she knew what she wanted, and she was just putting off making a final commitment.

Take the time.

Don't think about him.

Easy to say. He seemed to fill her world right now.

But she didn't want him to be her entire world. He was too dominant and she'd have to struggle every minute to hold her own against him. Very dangerous.

Yet when had she ever been afraid to face a challenge? And he might be the greatest one of all.

Be sensible. Give herself a chance to forget about sex and not let herself be carried away by that sheer magnetism that was always present.

And don't *think* about him.

CHAPTER 6

"IT'S UP THERE." Kendra pointed to a two-story building that blended with the desert around them.

It was the first sign of life they'd seen since pulling off the freeway ten minutes earlier and Kendra still wasn't sure they had arrived at their destination. "It's not what I expected."

"It used to be a junior high school," Lynch said. "It had been abandoned for years when Brock Limited took it over. It came in handy for training their agents in simulated hostage situations. School shootings, workplace violence . . ."

Her brows rose. "Isn't that the police's job?"

"In most places. But there are countries where local law enforcement just isn't very good at that stuff. It's easier for companies to recruit top talent for overseas positions if they can assure their safety. That's where Brock security comes in. They're not just bodyguards. They're trained to handle any dangerous situation that might come up."

"Even if it means stepping on a few toes?"

"It's amazing how a few thousand dollars to the right person can make local police forgive just about anything. Brock is famous for their little black doctor bags stuffed with cash."

"Institutionalized bribery. Great."

"Trust me, sometimes it's the easiest way to get the job done."

"So you give away little black doctor bags, too?"

"I prefer jackets with cash sewn in the lining."

She rolled her eyes. "You probably *should* be working for them."

"Absolutely not. My methods differ from theirs in a number of ways."

"The more you say that, the less I believe you."

"Believe me."

She did believe him. His voice was quiet but emphatic and she was suddenly curious what experiences had led to that very specific directness. "Still, Brock seems to think you'd be a good fit."

"If it gives us access, I'll let them keep believing it." He nodded to a tall bearded man standing in the building parking lot. "There's our welcoming committee. Josh Blake himself. As I told you, he heads this training facility at the moment."

She gazed at Blake appraisingly. "He doesn't look so tough. I thought he'd be one of those he-man, special forces types."

He shrugged. "He's no pussycat, but he actually has a corporate background. His value to Brock lies in the fact that he's both efficient and can be totally ruthless if the occasion demands." He pulled into the lot and parked.

Blake approached as they climbed out of the car. He was obviously amused at the sight of Lynch's Ferrari. "You're still driving this hunk of junk?"

Lynch shrugged. "There's nothing better."

Blake smiled, flashing a set of teeth that was slightly too white. He was tanned, fit, and appeared extremely sure of himself. "I'm joking. I own two Ferraris. But lately I've been tooling around in that Gallardo." Blake pointed to a bright green Lamborghini sports car behind them. "You haven't lived until you've driven one of those."

"I have driven one," Lynch said. "I just like a car that hugs the road a bit more."

"To each his own." He extended his hand to Kendra. "Josh Blake. And who are you, pretty lady?"

Lots of white teeth and his voice had lowered to what he must have believed was sexual intimacy. She tried not to look too repulsed by his smarmy charm as she took his hand. "Kendra Michaels."

He smiled as his hand tightened on hers. "Perhaps I can give you a ride and you can cast the deciding vote."

She pulled her hand away. "I always leave it to men to decide the relative merits of their sports cars and reproductive organs. It appears to be the two things you guys always seem to love talking about."

Blake laughed out loud and glanced at Lynch. "Wow. I would be offended, but I think she's probably right."

"Right about some of us more than others," Lynch said.

"I won't deny it." Blake cocked his head toward the facility behind them. "Shall we? I've been wanting you to see this place for quite a while."

They followed Blake around the other side of the building to what appeared to be a copy of an army basic training camp, with barracks, shooting ranges, and a challenging obstacle course. Every square inch of the facility was in use.

"This place is packed," Lynch said.

"We just can't hire all the people we need. Business is booming. The world's getting scarier every day and our clients pay us well to make it a little less frightening for them."

Kendra jumped at the sound of gunshots in the building behind them.

"Sorry about that." Blake motioned toward the building. "We're running a drill in there today. An elementary school hostage situation. In some overseas markets, we hold workshops for local law enforcement personnel."

"You're teaching them?" Kendra said.

"Where we can. It's all a part of being good guests in their countries. Our tactical teams actually have contracts with several foreign governments as well as with the U.S." He motioned for them to follow him to a small trailer parked next to the building. "You'll be interested in this."

They entered the trailer, which looked like the control room of a small television studio. Eight men sat at consoles, watching monitors that displayed what appeared to be a very authentic schoolhouse assault. One man spoke into his headset. "Attacker Two, move out of the stairwell."

On the screens, Kendra saw a black-garbed man with a rifle climb from the stairs and surprise an armed woman standing there. He fired his rifle, and the woman's armbands and baseball-style cap started flashing.

"That means she's dead," Blake said. "It's her first time in this simulation. She'll learn."

"I have to admit it's an impressive operation you have here," Lynch said. "How long is the training?"

"A minimum of sixteen weeks. It's a long time by the standards of our industry, but it separates us from our competitors. Our instructors are ex-special forces, FBI, and CIA."

"I know a few of them. You have some good people."

"The best. That's why we want you." He cocked his head toward the door and led them outside. He stopped and turned back toward Lynch. "But you know . . . Somehow I don't think you're looking for a job, Lynch."

Lynch nodded. "You're right about that. Not at the moment. Though I always keep my options open."

"And I'll try to make certain you keep us in mind when you see what a good team we'd make. So why are you here?"

"As it happens, we're helping the FBI on a murder investigation. I thought you might be of help."

Kendra stepped forward. "Elena Meyer. Did you know her?"

Blake thought for a moment. "Meyer . . ." He shook his head. "No."

"That's a little strange. Since she was part of the legal team that handled a case for you here in San Diego."

"Really? I know almost everyone on that team. Are you sure—?"

Kendra raised her phone and showed him Elena Meyer's portrait photo. "This is her. Ring any bells?"

He studied the screen. "Yeah . . . Yeah. But she was from another office. An assistant?"

"A paralegal. She was from the firm's Connecticut office."

He looked up from the screen. "She's dead?"

"Murdered," Lynch said. "Killed on a street downtown. You haven't heard about it?"

"If I did, it didn't make an impression. And I certainly didn't realize it was anyone I'd ever met."

"No one can tell us why she was here in town," Kendra said. "Was it something about your company's case that brought her back?"

"No. The case was over. It was actually one of the least contentious cases we've dealt with lately."

"You get sued a lot?" Kendra said.

"Goes with the territory." His white smile flashed. "When you're as successful as we are, there's a lot of jealousy. Hundreds of millions in income come from the government, so that opens us up to all kinds of oversight committees, congressional review, media scrutiny, you name it. If we're too aggressive in protecting our clients, we can get sued. If we're not aggressive enough, our clients might sue us for failing to deliver. We settle most cases, then go to court for the others." His smiled faded. "I'm being honest with you when I say there was nothing special about this case. Have you spoken with her firm?"

"We have," Kendra said.

"And?"

"They agree with you. They say the case—and the outcome—were strictly routine."

Blake nodded. "Still, it's a tragedy what happened to

her. We have some world-class investigators on our payroll. Why don't I put a couple of them on the case? It's the least I can do."

"We're fine," Lynch said.

"My people are good. You said so yourself."

"If we need help, we'll ask," Lynch said. "But thanks for the offer."

Blake raised his hands in surrender. "Fine. Just trying to help."

"You can help by asking the people in your organization if anyone has any idea who may have done that to her," Kendra said.

"Done."

"You know how to reach me," Lynch said. "If you think of anything—"

"Wait a minute. You don't get away that easily. I cleared my schedule because I thought I finally had a shot at reeling you in."

Lynch shrugged. "Sorry for your inconvenience."

"You can make it up to me."

"How's that?"

Blake smiled. "Walk with me just a few yards. To the target range."

"Why?"

"Your shooting scores at Quantico were through the roof. One of our guys was even in your class. He says it was quite a thing to behold."

"He was probably exaggerating."

"He wasn't. I've seen your scores."

Lynch cocked an eyebrow. "I thought those things were confidential."

"They are. I just happen to be extremely well-connected." He motioned toward the shooting range, which was set up to resemble a typical city street. "Please." His tone was wheedling. "It won't take you long and I want to see if you're worth the effort I've been exerting."

Lynch shrugged. "Whatever."

He and Kendra followed Blake to the range as he continued. "You've seen setups like this before. Life-size human-shaped targets will jump out periodically."

"Of course," Lynch said. "Kill the bad guys, spare the children and nuns. Fairly straightforward."

"The way I understand it, there's nothing straightforward about the way you shoot."

Blake reached into his shoulder holster and produced a large Walther semiautomatic handgun.

"I'd be honored if you would give it a shot."

Lynch took the gun. "No pun intended, I'm sure."

"None whatsoever."

Lynch ejected the magazine, checked it, and popped it back in. He turned the gun over in his hands. "Nice."

"She hasn't let me down yet."

Kendra smiled. "You're the first man I've ever met who thought of his gun as a 'she.'"

"Do I sense another phallic joke on the way?"

"No. But it does make me wonder about the relationship you have with women."

Blake smirked and shook his head. "If you're that interested, maybe I can show you."

She had let herself in for that one, Kendra thought. But she still had to look away to hide her disgust. Ugh.

Lynch nodded toward the practice range. "Where do you want me to start?"

"All the way at the left end. Work your way to the right as quickly as you can." He glanced at the button a few inches away on the side of the building. "All I have to do is press this button and the fun begins."

Lynch glanced into the gun barrel, then turned to angle it into the sun. He looked back up at Blake. "You have a problem."

"What's that?"

Lynch handed the gun back to him. "You have a barrel obstruction. A serious one."

Blake looked inside the barrel.

Lynch said with dangerous softness, "I don't need to tell you what might have happened if I'd tried to fire it. The gun probably would have blown up in my hands. I could have been killed." He glanced at Kendra. "And anyone close to me could have been killed."

"Killed? I don't know about that."

"You want to fire that gun? Go ahead. Just give us time to move away from you."

Blake inspected his gun more closely. "Looks like the inside of the barrel stripped and fused in a mass. Don't know how that could have happened. Sorry, Lynch. Let me get another one for you to use."

"I don't think so. Inefficiency annoys me."

"Aw, come on." He unfastened a walkie-talkie clipped to his belt. "I'll have another one brought over from—"

"No, thanks. I've decided I don't have the time." Lynch's gaze was ice cold. "Ask around, see if anyone has anything to share about Elena Meyer. If you dig up something for us, then maybe we'll come back."

Kendra was warily watching Lynch's expression as he turned away. He was usually cool and ultracollected in any situation. She had seldom seen him this close to an explosion.

Lynch turned toward Kendra and jerked his head toward the parking lot. As they started walking, Lynch called over his shoulder. "And get that gun repaired. Someone could get hurt."

The anger was still there. She could sense the explosion was still on the horizon.

She murmured, "Lynch?"

"It's okay. I just don't like the game he was trying to play with—" He broke off and stopped, standing very still. "Oh, what the hell! Why not?" He whirled on Blake, his eyes gleaming recklessly. "I've changed my mind. I *do* have the time." His fingers brushed under the lapel of his jacket and his semiautomatic was suddenly in his grasp. Before Kendra could comprehend what she had seen, he fired a spray of bullets at the large wall-mounted metal button. The block-long shooting range whirred to life.

Then he was on the move!

Kendra gasped at the figures that suddenly appeared on the street. They looked incredibly real from a distance, given away only by their gliding, rather than walking, over thin tracks in the pavement.

There was a postman, a little boy, a couple making out on a bench . . .

Lynch spun around and shot the young couple, blowing the tops of their heads away.

Only then did Kendra see that the figures were using their closeness to hide small assault weapons.

Several curtains and window blinds slightly parted, mimicking the effect of witnesses peering out from their homes and businesses.

BLAM! BLAM! BLAM!

Lynch fired at three of the second-story windows, leaving the rest undisturbed. Glass shattered and simulated blood sprayed across the windows. A gun barrel fell through one of the sills.

"Holy shit," Blake whispered. "He got all three." He looked at his tablet computer, which showed Lynch's rapidly-tabulating score.

More pedestrians appeared and Lynch extended his gun in front of him, holding it with both hands. He spun around as he moved down the street, keeping the entire target range in his field of view.

Next up was a police officer, a kid on a skateboard, an old lady carrying groceries . . .

BLAM!

Lynch shot the old lady, firing through one of the bags in her arms. The bag ripped, showing that it was covering a sawed-off shotgun aimed at Lynch. The lady target fell to the ground.

"An old lady with a *shotgun*?" Kendra said. "Seriously?"

Blake shrugged. "You never know where the next threat is coming from."

Lynch passed what appeared to be a homeless man. He ducked behind the figure and fired two shots through a shop window.

More breaking glass, more fake blood, and a "dead" sniper figure slumping though the opening. Lynch fired a shot into the homeless man's head, and the target flipped back to reveal he was wearing an explosive vest.

"Rough neighborhood," Kendra said.

"Yeah." Blake was looking in amazement at Lynch's score on his tablet.

Lynch spun around, ejecting the ammo cartridge and snapping another in place before the first even hit the ground. He fired two more shots at second-story windows. More splattered blood, and an *"Aieeee"* scream.

Kendra cocked her head. "I know that yell."

"That's because you've heard it in almost every movie ever made," Blake said absently. "It's called a Wilhelm. Our sound guy couldn't resist."

Lynch whirled toward a messenger carrying a large tube on a bicycle. He let the messenger pass but focused his attention on a white pickup truck moving down the street. The truck veered onto the sidewalk heading toward a group gathered around a small produce market. Lynch fired two shots into the drivers-side windshield. The glass shattered, and the truck veered harmlessly into a lamppost.

Then Lynch was running to the end of the street.

He raised his hands. "Time!"

Blake pushed a button on his tablet and looked at the result total. "Unbelievable."

Lynch holstered his gun and strode back to the start of the course. "Ready to go, Kendra?"

"Sure."

Blake held up the tablet. "Don't you even want to see your score? It's a course record."

"No, thanks. I'm done here." He took Kendra's elbow and nudged her toward the Ferrari. "I'm satisfied. We can leave now."

Kendra was looking over her shoulder at Blake standing dumbfounded as he gazed at the scores on his tablet.

"I don't believe Blake found the last couple minutes in the least satisfying," she murmured. "But I enjoyed them enormously."

"He irritated me," Lynch said. After they climbed in the car and shut the doors he added, "And it was a way of getting my own back without actually killing the son of a bitch. Though I would have been willing to go that route, too."

"You were . . . phenomenal." She was silent for a long moment. "You don't think that damaged gun was an accident, do you?"

"No."

"Neither do I. I'd say today was the first time that gun was in his shoulder holster. It usually holds a gun quite a bit smaller than that one. You could tell by the impressions in the leather."

Lynch smiled. "Well, *you* can tell."

"Anyone could tell, if they paid attention. Before this morning, that holster has probably held only one gun and it wasn't that one. That damaged Walther was there for you."

"That's what I thought. But for what reason? It could have been used to test me, one of Blake's little games, but that would have been risky. I don't respond well to games and Blake would know that. Or it could have been a warning." Lynch started the car and peeled out of the lot. "I tend to go in that direction. You know . . . outside of a government spy agency, if there was anyone capable of pulling off that cloak-and-dagger style attack on you, it was Brock Limited. And now, thirty-six hours later, the company vice-president puts what amounts to an explosive device in my hands."

"But why?"

"Obviously they don't want us pushing on this. I suspect they're more afraid of you than me. Elena Meyer was trying to get to you when she was killed. But there's more to it than just one dead woman on a city street."

"But where does this leave us? We still don't have anything on Brock."

"They'd make damn sure we didn't. They're good at what they do."

Lynch turned the wheel as they climbed a hill and took a curve in the road. The car sped up as they rounded the bend.

Kendra gripped the armrest. "Slow down. All that talk about Ferraris and hot cars did not impress me."

Lynch wrinkled his brow. "I know it didn't."

The car's engine raced.

Something was wrong. "What's happening?"

"Shit." Lynch gripped the wheel as his car spun dangerously around another curve in the road. He jammed his foot on the brake, but the car slowed only slightly as a metal-against-metal scream sounded from the undercarriage.

The car lurched forward.

"We have a runaway engine."

"A *what*?"

The wheel vibrated harder. "A runaway engine."

"That's a thing?"

"Afraid so. Bad oil seal, fuel injectors, maybe an on-board computer glitch." He pulled the emergency brake, but it only made the car even more difficult to control.

"Lynch . . . ?"

"We're in trouble."

They rounded another bend on the desert road, kicking up gravel as the left rear wheel skated over the edge.

"The brakes aren't working?"

"The brakes are the only thing keeping us from flying off the road at two hundred miles per hour right now."

The rear end fishtailed!

Kendra looked ahead, where the road climbed higher and even more curvy. "Lynch . . ."

"I see it. Shit."

The car sped up and went airborne as they jumped a small hill in the roadway. The front bumper struck the road as they landed. Lynch fought to keep the car on the pavement.

"It's getting harder to handle. Twelve cylinders is a hell of a lot of car."

The Ferrari roared over another bump in the road.

Kendra's looked at Lynch's face. She'd seen him in many dire situations before, but this expression was one she hadn't seen on him before.

Fear.

The steely focus was still there, but there was also perspiration on his brow and a clenched jaw. His sweaty hands tightened on the wheel. “This car isn’t stopping. At least not in one piece.”

“What do we do?”

“We need to get out without killing ourselves or anyone else. A little difficult to do at eighty miles an hour.”

His eyes flicked to a foothill towering over the road ahead.

“I’m going to try something.”

He drove for a moment longer as his face contorted into a grimace.

“That promising, huh?”

“Hold on to something. We’re about to leave the road.”

“What?”

“It’s going to get bumpy.”

She braced herself against the console. “Where are we going?”

He pointed to the ridge. “Straight up.”

“This is insane.”

“Probably. But it’s the only thing that can slow us down enough to jump out.”

“We could also flatten ourselves against it.”

“Trust me.”

“I do.” She moistened her lips. “It’s the laws of physics I have a problem with.”

"You have to do exactly as I say, *when* I say. Do you understand?"

She shook her head, her pulse leaping crazily. "Insanity."

"Do you understand?"

"Yes."

"Get ready . . ." He turned the wheel hard right and spun off the road.

She felt her teeth and spine vibrating in her skull. The Ferrari rocketed over—and through—brush and small stones on the unpaved hillside.

Rocks kicked up and peppered the windshield with spider-web cracks.

If anything, they seemed to be going faster.

"It isn't working!" Kendra shouted.

Lynch squinted to see through the cracked windshield. "I'm taking us up. Get ready to unfasten your seat belt."

Kendra placed her hands over the release and looked at the speedometer.

85 MPH.

80 . . .

70 . . .

Smash!

A large rock flew up and completely shattered the windshield in front of her face.

Kendra flinched, instinctively turning away.

"Are you all right?" Lynch shouted.

"Yes." She turned back toward the speedometer as more rocks struck the windshield.

60 . . .

55 . . .

50 . . .

Lynch swerved to avoid a pair of boulders embedded in the hillside.

45 . . .

40 . . .

"Unbuckle your seatbelt. Now."

Kendra looked at his face. This was the Lynch she knew. Calm in the face of overwhelming danger. Totally in control. As potentially deadly as their situation had become, his confidence was exactly what she needed.

She unbuckled her seatbelt.

"When we drop below thirty, open your door and jump. Roll away as fast and far as you can."

"What about you?"

"I'll be right behind you."

"Your seatbelt's still on."

"I'm staying behind the wheel until you get out."

"Lynch . . ."

"Don't argue."

The car suddenly felt as if it was travelling straight up, though she knew it was impossible. Gravity pulled her back into her seat.

"Get ready," Lynch said. "Thirty-five . . ."

He steered the car toward a grassy expanse of the

ridge. The engine roared as the tires slid and chewed up the soft earth.

"Now!"

Kendra threw open the door and jumped out. Her right hip landed hard on the hillside as she rolled away. She stopped herself and looked up just in time to see Lynch tumbling down the ridge above her.

She looked up to check the runaway car's trajectory.

The car.

It was rapidly approaching a sheer ninety-degree angle, which meant . . .

Oh, God.

It flipped backwards and flew downward.

Directly toward her!

"Kendra!" Lynch shouted.

There wasn't time to stand. She scrambled across the hillside, half-rolling, half-crawling, with no idea if she was moving toward or away from the car's path.

The roaring engine filled her ears.

Where in the hell was it?

Bammm. The car rocketed past her, tumbling down across the spot where she'd been only seconds before.

Her gaze followed the car down as it hit the bottom in a cacophony of twisted metal and broken glass. She smelled gasoline. Flames danced in the wreckage.

Lynch was climbing down to join her. "You okay?"

She wasn't sure. Her heart was pounding, her hands were shaking. "Yeah. I think so." She panted, "You?"

Lynch nodded. "Better now." Then he was next to her, pulling her into his arms. "Be still." The words were smothered in her hair. "Don't move for a minute. Just let me hold you. I was scared to death."

She wasn't about to move. She was clinging to him and the world was slowly beginning to right itself.

It took her a few minutes but she finally managed to let him go. She looked up at him. "It was Brock, wasn't it?"

"No question." Lynch stared at his burning car. "I'm sure of it."

"But we were only away from the car for ten or fifteen minutes."

"I've known people who could do far more in far less time." Lynch reached into his pocket. "I'll call Griffin. We'll have the FBI tow in my car and inspect it. Not that it will probably do much to—"

The Ferrari exploded, casting chunks of burning debris hundreds of feet!

Lynch sighed. "Or at least inspect what's *left* of it."

THE FBI EVIDENCE RESPONSE Team arrived within ninety minutes and Griffin and Metcalf arrived soon afterward.

Griffin stared at the burned-out husk of Lynch's car at the base of the ridge, forty feet from the road.

"Wow," he murmured. "Adam Lynch without his Ferrari. Only now do I realize that my mild annoyance at seeing you in that car was rooted in pure envy. Lord, it was a beautiful machine."

Lynch looked at him in surprise. "And here I thought you just came out here to gloat."

"I may have. But the sight of that wrecked car put things in perspective."

Metcalf joined them and nodded solemnly. "Tragic."

Kendra looked in disbelief at the three men staring so forlornly at Lynch's car. "You're joking, right?"

They weren't joking.

Kendra stepped between them and the car. "Forgive me for not giving that Ferrari due appreciation at this automotive wake. But, in case anyone's forgotten, this is the scene of an attempted murder."

"We realize that," Metcalf said. He motioned toward the car. "You're right, but that beauty deserves a little respect, please."

The twinkle in his eye told her he wasn't being entirely serious.

"Look, I expect Lynch to go into mourning, but there's no excuse for anyone else here," she said impatiently. "I've seen some of these same Evidence Response people making jokes while stepping over dead bodies. But for a smashed-up Ferrari, they're downright grief-stricken."

"Okay, okay," Lynch said testily. "I know you've never understood. It takes a certain mind-set." He looked between Griffin and Metcalf. "Any theories about what may have happened here?"

Griffin approached the still-smoldering car. "I talked to Jerome in the garage. He won't know until he looks at it, but he thinks it could have been a computer hack."

"I had the same thought," Lynch said.

"You think someone hacked your car?" Kendra asked.

"Most modern cars have computers more powerful than anything we have in our homes. If someone can access them, they can do a lot of damage."

"But how could they access it? I know how you coddle that car. That Ferrari was locked and alarmed tighter than a Brinks truck."

"Much tighter. It was a custom alarm system made especially for me. The key fob and my phone would shriek if anyone even attempted to break in, no matter how far away I was."

"And we were never more than a hundred yards away from your car while you were playing Superman. Wouldn't we have known if anyone tried to tamper with it?"

Metcalf looked intrigued. "Superman?"

"You would have had to have been there," Kendra said.

"It's good they weren't. We didn't need anyone else to stumble over when we were dodging that runaway car chasing us down the hill." Lynch knelt beside a charred object that may have been a headrest. "And we wouldn't necessarily know about any tampering. You've enjoyed my car's onboard Wi-Fi. Even though I had CIA-level encryption, nothing's uncrackable. They could have hacked in and burrowed into my car's computer system from a mile away."

"That's scary."

Lynch frowned. "I took every precaution, but I guess the only thing that would have worked is if I'd bought that 1963 Aston Martin DB5 I was looking at."

Metcalf, who had been looking through the rubble, instantly raised his head. "If you get one, can I drive it?"

"We'll see."

"Just once, Lynch."

"We'll see. In any case, I think a breach of my car's computer system is a good guess."

"And can you guess who might have done this?" Griffin asked.

"Kendra and I both have a guess. That's not the same as proof."

Griffin looked back at the training center. "Brock?"

"Possibly. It's too great a coincidence that this happened on their doorstep."

Griffin nodded. "I agree. And I'm surprised that explosion didn't bring them running. We'll go talk to them in a few minutes."

Lynch glanced behind him. "Or now?"

Kendra turned to see Josh Blake's green Lamborghini Gallardo pulling over to the roadside, just a few yards from where they stood.

Blake climbed out of his car, clutched his heart, and gave Lynch a sympathetic look. "Dude!"

"Not the reaction I was expecting," Kendra murmured.

Blake started to join them, but Griffin raised his hand. "You'll have to stand back. This is a crime scene."

Kendra moved toward Blake and made the introductions. "FBI agents Michael Griffin and Roland Metcalf, this is Brock Limited VP Josh Blake."

"Crime scene?" Blake said. "You're joking. One of my instructors drove by and told us there had been an accident involving a Ferrari. I was worried." He grimaced at the sight of the burned-out wreck. "You're lucky to be alive, Lynch."

Lynch fixed him with a cool stare. "Yes. We are. Twice in one day. How could that happen?"

"But a crime scene?" He shook his head. "It sounds a bit paranoid. Did someone force you off the road?"

"Paranoid?" Lynch's expression was no longer cool but icy, Kendra thought. He took a step forward as if he was about to demonstrate the head-twist-neck-break move on Blake.

Griffin probably thought so, too. He quickly stepped between them. "Mr. Blake, we'll be happy to fill you in.

But we need to talk to you about what happened here today."

He looked puzzled. "Why?"

"Just a few questions. Would you mind if we stopped by your facility in a few minutes?"

"I'd be delighted. But I'm afraid that conversation can't happen until I have one of our attorneys present."

Griffin stared at him in disbelief. "What?"

"Company policy. Brock Limited employees can't speak to any law enforcement officer about anything without an attorney."

"You spoke to us," Lynch said.

"If I'd known the purpose of your visit, our attorney would have been there." He turned back to Griffin. "I'm happy to cooperate in any way I can, but first we'll have to make arrangements for counsel."

"Do you realize how suspicious this makes your company look?" Kendra asked.

"It shouldn't. It's been our company policy for over a year. Check it, you'll see. I'm afraid my hands are tied."

"Such a shame," Lynch said.

"Well, I'm glad the two of you are all right. That's what's important." His smile was beaming. "We have a helicopter heading downtown in a few minutes. If you'd like to hitch a ride, there are two extra seats. I don't think that Ferrari is going to get you very far."

"No, thanks," Lynch said. "We have a ride."

Blake looked at the Evidence Response Team sifting through the wreckage and his smile didn't falter. "Of course. Enjoy the rest of your day." He turned and walked back toward his car.

"Huh," Kendra said quietly to Lynch as her gaze followed Blake. "Can't imagine why you wouldn't want to work for that guy."

Lynch turned back toward Griffin. "How quickly can your people take a look at my car's computer system?"

"Assuming there's anything to look at, I'll have them start this afternoon. And if we have to send it to Washington, we can have it there by early tomorrow."

"Good."

"Any news on Elizabeth Gelson?" Kendra asked.

"None. Her husband was supposed to have gotten back from Asia today, so we'll talk to him. We've pulled some traffic cam footage of her neighborhood and our people are combing it for a silver SUV or van. No leads yet."

Kendra turned back to watch Blake climb into his car and speed away. "What in the hell are they hiding?"

Lynch shook his head. "I have no idea. But they don't deal in small change. And whatever it is, they appear to believe it's worth killing both of us to protect."

"And maybe Elena Meyer?"

"Maybe."

Kendra thought for a moment. "You have some contacts in the Justice Department and the Department of Defense. Can they tell us more about Brock Limited?"

"I actually reached out to them last night. We'll see what they come up with."

She smiled. "I just remembered that I have a source, too. One with a military background who has an uncanny habit of knowing where bodies tend to be buried. She might be able to dig up something on them."

Lynch raised an eyebrow and then his lips suddenly lifted at the corners. "Sounds very familiar. Anyone I know?"

"Oh, yes." She met his eyes. "Don't you think it's time to call Jessie Mercado?"

DEREK LOOKED AT THE VIDEO playing on his van's in-dash DVD player. It was the only movie he'd watched in the past few weeks, but he still wasn't even close to growing tired of it.

There was a momentary video glitch as the maid of honor lifted her glass to her friend, the bride. "Lizzie and I have shared everything . . . a dorm room in college, eyeliner, study notes, and our embarrassing affection for sappy Kelly Clarkson songs."

The crowd generously chuckled.

People would always smile at Barbara Campbell, even though she had violated a cardinal rule of maids of honor.

She was prettier than the bride.

Barbara couldn't help the fact that she was a natural beauty, but she had obviously spent a lot of time with her hair, makeup, and tanning for the wedding. She was positively luminous.

Bad girl, Barbara. Mustn't upstage the bride.

He'd have to discuss that with her. And he would, very soon.

Derek looked up from the console screen. He was parked on Collins Drive, across from the clothing boutique Barbara owned with her sister. It was almost closing time, which meant Barbara would soon be locking the store and walking around the corner toward her blue MINI Cooper.

"What can I say?" Barbara's voice sounded tearful as she continued on the video. "Lizzie, you'll always be my best friend, my partner in crime, my soulmate . . ."

Lies. All lies. He knew they never saw each other anymore. But that was okay. They would soon be reunited.

The boutique's glass door swung open. It was her!

Derek started the van.

It's showtime, Barbara!

CHAPTER 7

Beverly Hills, California

10:30 P.M.

LYNCH LOOKED UNCERTAINLY at the dark street as Kendra parked her car. "Here?"

Kendra checked her phone again. "This is the place. Jessie told me to park here and walk about half a block up. She didn't want us to blow her stakeout."

Lynch looked around at the large Hillcrest Road estates. "These are ten-million-dollar houses. What kind of case is she working?"

"She didn't say. Just that it was a well-paying client and that if we wanted to talk to her tonight, this was the only way it could happen."

They climbed out of her car and walked down the street. Kendra looked at the street address numbers on the curb. "We should be at the right place."

"You are," a familiar voice whispered. "Though I've been wondering all night if I am."

Kendra and Lynch spun around to see a young woman stepping from the shadows. It was private investigator Jessie Mercado. She wore dark clothing and a pair of headphones and looked her usual sleek, vibrant self.

Kendra gave her a quick hug. "Sorry to crash your operation."

Jessie made a face. "I believe that's a misnomer." She was in her early thirties, but she could easily pass for a decade younger. Her short brown hair attractively framed her face in a pixie cut and her large brown eyes glistened in the moonlight. "Whatever this is, I'm not sure it can be called an 'operation.'"

Lynch bumped fists with her. "Then what is it?"

"Just another day, another dollar." She cocked her head toward a black Land Rover parked across the street. "Get in. We can talk in there."

Jessie took the driver's seat, Kendra took the passenger side, and Lynch climbed into the cluttered back seat.

"Sorry about all the junk," Jessie said. "Tools of the trade. Be careful, you may be about to sit on a stun gun."

"Now you tell me," Lynch said.

"Man up. The worst that'd happen is that you might wet your pants and froth at the mouth a little."

Kendra laughed. "Now I'd pay to see that."

"We'll talk later," Jessie said. "My rates are quite reasonable."

Lynch picked up a stun gun and a pair of binoculars and carefully placed them on the seat next to him.

Kendra peered out the windshield. "So what are you working on?"

"My current client is a movie studio that's bankrolling a two-hundred-million-dollar action film starring one of the biggest stars in the world. Said star recently lost his driver's license due to one too many DUIs. The star can afford every chauffeur in town, yet he still prefers to drive. Trouble is, if the cops catch him behind the wheel, the star goes to jail and the film gets put on a costly hiatus."

Kendra nodded. "So it's your job to make sure he doesn't drive."

"Yep. He's at a party in that white house at the end of the block. If he so much as climbs behind the wheel of his car, the studio has authorized me to block him and yank him out of the vehicle."

"Are you sure you can handle that?" Lynch asked. "You said he was a big-time action star."

"Big-time action star, surprisingly little guy." She gave him a sly glance. "But I think I've shown you that I'm capable of handling guys twice my size."

"True," Lynch murmured. "My ribs still haven't recovered."

Jessie smiled. “My confidentiality clause prevents me from telling you who this movie star is, but if you hang around long enough, you’ll soon see him. He’ll probably leave the party with at least two or three women who look like Victoria’s Secret models.”

“Tempting,” Kendra said. “But we have something else we need to talk to you about.”

“I figured you didn’t come all this way to watch me babysit Hollywood’s action hero du jour.”

“We’re working a murder case in San Diego.”

“Show-off.” She grimaced. “As if I wasn’t already feeling embarrassed by this job.”

“You said you were being well-paid,” Lynch said.

“Ridiculously well-paid. But it seems a little trivial when you’re probably making the streets safe from a monster.”

“We could use your help,” Kendra said.

Jessie leaned back in her seat and turned to more fully face her. “What’s the story?”

Kendra brought her up to speed on Elena Meyer’s murder and the trail that led them to Brock Limited.

“Brock?” Jessie practically vomited the word.

“I thought you might know them,” Kendra said.

“You could say that.” The sour look still hadn’t left her face. “They had a heavy presence in Afghanistan when I was there. Trust me, every soldier knew who they were. You’ll have a hard time finding anyone with anything nice to say.”

Kendra nodded. "I read a couple *Rolling Stone* articles today."

"You mean in the hours since they tried to kill you?" Jessie's flush of anger was visible even in the dimness of the car. "Believe me, they've managed to keep the worst stuff quiet. They took chances they never should have and we had to risk our lives to pull them out of some tough spots. Two good friends of mine died because of them."

"I never heard about this," Kendra said. She turned toward Lynch. "Had you?"

"Just rumors," Lynch said. "It probably wasn't unique to Afghanistan."

Jessie was getting even more visibly upset. "By the time these stories hit the media, it was presented that Brock Limited was pulling U.S. military forces out of harm's way instead of the other way around. To make things worse, our base commanders wouldn't even let us set the record straight. They said it would disclose confidential strategies and troop movements and that we could be court-martialed for treason if we spoke about it at all."

"Nice," Kendra said. "Looks like we came to the right person."

"I don't know about that. I'm not very objective where Brock Limited is concerned. I'd give anything to pound Vivianne Kerstine into the ground."

"She's their CEO, right?"

"Vivianne Kerstine was head of Brock's operations in Afghanistan when I was there. She was a tough and brutal woman and her own employees were terrified of her. But Brock must have liked what she was doing because she's now head of the entire company. And their fortunes have only skyrocketed since she became CEO."

Kendra took a deep breath. She hadn't expected such a strong emotional reaction from Jessie. In the short time she'd known her, nothing had seemed to faze her. "We think they're involved in this murder in San Diego. And maybe even this abduction. Will you help us?"

Jessie tensed her jaw. "Just try to stop me. What do you need?"

"Elena Meyer's only connection to San Diego was through her law firm and the Brock Limited case. Can you dig up anything on this case and what Elena might have gotten herself into?"

"I'll see what I can find out."

"Thanks, Jessie."

Jessie leaned back to address both Kendra and Lynch. "Listen . . . you think you know what Brock is capable of. But trust me, you have no idea."

"I think we do," Lynch said. "We almost died today, remember?"

"It won't stop there," she said curtly. "You need to watch your back."

Lynch nodded. "That's the plan."

"And if those guys are as bad as you say, you might take your own advice," Kendra said. "If you're poking around Brock Limited, you could find a target on your back, too."

"Believe me, that's nothing new. I might as well get a target tattooed back there." But she was suddenly smiling recklessly. "And as far as I'm concerned, Brock can do their damnedest. I've been waiting for the chance to bring some serious pain down on them."

KENDRA AND LYNCH TOOK Sunset Boulevard back to the I-405 and headed back to San Diego. Kendra finally broke the silence. "I admit I didn't expect Jessie to have such strong feelings about Brock. She's usually very cool and analytical."

"Neither did I. But then how much do we know about Jessie? She only lets us see what she wants us to see. We're probably lucky that she permits us to get past the first barriers."

"What? Barriers?" Kendra looked at him, startled. "Jessie doesn't try to hide anything. She's always been open with us."

Lynch shrugged.

She didn't understand this. "You *like* her. You admire her." She added in frustration, "Now you're saying that she might not be what we think she is?"

"I'm saying that Jessie's a very complicated woman." He smiled. "And I like what I see. I'm just not sure what else is beyond that first barrier. I'm looking forward to finding out."

"First barrier," Kendra repeated. "You said that before. You make her sound so guarded. You don't believe that what you see in Jessie is what you get?"

"I don't believe anyone is what they seem. That's what makes life fascinating, exploring the potentials." He chuckled. "You're frowning. I'm not attacking Jessie. I knew you'd probably be offended that I even hinted she might not be everything you think she is. You're very loyal and you consider Jessie your friend. But did you ever think that she might be even *more* than you think she is? Potentials, Kendra."

And she shouldn't be this surprised, she thought. Lynch was considered a world-class expert at not only identifying but pulling the strings of everyone with whom he came in contact. This kind of cool, judgmental analysis was his stock in trade. She'd just never thought it would be applied to someone she liked and respected.

"Actually, I was complimenting her," Lynch continued. "Complicated women are much more interesting." He met her eyes. "I have a passion for them."

She tore her gaze away. "Why can't you just accept people as you find them? Why do you have to analyze and tear everyone apart?"

"You've already figured that out. Perhaps for the same reason you tear a crime scene into impossibly small pieces until you know exactly what happened there." He added, "But Jessie's response wasn't all that unusual considering her background. There are mixed feelings about Brock in the intelligence community, but for soldiers on the ground it's obviously much more personal. It was a good idea to go to her. She'll be extremely motivated to find out what she can about them."

"More than I ever guessed she would."

"And you were also smart to warn her about them. It's a warning you should take to heart yourself, especially after what you've been through in the past couple of days."

Her brows rose. "Is this another play to get me to stay with you at your house?"

"Not a play. Just good advice. You know there's no place safer. And if someone does manage to penetrate my house's defenses—not damned likely—you have the security of knowing I'm in the next room." He grinned. "You might even get to see me perform the head-twist-neck-break maneuver on some unfortunate intruder. That alone should be incentive enough."

She frowned. "I'm not sure I'd really want to see that."

"Sure you would. Especially if was someone who was coming after you."

"My place will be fine, thank you."

"Oh well, you have about eighty-five minutes to change your mind. Think about it."

Less than thirty minutes had passed when Kendra's phone rang. She glanced at the Caller ID display on her console screen. Metcalf. She punched her steering wheel button to put him on speaker. "Working late for that government paycheck, Metcalf? You're on speaker with me and Lynch. What's going on?"

"Plenty." Metcalf's tone was grim. "It seems the scope of our investigation has changed, Kendra."

"What are you talking about?"

"A woman disappeared tonight. It looks as if she was taken near her workplace downtown as she was getting in her car."

Kendra felt that familiar knot in her stomach. "And you think she's connected with our case?"

"Oh, yes, almost certainly. Her name is Barbara Campbell."

"Who?"

"Barbara Campbell. You've seen her. Kendra . . . She's in the wedding video."

Kendra shared a quick glance with Lynch. He mouthed an expletive.

Kendra said it aloud. "Shit."

"Yeah. She was the maid of honor. But I'm afraid that isn't the worst of it."

"It gets worse?"

"I'm afraid so. Like I said, we think she was taken near her car." He paused. "And we got another unpleasant surprise."

A chill raced up her spine. Please, please don't let it be what she was thinking . . .

"It was the corpse of the first kidnap victim," Metcalf said. "The bride. Elizabeth Gelson. She was in the back seat."

Kendra inhaled sharply. "I was afraid of that. But that's crazy, isn't it? Why would—" She was trying to think. "Could we be looking at a serial killer?"

"It's still too early to tell what we're dealing with here, but we're already working through the possibilities. We're holding a powwow at the office tomorrow morning at 9:00 A.M. You and Lynch should be there. But before that, do you think you can get yourself to the crime scene before it's broken down?"

"We're on the road from LA. We can be there in an hour."

"Good. For the moment, we're sharing jurisdiction with San Diego PD. Evidence Response is finishing up right now and the ME is already playing Words with Friends on his iPhone. We'll hold the scene until you can take a look. We're at Collins and Broadway."

"Thanks, Metcalf." She shivered. "As always, you know how to show a lady a good time."

"It's what I do."

Kendra had a sudden thought. "One more thing. What are you doing to protect the other people in that video?" she asked. "If this is a serial killer, any of them could be next."

"We're on it." He added, "It's not easy. It was a huge wedding even without the immediate bridal party. Both bride and groom had large families, and the place was brimming with business guests as well. We decided we had to narrow it down to the bridal party and identified fourteen potential targets and reached out to them. The bridal party, parents of the bride and groom, and the officiant. There's still a couple we haven't been able to contact."

"Who?" Lynch asked.

"A bridesmaid and a groomsman. They're both out of town, but we left messages for both."

"This might be an opportunity to draw our perp out," Lynch said slowly.

"You want to use them as *bait*?" Kendra asked.

Lynch shook his head. "But they may already be targets. It makes sense to use it to our advantage."

"I'm sure it will be on the agenda tomorrow morning," Metcalf said quickly. "We'll talk when you get here."

He cut the connection.

Kendra glanced at Lynch. "Metcalf wasn't thrilled with your idea."

"He knew *you* weren't thrilled. He wanted to duck out before the fireworks started."

"No fireworks. It's just that putting innocent lives in jeopardy is never my first response."

"They may already be in jeopardy. If we can find a

way to protect them without calling attention to ourselves, it might be an opportunity to get this lunatic off the streets. That's our priority, isn't it?"

"It's not that simple." Her lips thinned. "You and I have both been part of investigations where plans like that have gone south."

"Horribly so. I admit it." He added quietly, "But if we don't act fast, we know that the chances are that more people are going to die. That's true, too, isn't it?"

Kendra didn't want to admit it, but she had a terrible feeling that he might be right. "Maybe. But I'm not ready to take that chance yet," she said unsteadily. "I'm not like you. I can't study a person or situation and analyze 'potentials' and decide if it's worthwhile to risk a life just because it *might* be a good idea. These are people we're talking about."

"I know that, Kendra," Lynch said. "And I'm not pushing. I'm just saying that there will come a time when you'll probably have to make a decision." He paused. "Or let me do it for you."

"The hell I will."

He chuckled. "Well, that was the response I thought I'd get. You were getting a little shaky. I'm glad to know you're back to normal. Now suppose we just wait until we get to the crime scene and see what we decide after we listen to what the ME says."

* * *

KENDRA AND LYNCH ARRIVED at the scene fifty minutes later. Barbara Campbell's MINI was parked on a side street, illuminated by a pair of work lights. The medical examiner's van was a few yards away, competing for space with an enclosed transport vehicle that would soon move the car to the FBI's garage. Two police cruisers were also parked nearby and four uniformed officers stood by at the periphery of the scene.

Metcalf greeted them with a weary shrug. "Hell of a day."

"Tell us about it," Lynch said.

Metcalf cocked his head toward the car. "We're about to let the ME take the body. You wanna take a look first?"

Kendra nodded.

She found her gait slowing as she approached the MINI. Damn. As many murder cases as she'd tackled, it never got easier. As she'd told Lynch, these were *people,* and life was precious to each and every one of them.

Kendra froze.

But maybe this was even harder than ever before.

Because there was Elizabeth Gelson, scrunched in the back seat. The pretty bride who had been so happy, so full of life in that video. So loved by her father, who was out of his mind with worry at the mere thought that his little girl might be in trouble.

Now, she was gone.

The victim was wearing a skirt, white blouse, and dark jacket, probably as she had dressed for work the previous morning. Her shoulder-length hair was surprisingly well coiffed and the only obvious evidence of her trauma was the severe bruising on her face and the tear stains of eyeliner running down her cheeks.

Kendra cleared her throat and turned to Metcalf. "Cause of death?"

"Strangulation, most likely. Burst blood vessels in the whites of her eyes."

Kendra knelt beside the open door and examined the skirt. Lightly splattered with what appeared to be orange juice, confirming the kitchen abduction as she'd envisioned it.

"Has the ME been able to pinpoint a time of death yet?"

"Twelve hours, give or take."

"So he held her captive someplace for over twenty-four hours before killing her. That explains the zip tie marks on her wrists and ankles." She examined her face. "There's also a rawness on the skin around her mouth. Maybe from duct tape."

Kendra glanced around at their surroundings. Although the side street was relatively secluded, they were less than fifty feet from the somewhat busier Collins Avenue, home to several restaurants, strip centers, and mini-malls, all now closed.

Kendra looked back toward the car. "Tricky. . . .

Abducting someone while at the same time leaving behind the body of your previous victim, all on a downtown city street."

Lynch nodded. "It was dark and these businesses near the car were closed. If he had a large vehicle like a van, he could have shielded himself from Collins Avenue where someone may have spotted him."

"That's how we figure it," Metcalf said.

Kendra stepped back, trying to take in the entire scene. "The body was put in the car first, before Barbara Campbell even left her store . . ."

"Most likely. The second he grabbed her, he would surrender some control of the situation. He probably wouldn't want to spend time moving the body inside her car while also having to contend with his newest victim."

"Unless he'd already killed her," Lynch said.

Kendra shook her head. "He hadn't. Barbara Campbell was alive, but unconscious."

"How do you figure that?" Metcalf said.

Kendra walked toward the car. "The driver's side door was ajar like this?"

Metcalf followed her. "Yes. And the bank deposit bag was on the street."

"Keys?"

"No. But her purse and cell phone were on the passenger seat."

Kendra glanced around. "Security cameras?"

"Only two nearby. One at the jewelry store across the street, another at the ATM down the block. Neither appear to be aimed at the car. We'll be checking the footage, of course."

Kendra turned back toward the MINI. The interior of the car was clean except for the slight traces of fingerprint powder still on the steering wheel and dashboard. Kendra pulled out her phone, activated the light and shone it on the side of the car. She worked her way around the vehicle, studying it as she completed a full turn.

"Anything?" Lynch said.

"Maybe." She turned to Metcalf. "Are there security cameras in her store?"

"Two. One on the floor, one on the cash register. The video feeds are stored in the cloud. We got the access codes from her sister-slash-partner just a little while ago. We'll examine the feeds to see if there were any creeps lurking about, if that's what you're thinking."

"It's not. I want to see what she was wearing when she left tonight."

Metcalf crossed his arms, his eyes narrowed on her face. "Why?"

Kendra kneeled beside the MINI. "This car is dirty. It hasn't been washed in a while. There's a thin layer of grime, undisturbed everywhere but just in front of the driver's side door." She aimed her light at the panel. "It looks like there was a scuffle here, like someone may have been thrown against the door. There are two fresh scratches here about five inches apart."

Metcalf looked at the scratches. "From keys or a weapon?"

"I'm thinking metallic buttons from a jacket, and they left these scratches during the struggle. If she's not wearing one, then it might be her abductor's. Then that's what you could look for on the security video. But it could just as well be that she was slammed against the door from behind, then rendered unconscious."

"By a choke hold?" Metcalf said.

"Probably ether. Look at those dried droplets on the driver's side window." Kendra moved the light to show the droplets. "Make sure your lab swabs for it."

Metcalf hunched over to see for himself. "How do you figure ether? Smell?"

Kendra nodded. "Yes, but there's something different about this scent. Still, it's an extremely recognizable odor. I'm sure it's ether."

"Okay. Anything else?"

She glanced around once more. "That's all I got. Let me know what your AV guys get off the store video, will you?"

"Sure. They may not have anything by our meeting tomorrow morning, but I know somebody's already on it."

Metcalf gave the twirling-finger "wrap it up" sign to the medical examiner, who nodded to an assistant still in the van. They began the grim task of removing the corpse from the car's back seat.

Kendra walked a few feet away and sat on the curb.

Lynch sat next to her. "You okay?"

She stared at the car a moment longer. "I still think I'm missing something here. Maybe something that might have helped protect Barbara Campbell."

"You're doing everything you can. You put Jessie to work on the Brock Limited angle, and for now we'll see where this side of the investigation takes us." He lifted her chin. "And if we're going to make that meeting tomorrow morning, I should get you home."

"I'll get myself home, after I drop you off at your house. I'm driving."

He made a face. "I keep forgetting."

She frowned. "Sorry about your car. I know how much you loved that thing."

He shrugged. "In the end, it was just a thing. The entire time it was being destroyed, all I could think about was you. Keeping you safe. And here you are, which counts as a win in my book. That alone makes it a good day."

He stood and extended a hand down toward her. "Let's go. I have a feeling tomorrow is going to be another long day."

CHAPTER 8

"WHO ARE WE waiting for?"

It was 9:15 A.M. and Kendra was getting impatient with the small talk with Metcalf, Griffin, a half-dozen FBI agents, and a pair of San Diego police detectives. They were in the fifth-floor FBI conference room, surrounded by freestanding bulletin boards plastered with photographs of the two abduction scenes. One board was entirely devoted to shots of Elizabeth Gelson's corpse, including several pictures that had obviously been sent over from the morgue in the past few hours. Kendra found herself averting her eyes from that board. She hated morgue shots. With no clothing, makeup, and hair pulled back, the photos stripped the victim of whatever had been left of her personality.

"Who are we waiting for?" Kendra repeated. "Can't they just join in later?"

Metcalf looked at Griffin. "Do you want to tell her or should I?"

"I'll take this one." Griffin smiled and turned toward Kendra. "Based on his performance on a previous investigation, I wrote a recommendation for a young man who applied to the Bureau. He put in some good work with the Florida Department of Law Enforcement and I thought his talents could be put to good use as a profiler in Washington. He's just come out of Quantico, and the Washington office is pretty well populated with profilers already. So he's joining us out here. His paperwork isn't even dry yet, but I asked him to take a look at this case."

"The FDLE," Kendra said suspiciously. "You couldn't possibly be talking about—?"

"Sorry I'm late everybody!"

Trey Suber walked into the conference room.

Kendra felt her jaw drop. "I'll be damned. Not our serial killer geek?"

Trey smiled. "I prefer serial killer *enthusiast*. Hello, Kendra. Good to see you again."

She smiled. "Hi, Trey." Trey Suber was in his mid-twenties, but he wouldn't have looked out of place in the halls of any high school. The thin, bespectacled man had assisted in her most recent case as part of a "dream team" of investigators who had flown in from all over the country. Since his teenage years, Suber had managed an online serial killer compendium that rivaled even the most comprehensive law-enforcement databases, giving him an encyclopedic knowledge of cases from around the world.

Lynch shook his hand. "Welcome, Suber. I'm still waiting for you to put out that set of serial killer trading cards."

Suber pushed up his glasses. "I think you're probably joking, but that's already a thing. I have several sets."

Lynch stared at him blankly. "I was joking."

Suber shrugged. "I'm in the market for a mint condition Eclipse 1992 Jeffrey Dahmer if you run across one."

"I sincerely hope I don't."

Kendra shook her head. "The Bureau is crazy not to keep you in D.C., Trey."

He smiled. "I think so, too. I may have spooked some of them. Serial killers is one area of expertise in which it's possible to be a little *too* good at your job."

"You'll show 'em," Kendra said.

"He's going to show us right now," Griffin said. "After I bring everybody up to speed on the investigation, I'm turning things over to Suber for his thoughts."

Metcalf patted Suber's arm. "Nothing like throwing you in the deep end, huh?"

He smiled cheerfully. "I'm ready."

Griffin stepped toward the head of the table. "Then let's begin."

Kendra and Lynch joined the others at the conference table and watched Griffin as he steered the team through the particulars of the case to date. Although Kendra had already been immersed in it, she appreciated Griffin's concise summary, including updated information about the murders of both women. The ME final report on Elena Meyer indicated that she had been shot from several yards away with a 9mm handgun that had also grazed her backside, indicating a pursuit before she bolted out onto Fifth Street. Elizabeth Gelson had been strangled by a small-handed attacker who probably placed a knee against her ribcage as he squeezed the life from her. No sexual assault, but there were some signs of bruising and torture. Her time of death was estimated as being only hours before her body was discovered.

Griffin displayed several shots of Barbara Campbell's car, both on the street and in the FBI garage. DNA swabs had been taken from several interior spots and outside the driver's side window, where forensics analysts backed up Kendra's observation that a scuffle had taken place.

After Griffin finished, Suber stepped up and plugged his own thumb drive into the laptop on the conference table. "Hello, everyone. I'm Special Agent Trey Suber. There are certain ritualistic aspects to this case that indicate we may be dealing with the start of a serial murder pattern." Suber pressed a tiny remote in his hand to bring up side-by-side photos of Elizabeth Gelson and

Barbara Campbell, which Kendra recognized as frame grabs from the wedding video. "We have two women abducted in the middle of their daily routines. They were connected by their friendship, but also by the wedding video in the possession of the third victim, who had no connection with the other two. And Elena Meyer was not abducted prior to her murder."

Suber displayed the shot of Elizabeth Gelson's corpse in the car. "This is extraordinary, for the murderer to place the corpse of the previous abductee at the scene of his new abduction. If the pattern continues, it will be something we've never seen before in the history of serial killers."

Suber's eyes were widening in a way that showed more enthusiasm than revulsion, Kendra thought. It didn't surprise her that some people were creeped out by him.

He displayed old crime-scene shots of Polaroids littered on sidewalks and parking lots. "This is the closest we've seen, in a 1974 case in which the killer left behind Polaroids of his victims' corpses. But our case obviously requires a much higher level of sophistication, planning, and just plain nerve. Our killer falls into the highly organized category, intelligent but not necessarily highly educated. He has difficulty forming personal attachments, but he may exhibit highly developed social skills when it benefits him. He's most likely aged twenty to thirty-five. The fact that his victim was killed only shortly before being deposited at this scene suggests that his latest abductee is probably still alive."

"Until he's ready to snatch someone else," Lynch said.

Suber nodded. "If the pattern holds."

The words sent a shiver through Kendra, even though the thought had already occurred to her.

If the pattern holds.

She turned to Griffin. "He probably has his next victim already picked out. That means she may have only hours to live."

"We're doing everything we can, Kendra."

"And the other members of that bridal party are still being protected?"

"Yes." Griffin nodded toward a pair of police detectives at the far end of the table. "San Diego PD is helping out with that."

Kendra thought for a moment. "And have you considered the possibility that one of the bridal party may be our killer?"

"Of course," Suber interjected with an offended tone. "Just before this meeting, I gave Griffin my evaluation of the most likely suspects in that group. Two groomsmen are especially worth looking at."

"We've already begun interviewing everyone who was at the wedding," Griffin said. "We have the entire guest list."

"Good." Everyone was being so very reasonable and competent, but Kendra couldn't shake the thought of Barbara Campbell imprisoned somewhere, at the mercy of a psychopath. How helpless she must feel.

And every wasted second would bring the woman closer to a horrible death.

"I want to talk to Elizabeth Gelson's husband. Is he back in town?" Kendra asked.

"He arrived from Beijing late last night," Metcalf said. "We had someone meet him at the airport with the news about his wife. He was devastated, as you can imagine."

Kendra *could* imagine. She was still haunted by the memory of Elena Meyer's parents at the medical examiner's office, of John Hollingsworth the morning his daughter was taken, and of dozens of other grieving relatives in the cases she'd worked.

"I'm sure it's hard for him to even function," she finally said. "I'm sorry. But I'd still like to speak to him. Today, if possible."

Lynch took a step closer to her. "It's possible. Make it happen, Griffin."

"You don't run things around here, Lynch. I'm not one of your Justice Department cronies. How many times do I have to remind you?" Griffin growled. "I thought she'd want to see him. I've already made arrangements."

* * *

"MR. GELSON?"

Kendra, Lynch, and Metcalf stood in the driveway of the Escondido home they had visited with Elizabeth Gelson's father only two days before. They had driven straight from the FBI building.

A parked Honda CRV was running and Kendra instantly recognized the driver from the wedding video. It was Jeffrey Gelson, the recently widowed groom. He was sitting in his car, staring dully out the windshield.

Kendra motioned for him to power down his window, and he complied.

"Mr. Gelson, I'm Kendra Michaels. I'm working with the FBI on your wife's case. I wonder if I could talk to you."

Gelson nodded. "Whatever." He looked stunned. "I . . . spoke to the FBI last night."

"I'm sorry. I know this is the worst possible time. Are you going somewhere?"

He nodded. "Funeral home. I'm supposed to make arrangements. My in-laws are meeting me there." He rubbed his temple. "It's the last thing I want, but I think we're in for a fight."

"You don't get along with your wife's family?" Metcalf said.

"Usually we do, but we have different ideas about how to handle . . . this. Liz wanted to be cremated and her ashes spread in Hawaii. She loved Hawaii . . . But her parents want her in a $30,000 mahogany coffin in Point Loma Cemetery." Gelson shook his head bitterly. "But I'm only the husband, right?"

"I'm sorry," Kendra said. "I know this is a bad time all the way around. We just have a few questions."

Gelson shrugged. "Go ahead. I'm in no hurry to get there, believe me."

Metcalf stepped forward. "I know the agents asked you about this last night, but now that you've had some time to think about it . . ." He hesitated. "Is there anyone who might want to target you or your wife?"

He frowned. "Like who?"

"You tell us," Metcalf said quietly. "Someone appears to have zeroed in on your wedding for some reason. Are there any exes—from you or your wife—who might be harboring bad feelings?"

"Bad enough to kill my wife and her maid of honor? No. There's no bad blood between me and my old girlfriends. And two of Liz's ex-boyfriends were actually at the wedding. With their wives." He cleared his throat. "No bad feelings. I don't think you'll find any suspects there."

Metcalf handed him his business card. "Just to be sure, I'd appreciate it if you would email me their names and addresses later today."

Gelson looked at the card. "Okay. Sure."

Kendra leaned in closer. "And there's one thing we haven't found out yet. We ran across a video of your wedding. It was shot with a phone by a tall man in a tux. We still don't know who it was who took that video."

Gelson thought for a moment. "Oh, that was a guy I went to college with. Paul Tate. He shot and edited that as kind of a present for us." He shrugged. "Liz loved it."

"It was a nice gift," Kendra said. She turned to Metcalf. "We have Paul Tate's information?"

Metcalf nodded. "I remember his name from the guest list."

Lynch took a step closer to Gelson. "Do you know a woman named Elena Meyer?"

He shook his head. "No."

"She was a paralegal from Connecticut," Lynch said gently. "She was killed with a copy of the video on her. That's how it came to our attention."

For the first time, Gelson seemed to emerge from his fog. His face was registering surprise.

Kendra spoke softly. "Do you have any idea how this woman came to have your wedding video on her?"

"No idea. But I know Paul put it up on YouTube for a few weeks so that everybody could see it. Especially people from out of town who couldn't make the wedding. We sent the link out to everyone on our invitation list. I don't think it was a private link or anything, so I guess anyone could have seen it and downloaded it."

"Probably so. Thank you, Mr. Gelson. We won't take any more of your time."

He nodded. "Is there any word about Liz's friend Barbara?"

"Not yet," Metcalf said.

"You gotta find this guy," Gelson said hoarsely. "Whatever it takes, whatever you have to do."

"We'll find him," Lynch said. "Trust me."

He spoke with such certainty, such authority, that Gelson seemed to take comfort in his words. He nodded jerkily, then backed his car out of the driveway and drove away.

Kendra turned to Lynch. "That's why I could never make this my life's work. It tears me apart to see people like that man."

"You're helping them. Whatever peace and closure there is to be had, you're getting it for them."

"It's not enough."

"It can never be enough for them. But it's something. And you're keeping others from feeling the pain he has." He added quietly, "And that's everything."

Kendra's phone vibrated in her pocket. She fished it out and looked at the screen. "I just got a text from Jessie. She may have something for us."

"Jessie Mercado?" Metcalf said. "You brought *her* into this?"

"Yes."

"Why?"

"Why not? She has a way of getting back-channel

info that would take your office weeks to get through official channels. We don't have time to waste." She gazed at him with a hint of belligerence. "Do you have any objections?"

Metcalf blinked. "No, just asking."

Kendra scrolled down to read the rest of Jessie's text. "She'd like us to meet her in her office this afternoon."

"That was fast," Lynch said.

"She doesn't let the grass grow beneath her feet. You know that about her." She looked him in the eye. "And you also know how damn good she is."

"I do." He was smiling faintly. "I'll never argue that with you. I wouldn't dare. Where's her office?"

"Santa Monica." She tilted her head. "What do you say? Wanna go to the movies?"

Lynch looked at her quizzically. "What?"

KENDRA AND LYNCH ARRIVED at Santa Monica's Montana Avenue a few minutes before 2:00 P.M. They parked on a block of shops and restaurants, directly in front of a 1940s-era revival movie theater. The neon-lined marquee announced that the current attraction was a pair of *Thin Man* films.

They climbed out of the car and Lynch looked with interest at the box office. "Her office is in the movie theater?"

"No, it's *over* the theater. You can't even get to her office from inside there."

"Then how do you get to it?"

"Follow me."

She led him around the corner to a large door on the building's east side. She tried it. Locked.

"Are you sure this is the right place?" Lynch asked.

Kendra pointed to a small, sun-faded plaque that read "MERCADO INVESTIGATIONS." There was a button below, but before she could press it, there was a buzzing sound. Kendra pulled the door open and pointed to a camera mounted just under the theater's roofline. "She's already seen us. Let's go."

They moved through the door and climbed a long, dark stairway. They emerged at a reception area with a mission-style desk, shelves, and a leather couch. No one there.

"Come in!" Jessie's voice came through an open doorway.

Kendra and Lynch stepped into Jessie's office, which was dominated by art deco shelving and a large, beautifully restored wooden desk that was probably as old as the theater. Wood shutters covered the windows. Jessie was seated at her desk, scrolling through photos on her camera's screen. "Welcome."

"Still no receptionist?" Kendra said.

Jessie didn't look up from her camera. "I've had three since you were here last. I had to fire all of them. One was never on time, another spent hours every shift flirting with the ticket taker downstairs, and the other decided to direct my prospective clients to her stoner boyfriend, who undercut my price by half."

Kendra shook her head. "Wow."

"Yeah. The dumbass almost got himself killed tailing a cheating husband. Anyway, I've been too busy to interview more candidates."

Lynch stared at a wall of photographs of Jessie at different times in her varied and interesting life. There were pictures of her in uniform in Afghanistan, as a contestant on the *American Ninja* television show, and as security director for a teenage pop star.

"Nice office," Lynch said. "I've never seen one like it."

Jessie finally looked up from the camera. "That was the idea. It's all me. Thanks."

"Do you ever see the movies downstairs?"

Jessie smiled. "The owners say I can go for free whenever I want. A perk of my rental agreement, I guess. I've been too busy to take advantage of it."

"And we've made you busier," Kendra said. "Sorry about that."

"Don't worry about it. Some jobs are worth a little hassle." She rifled through a stack of papers on her desk. "In your investigation so far, have you ever run across the name Ryan Facey?"

Kendra and Lynch shook their heads.

Jessie showed them a photo printout of a narrow-faced man with a gray-black beard. "Ryan Facey. Ex-Special Forces, for the past four years he's been a so-called security specialist for Brock Limited. He works out of the San Diego office."

Lynch studied the photo. "You think he may have something to do with our case?"

"I'm not sure. But I do know that he's gone missing in just the past few days."

"Missing? You think he may be another victim?" Kendra asked.

"Don't know. It seems different than that. There's been no police report filed. The only reason I found out about it is that a couple of Brock's people have been making a lot of noise looking for him. They've been leaving their business cards at his usual haunts—with his building doorman, at his gym, even at his dentist, where he missed an appointment yesterday."

"You found all this out today?" Kendra asked.

"I'm used to working fast. In my business, time is money." Jessie shrugged. "You wanted information on Brock, so I ran all their San Diego operatives through the activity databases. Even a few that the general public can't usually access. I thought it was strange that Brock Limited was searching for arrest, hotel, and airline information for someone who worked for them. I followed up by looking for Facey myself. That's when I found out that Brock's agents have been leaving business cards and fifty-dollar bills around for anyone who might run across the guy."

"And who are these Brock people?" Lynch said.

Jesse turned her camera screen around to show a pair of Brock Limited business cards she'd photographed on a countertop.

"Gilbert Billings and Lawrence Gaines," Kendra read.

"Know either of them?" Jessie asked.

"Gaines is an ex-Army Ranger," Lynch said. "He spent some time freelancing before going with Brock. I don't know Billings."

"Well, I started scanning their names on all the databases and I got an immediate hit. The two of them got on a plane for Portland this morning. I have no way to tell if it had anything to do with Ryan Facey, but it looks like they've been doing little else lately. And here's something else . . ." Jessie pulled another sheet from the stack on her desk and handed it to Kendra. "Facey flew to Connecticut last week. That's where your first victim, the paralegal, lived. Right?"

Kendra nodded. "Yes."

"Hard to say if he had any contact with her, but it raises the question that his disappearance and their search for him might be related."

"Yes," Lynch said. He turned to Kendra. "I think we need to find Ryan Facey. Before Brock does."

"How do you propose we do that?

Lynch thought for a moment. "I'm going to Portland."

"What?"

"That's where the trail is leading. Jessie can keep

helping with any more information she uncovers and I'll make use of my own sources."

"I can't go to Portland," Kendra said impatiently. She was suddenly remembering the sight of Elizabeth Gelson in the back of the MINI. "There's too much going on here."

"I realize that you're too busy. I don't want you there anyway. You'd probably get in my way. You're not aggressive enough to deal with Brock's agents. You tend to be a little too polite. I told you that they can be very nasty characters."

"I can vouch for that," Jessie said sourly.

Lynch smiled teasingly at Kendra. "Besides, Metcalf will be happy to have you all to himself anyway."

Jessie stood from behind her desk. "He won't have her to himself," she said curtly. "I'll be there."

Kendra frowned as she turned toward her. "You? I thought you were busy babysitting that movie star."

"No, that's done. He leaves for Abu Dhabi tonight for six weeks of location shooting. The studio asked me to go, but I politely declined. He'll be someone else's problem." She shrugged. "I was going to spend some time at my place in Vancouver, but this sounds a hell of a lot more interesting."

"Yes, doesn't it," Lynch murmured. "I'll be sorry to miss out watching the two of you bond. I imagine it might be an exploration of potentials that would be totally unique."

"What the hell are you talking about?" Jessie asked bluntly, her gaze narrowed on his face. "That sounds weird as hell. Don't you want me on this job, Lynch?"

"Absolutely. Isn't that what I said?"

"It's hard to tell through the double talk." Her gaze was still searching his expression. "But I believe that there's something else going on here other than the obvious. I don't have time to play games. I want Brock. Are you going to trust me to find a way to get them?"

"Forget Lynch," Kendra said curtly. "Of course, I'm going to trust you. Why else did I hire you? And that's all that's important. Lynch probably trusts you, too. But you're right, he tends to play stupid games."

"Not stupid." Jessie was still looking at Lynch. "He's never stupid. Are you going to trust me, Lynch?"

"Oh, yes." He smiled. "Think about it. I'm leaving you with Kendra. Do I trust you?"

Jessie gazed at him a moment longer. Then she turned away. "Someday you're going to tell me what that was all about. Right now, both of you get out of here so that I can get back to work. I'll call you later, Kendra."

"Right." Kendra was already out of the office and going down the stairs. She glanced back at Lynch. "Was that necessary?"

"No, but you learned a lot about Jessie from just an enigmatic few words from yours truly." He cocked his head. "Let's see, she's so sharp that she can sense every nuance, she reacts with boldness instead of caution when she feels threatened, she's studied both of us enough to get a grip on who we are and how we'd behave in a given situation." He glanced at her. "And she's completely aware of how I feel about you and the consequences if she doesn't take good care of you while I'm gone."

"I don't need either one of you to take care of me," she said through set teeth. "For heaven's sake, we're involved in an investigation and I usually manage to survive, don't I?"

"Are you going to throw that twenty-six number at me again?" He shook his head. "Won't work. You have your areas of expertise and I have mine. It's only sensible to stick to what you're good at. Would you care to go over my numbers?"

That's the last thing she wanted. She'd seen some of the scars on his body and those numbers must be in the legend category. "I probably couldn't count that high." She paused. "Just how nasty are those guys you're going to be searching for in Portland?"

"Probably just enough to be entertaining." He held the car door open for her. "I'd bet Jessie's secretly jealous that I get to go instead of her. You'll have to tell me when I get back."

"How would I know?" She got into the driver's seat. "I have no intention of probing into who she is or what she's feeling. That would be an intrusion into her privacy. I told you, I don't play those games, Lynch."

"Not intentionally." He was around the car and

getting into the passenger seat. "But now you know what to look for and how to interpret. Are you going to be able to resist getting the entire picture of Jessie Mercado?"

"I sincerely hope I can," she said.

"I know you do," he said gently as he reached out and touched her cheek. "And I hope you can't. I kind of like the idea of you being surrounded by friends and people who care about you. It makes me feel safer about going off and leaving you. But you tend to be very careful who you choose to accept into that circle, and one of those prerequisites is total honesty. You have to really *know* them." He shrugged. "You really *like* Jessie Mercado, that's why I thought it might be worth your effort to get beyond that first barrier."

"Which I'm sure doesn't exist," she said shortly. "You're making this sound like an audition, which is totally ridiculous. You can just do your own probing and analyzing, if you're not afraid she might deck you."

He threw back his head and laughed. "There's always that danger. You might be close to that point now. Are you too pissed off to take me to the airport?"

"I guess not." She backed out of the parking space. "At the moment, the idea of you soaring out of my life and into the blue has a certain appeal."

He was still laughing as he leaned back on the seat. "Then, by all means, get me to that airport so that I can oblige you."

But when she dropped him off at the airport, he would be boarding that flight that would take him to Portland and she wasn't going with him. It didn't seem right. She'd refused to go, but in spite of what he'd said, maybe she'd been wrong to refuse. She didn't want him to be alone, dammit. He was always alone and accepted it without a second thought. Hell, he enjoyed being a loner.

She was the one having trouble with it and it was probably stupid and unreasonable, but she couldn't shake the feeling that it was wrong.

I kind of like the idea of you being surrounded by family and friends.

But when did he ever have that comforting sense of someone watching over him? The idea was almost laughable. Yet she wasn't laughing. She should be able to do something, anything, to help him, keep him from being that alone. . . .

CHAPTER 9

FORTY MINUTES LATER Kendra drove into the short-term parking lot at Los Angeles International, parked and got out of the driver's seat. "Don't just sit there. Let's go. I need to get back to San Diego sometime today."

"Sorry to inconvenience you." He got out of the car and strolled toward the exit. "I was just surprised. I thought you were just going to drop me off. I didn't expect you to actually deliver me to my gate."

"Don't be ridiculous. The closest I could get would be security." She stopped before crossing the street to the terminal. "It just occurred to me that you weren't exactly prepared for this trip. You don't even have an overnight bag." She added, "And you don't have a reservation yet. What if you can't get a flight out? It might be better if you had someone available to run you to another town or airport if you have trouble."

"Very wise," Lynch said solemnly. "And Los Angeles has so few choices in air service. I might be left high and dry."

"It could happen." She didn't look at him as she crossed the street. "I'm just being efficient. Stop being so damn arrogant. I know you think that you can handle anything that comes along from Beijing to Tehran. You probably can. But why not occasionally take a little help? It wouldn't hurt you. I'll just go in with you and check it out and then turn and leave if—"

"Hush." He took her arm and spun her to face him as they reached the terminal. "I'm not arguing. I have no pride where you're concerned." He was smiling gently. "Go ahead. Be efficient. Take care of me." His gaze was on her face. "But do you mind telling me where this came from? One moment you were ready to jettison me into the stratosphere, and the next I'm being cosseted like one of the kids at your studio."

"No, you're not," she said curtly. "Because my kids would never be as self-destructive as you are. They'd never think it was fun to go up against murderers and sickos. And they'd accept my help if I offered." She frowned. "That last wasn't quite true. I meant, once I explained and found a way to reach out to them."

"Yes, by all means, qualify that. I've seen how hard

you work to reach those kids." He tilted his head. "Now can we get down to why this is applying to me?"

She shrugged. "On the way to the airport I just started thinking how you want to run everything in your world, but never let any of your rules apply to yourself. First, I found myself actually fretting about it. Then I began getting pissed off."

"I thought I was getting mixed messages. Elaborate."

"All this crap about how it would make you feel better if I had more friends around me so that you wouldn't have to worry. Too bad, Lynch. Not only is it not your business, how many people do you allow to reach out and help you? You cheat all of us."

"Am I bad?"

"It's not a joke." She added wearily, "Or maybe it is to you, but it's not to me. It just shows we're not even on the same playing field. I thought this time that I'd try to see how far I could get before you shut me down. It wasn't very far, was it?"

"I just had to see where you were going," he said quietly. "If it's bothering you, we'll work on it." He smiled mischievously. "Now do you want to come in and make me reservations and then buy me an overnight bag?"

"No." Then she added fiercely, "I only want you to not get yourself killed in Portland because you think you're made of Kevlar and you don't need to call anyone for help."

"I can handle that. No problem. Much easier than—"

His phone was ringing and he glanced down at the ID. "Dr. Alan Fletcher at the naval hospital. I should take it."

"Yes, you should." She started to turn away. "I think we're done here."

"No, we're not." He put his hand on her arm. "Not nearly. Wait." He answered the call. "Alan, I'm in the middle of something. What is it?" He listened for a moment. "No, I can't come, but I'll send Kendra. Leave two passes for this afternoon. I'll have her call you." He cut the connection. "It's something about the chemical he found in your system. I thought you and Jessie might want to talk to him."

"Yes, I do." She tried to break his grip on her arm. "It sounds much more productive than the discussion we've been having. Though I knew that was the way it would turn out." She held up her hand as he started to speak. "I know you can't change who you are. I shouldn't have tried. I don't even know why I thought it would be worth it."

"I don't either." He paused and then looked down into her eyes. "But I'm glad you did. It made me feel . . . valued."

She couldn't tear her gaze away. She tried to joke. "Valued? Says the man who charges fees that stagger the imagination. I'm sure that it was only a temporary aberration."

"And I'm not at all sure. Now do you want to come

inside and hold my hand until I get on my way or do you want to go see Fletcher and trust that I'll be able to handle this on my own?"

"Don't be ridiculous. I told you that I'd made a mistake and that—"

He kissed her. "That's once. Everyone expects people to be kissing at airports. I thought I might as well get something out of it." He kissed her again. "That's twice. I'll call you when I get to Portland, providing I manage to make it out of this tiny, completely uncivilized airport at a decent time."

He turned and walked toward the entrance.

Her lips were tingling and her heart was pounding and she wanted to follow him into that terminal. "Damn you, Lynch."

He looked back over his shoulder. "I meant it," he said softly. "Valued, Kendra."

Then he disappeared inside the terminal.

She drew a deep breath and then turned and started back toward the parking lot.

She didn't know quite what had happened to her during these last hours. Lynch always managed to disturb and turn her day into chaos. This had just been a different sort of chaos.

It made me feel . . . valued.

But she did know that those words had touched her and warmed her and made her also feel valued.

And she'd better forget about them because she had work to do. She couldn't be thinking about Lynch and what he might or might not run into in Portland. That nonsense had been what had led her into that emotional, idiotic scene after they'd arrived here at the airport. Totally unprofessional.

She dialed Jessie the minute after she got back to her car. "Lynch got a call from Doctor Alan Fletcher, who treated me for that poison attack we told you about. He has new information about something he found in the chemical in my system. Want to go with me to talk to him?"

"If you think he's worthwhile seeing."

Kendra had a sudden memory of Alan Fletcher the last time she'd seen him. She chuckled. "There's not a woman in the universe who wouldn't think Fletcher's worthwhile seeing."

"What's so funny?"

"Not to objectify the man, but he's rather spectacular."

"How spectacular?"

"Over the top."

"And he's a physician?"

"Yes."

"And totally brilliant?"

"All in one package. Do you want to go along?"

"Let's see, go visit a spectacular-looking physician

who's also totally brilliant. Can you give me a minute to consider it? Never mind. I feel it's my duty. When and where?"

"I'm on my way to the naval hospital now. Do you want me to pick you up?"

"No, I'll take my Harley down to San Diego. I'll need it anyway. I'll meet you at the naval hospital. See you there."

"LYNCH MANAGED TO GET a flight out to Portland?" Jessie asked when she met Kendra in the parking lot in front of the hospital.

"Probably." She didn't look at Jessie as she locked her car. "I didn't stick around to see. He usually finds a way to get whatever he wants."

"I've noticed that." Jessie grinned. "And why should you hang around to watch the inevitable happen?"

"Exactly." Kendra turned and walked briskly toward the front entrance of the hospital to get their badges. "He doesn't need anyone. And he was almost rude to you today. I felt like socking him."

Jessie laughed with genuine amusement. "I can take care of myself, Kendra." She shrugged. "Though I was a little confused about his attitude toward me today until I figured it out. He was a little uneasy about taking that trip to Portland. I think maybe there was a lot of things going on inside that devious brain of his, but he was basically telling me that he trusted me to take care of you. But that I'd better do it right or face the consequences."

"Ridiculous. You weren't hired to take care of me. We have a job to do together."

"Right." Jessie paused. "I'm not certain he has that straight. But I do know he's well aware what bastards those guys at Brock can be and how I feel about them. It was a clear warning to keep my focus straight on what he considers important." She chuckled again. "And in his view he's the only one who should control what's important and what's not. Though from what I've heard about him he seems to have convinced half the world's intelligence community of the same thing."

"The *entire* intelligence community," Kendra said sourly. "Even Griffin thinks twice about going against him and he used to work with him. I've never understood the dynamic. But then I've never understood anything going on with Lynch. How could I? For instance, he never even talks about the past, it's always the present."

"Not even to you?"

"Only if the past influences our present."

"Interesting." Jessie was presenting her ID to the agent at the security desk who was handing her a badge. "And disappointing. I'd bet he has some fascinating tales to tell."

"That's what he thinks about you," Kendra said as she took her badge and fastened it on her jacket. "He said I should explore what's beyond 'the barriers' with you. I told him if there were barriers then what was behind them wasn't my business."

"There *are* barriers." Jessie smiled. "And I can see that Lynch would want to make sure there aren't also thorns that could sting you. You're far more trusting than he is."

"Good. I wouldn't like to live in his world." She didn't know why she had even gotten into this conversation with Jessie. She'd had no intention of doing so. But then nothing was going as she'd intended today. She changed the subject. "We need to go to the auxiliary structure adjacent to the main hospital."

"Right." Jessie adjusted the badge on her leather jacket as she followed her to the annex. "I've been in this hospital before. They don't usually make you wear these things when you visit a patient."

"I think there are a lot of labs in the auxiliary building. NCIS uses some of them for forensics work, that kind of stuff."

"And how does Lynch know this doctor?"

Kendra shrugged. "It's kind of mysterious, like all things Adam Lynch. I got the feeling that they'd worked together on some things neither of them are too anxious to talk about."

"But you didn't ask him questions." Jessie's lips were twitching. "Because it wasn't your business." She held up her hand. "I'm not making fun of you. I'm just accustomed to asking questions of everyone. It's how I make my living. I'd starve if I was as sensitive as you about—" She broke off, her gaze fixed on the hall ahead. "That *has* to be him."

Kendra looked toward the end of the corridor and sure enough Dr. Alan Fletcher was holding court with two nurses and an orderly. The staff members were smiling and hanging on his every word. "That's the guy. And I guess he travels with his own fan club."

"You're right, he's very good-looking. Even spectacular, as you said." Jessie studied him for a moment. "But he may be a little too much of a pretty boy for my taste."

Kendra nodded at the nurses and orderly. "Doesn't seem to bother them. To each his own."

Alan had spotted them and waved off his adoring staff members. "Excuse me." He turned toward Kendra and Jessie. "Thanks for coming. I was hoping Lynch would be able to run down here, but it's kind of you to fill in." He made a face. "That was rude. Forgive me, I know how prestigious you are in your field. I'm just used to Lynch."

"You're forgiven." Her gaze was still on the departing nurses. "But I'm afraid that blond nurse isn't going to forgive *me*. She seems heartbroken that you've dismissed her."

"Her?" He shook his head. "She's married."

"So?"

"You're mistaken. She's just being nice. We're all a team here."

And he might actually believe that. "Great." She gestured to Jessie. "Dr. Alan Fletcher. Jessie Mercado. You'll find she's a great team player, too. She's a private investigator."

"Really?" Alan shook her hand. "Lynch doesn't usually deal with the private sector."

"Well, I'm the exception to most rules," Jessie said. "And this case was too interesting for me to pass up. I get to do my part in cleansing the environment of scum." She grimaced. "And it beats most of the other assignments I get."

"I hear you." Alan's eyes were twinkling. "When I'm done here, I need to get back to my office to check the results of a patient's stool sample labs."

Kendra smiled. "Glamorous. What do you have for me?"

Alan motioned for them to follow him down the hallway. "I decided to take a closer look at the toxin that was sliced into you the other night."

"I thought you already knew what it was."

"We do. Tribuxin. But it was another substance, a synthesized protein, we didn't immediately recognize. It took a while, but I finally identified it. It's a carrier protein used to speed absorption of drugs into the bloodstream. That's why the toxin acted so quickly on you."

Alan led them through a set of double doors to a long narrow lab populated by a half-dozen workers in scrubs. He stopped in front of a large monitor mounted above a console. He pressed a few buttons on the keyboard until the screen flickered and displayed two side-by-side images, each with a series of splotches that had absolutely no meaning for Kendra. Alan proudly cocked his head toward it.

"I'm sure I should be impressed, but I don't know what I'm seeing," Kendra said.

"Sorry," Alan said. "I forgot my audience. If you were a pair of research scientists, you'd be bowing down before me right now. Maybe even erecting a statue or sculpture garden in my honor."

Jessie nodded. "Or building a towering monument to your humility."

"I've already been through that with him," Kendra said. "You'll find no shame there."

"Absolutely not," Alan said. He pointed back to the screen. "This carrier protein that we found in you is an exact match for one that comes from one place and one place only: Gensyn Labs, right here in San Diego. They manufacture it and they own the patent on it. There are other similar ones, but none with these specific characteristics."

"But couldn't they have sold it to anyone?" Kendra asked.

"I'm sure they'd like to, but the FDA hasn't approved it yet. As far as I know, it's only been made available for research purposes."

Kendra studied the screen. "They created the poison cocktail that threw me for a loop?"

"It's a pretty good bet."

Kendra turned back toward Alan. "Does the FBI know this?"

"I sent this over right after I called Lynch. The FBI lab in Washington is working on its own analysis, but of course they're quite a bit slower than I am. Griffin doesn't want to approach Gensyn until the FBI lab results come back."

Kendra muttered a curse beneath her breath. "Does he know who you are?"

"Same question I asked. Incredibly, he still wants to wait."

"What's the name of the lead researcher who developed this?" Jessie asked.

"It was developed by Gensyn's Pharmacological Research Group."

"Can you give me a name?"

Alan checked a note pad lying next to his work station. "The support papers were written by Gregory Farnsworth. He's probably the man in charge."

Kendra pointed to the side-by-side images. "Please print these out for me, Alan."

"Sure." Alan pressed a button on the keyboard and a

printer whirred behind them. "May I ask what you're planning on doing with it?"

Kendra and Jessie shared a quick look.

"It's probably better if I don't tell you," Kendra said.

"Really?" Alan's face was suddenly beaming. "That's truly marvelous. I could tell at the hospital that you and Lynch were kindred souls. Do let me know if I can be of any further help." He turned and strode out of the lab.

"Maybe he's not as pretty as I thought he was," Jessie murmured as she watched him leave. "He's definitely growing on me. I think I like him."

JESSIE CLIMBED INTO the passenger seat of Kendra's car and pulled the door closed with a lingering look back at the hospital. "Well, he actually is too pretty, but he's smart and funny and that takes some of the edge off."

"And he obviously made an impression on you, if you're still thinking about him."

"I just appreciate the fact that he can rise above a handicap like that. Can you imagine having to push women out of your way on a twenty-four-hour basis?" She chuckled. "Who the hell would want to take on a task like that?"

"I'm glad he amuses you. Any ideas about where to go with the information he gave us? He might have given us his subtle seal of approval, but he clearly left the execution up to us."

Jessie thought for a moment. "I'm sure your immediate inclination is to go straight to Gensyn Labs and demand information. That's what anyone would do if they had the full force of the FBI behind them." Her lips quirked. "Though I'm sure you'd be courteous and polite with any demand in case it wasn't your business."

Kendra scowled. "Knock it off, Jessie."

"Sorry, I couldn't resist. But the FBI isn't behind you, at least not yet. And I take it you don't want to wait on their lab?"

"Hell, no. There's a killer out there who still has Barbara Campbell." She only hoped that the woman was still alive. "I don't know how much time we have."

"My feelings exactly. And since you can't rely on the FBI just yet, I thought we'd play it the way I usually do. By taking it a little more street level."

Kendra thought for all of three seconds. "I like it."

LESS THAN HALF AN HOUR LATER, Kendra slowly drove up and down the rows of parked cars in front of the three-story Gensyn Labs complex. "Anything?"

Jessie glanced down at her phone. "The DMV records tell us that Dr. Farnsworth owns a silver Mercedes AMG. We've seen two black ones so far, but no silver. It's almost five, so he may have already gone home."

"Or he may be on vacation," Kendra said. "Or he just bought a new car and it hasn't been registered with the DMV yet."

"All strong possibilities."

"Frustrating possibilities. If this doesn't work, I guess we can try his home. You have his address there, right? Or maybe we can—"

"Just a minute," Jessie interrupted. "There's a guy over there that looks a lot like his driver's license photo. And he's walking toward—" Her eyes lit up. "It's a silver AMG."

Kendra stepped on the gas.

"Circle around," Jessie said. "Block him in."

Kendra rounded the corner and raced back up the aisle. She jammed on the brakes. Then she and Jessie jumped out of her car and converged on the parked Mercedes.

Inside the car, a nervous, balding man in his fifties looked up at them in bewilderment. He slightly lowered his window. "What's wrong? Has there been an accident? What's happening?"

"No accident." Get his attention, Kendra thought. Take him off guard. He was a scientist, hit him with his own work. She slapped the printout Alan Fletcher had given them on his driver's side window. "This is happening. We need to know why."

Farnsworth blinked, but his gaze was instantly drawn to the printout. He frowned. "This isn't right . . . Where did you get these?" Then he shook his head. "But I don't know if I should even be talking to you. I'm not accustomed to being confronted in my company's parking lot.

Perhaps you should go inside and explain what you're doing here."

"I'm afraid we don't have time," Kendra said. "I can see why you might be uneasy, but I assure you that we're not some kind of criminals. I'm Dr. Kendra Michaels and this is my associate Jessie Mercado." She handed him her credentials. "We only want answers. You're a scientist, this is your work. You should want them, too. What isn't right about those printouts?" She pinched one of the pages and held it before his eyes. "Shall I tell you? This was *inside* me." She showed him the other one. "And this was the one you made. See the similarity?"

Dr. Farnsworth nodded slowly. "Of course, I do. But I don't understand this." He was staring at Kendra's printout. "And I certainly don't know how you got hold of this one. It's a complete mystery to me."

"Trust me, it wasn't anything I asked for. Your carrier protein helped deliver a Tribuxin dose right into my bloodstream. It's a combo only this lab could have created. We need to know who you made it for."

"I don't know what you're talking about. We're still waiting on regulatory approval. It won't be ready for another year at least."

"But you are conducting some field tests?" Jessie asked.

"Yes." Dr. Farnsworth climbed out of his car and was still frowning as he examined Kendra's psychologist license and business cards. "Dr. Michaels, you're a music therapist." He handed her credentials back to her. "How is this any of your business?"

Jessie stepped forward. "It became her business when she almost died after ingesting your protein. She was assisting the FBI on a murder investigation at the time. Your creation was used against her for some reason. Don't you think she has the right to ask why?"

Farnsworth's eyes widened in shock. "Murder? You have to be mistaken about—"

"Is everything okay, Dr. Farnsworth?"

Kendra and Jessie turned to see an attractive young woman approaching the car parked next to his.

Farnsworth nodded absently. "Yes, Anita." He added, "Thank you."

She looked doubtfully at Kendra and Jessie. "Are you sure?"

"Yes. Have a good night."

Anita stood there for a moment longer. Then she finally climbed into her car, started it up, and drove away.

"My assistant," Farnsworth said. "She's very protective."

"Good employee to have," Jessie said.

"Exceptional." He shrugged dismissively. "But as I was saying, you have to be mistaken. I don't know what was happening, but it couldn't have been my work."

"Then who else had this formula?" Jessie asked.

Farnsworth grimaced. "It sounds as if you'd like a peek at our records." He was suddenly defensive. "That's not going to happen. You might be a rival lab or just some nutcase."

"It's not necessary that we examine records. I can see that might be awkward," Kendra said. "We only have a few questions. Just tell us what we need to know."

"Perhaps you should come back with a warrant," he said belligerently.

He was obviously going to stonewall them, Kendra thought. But maybe she had a way around it. "I told you, we don't have time. Maybe you just talk to me and trust that I'm exactly who I said I am."

His lips curled. "And why should I do that?"

She said softly, "Because you're going to hope I don't tell your wife and coworkers that you've been sleeping with your assistant."

Dr. Farnsworth inhaled sharply. "What did you say?"

"You heard me. I'm not a fan of blackmail, but I almost died a couple days ago. I'm a little annoyed that you're being so stubborn."

Jessie coughed in a futile attempt to hide her laughter.

"You're guessing." Farnsworth eyed Kendra uncertainly.

"I don't guess. I observe."

"What makes you think I'm having an affair?"

"I'll tell you after you've told us what we need to know. And believe me, you'll want to hear this. If I can pick it up, your wife sure as hell will. If she hasn't already. It may already be too late for you."

His forehead was suddenly perspiring. "Tell me."

"Later. You talk first."

"There isn't much to tell. It's clear someone's made some kind of mistake."

"Shall I talk to your human resources department? Then maybe your wife?"

"I'm being honest with you." His tone was pleading, almost desperate.

"Then stop telling me I've made a mistake."

"Listen, this formula is only being tested on a U.S. military installation in Torii Station, Japan."

"Japan?" Kendra said.

"Yes. On Okinawa. No way it could have been used on you here."

Kendra looked to Jessie for a reaction, but she was already madly thumbing her phone screen.

"I'm being totally honest with you," Farnsworth said. "You have to believe me."

"I'm inclined to believe you. Though a man who would cheat on his wife can't really be trusted," Kendra said. "I'm just trying to make sense of it."

"While you make sense of it, maybe you can tell me why you thought—" He moistened his lips. "You know."

"Your affair? There's a drink in your car's cupholder. Your assistant's lipstick is on the straw."

Farnsworth looked down at the console. "It could be my wife's lipstick," he said defiantly.

"Could be, but not likely that your wife also happens

to use Revlon Lustrous Primrose lipstick that I see on that straw. I also just saw it on your assistant's mouth. By the way, I also see long, shiny strands of her pretty blond hair on your front passenger seat and several more on the folded-down backseat of your SUV. It doesn't seem very comfortable back there, but I guess it's cheaper than getting a hotel room each time. There's a bit of fresh mud caked on those tires, which tells me that you went off road for one of your recent trysts."

Dr. Farnsworth glanced back at his car. "*Shit.*"

Jessie patted Kendra's arm. "Let's go. We got what we need."

"We did?"

"Yes." Jessie glanced at Farnsworth as she nudged Kendra toward the car. "Thank you for your cooperation, Doctor."

Kendra looked back at him over her shoulder. "I may not see you again, but you'll probably be visited by the FBI soon. If it makes you feel better, you can mention me to them to assure yourself that I'm legitimate. I hope you'll be as forthcoming with them as you have been with me."

Farnsworth looked dazed. "Sure."

He was still standing there as Kendra and Jessie climbed into Kendra's car and sped away.

CHAPTER 10

"THAT WAS TRULY EXCELLENT," Jessie said to Kendra as they left the parking lot. "I enjoyed it thoroughly. You definitely have an affinity for street level."

"As I told him, I don't like blackmail, but he gave me no choice." She changed the subject. "Does Torii Station, Japan, mean something special to you?"

"It didn't at first, at least not until I looked it up."

"And?"

"Several U.S. contractors share space at that installation. Including one that you and I both know."

"You mean your favorite scumbags?"

She nodded. "Brock Limited."

"But did they have access?"

"I've spent time on military bases, remember? Things

go missing from supply depots all the time. If they wanted something, Brock could have gotten it."

"Good to know something definite." Kendra grimaced. "This is like one huge puzzle with half the pieces missing. What the hell could Brock Limited have to do with the murders of those wedding guests? Brock Limited is obviously all about corruption, money, and power. Yet those murders had a profile that didn't reflect any of those things. They were definitely closer to that of one of those highly organized, patterned serial killers." She shivered. "Putting that poor bride in the back seat of that MINI . . . Where's the damn connection?"

"Lynch is on his way to tracking down one of those connections right now," Jessie said. "Ryan Facey, the man who probably made contact with the woman in Connecticut who sent you that video. And who is now quite possibly on the run from Brock's men." She shrugged. "All the connections will come together, Kendra. One by one."

"Yet we still don't have proof that Brock is involved."

"Of course not. But it's one more piece that confirms you're on the right track with them. The evidence is stacking up as we speak." Her lips tightened. "Now all we have to do is find a way to push them off that stack and hang the bastards."

Kendra's gaze was on Jessie's face. "You really do hate them."

"They hurt my buddies and they got away with it.

It's bad enough that we had to go through all that hell in Afghanistan. There should be some justice in this world."

"And you're going to find it for them," she said quietly.

Jessie nodded. "You bet I am." She smiled. "With a little help from my friends. I'm curious to see what Lynch comes up with in Portland."

"He said he'd call me when he got in. I don't know when that will be. It's already almost six. I'll let you know when he does. What do we do now?"

"You take me back to the naval hospital to pick up my bike. Then I go out to the base here and see what I can gather about Brock's activities in this area. Tomorrow we should probably go and question Barbara Campbell's husband to see if he knows anything. I'll be at your condo around eight."

"You know you could stay at my place."

She shook her head. "I never know where I'll end up once I'm on a case. I'm better off on my own. Thanks, anyway."

She was almost as much of a loner as Lynch, Kendra thought. Was it the life they had lived that had made them trust only themselves? "If you change your mind, just call me."

"I will." Jessie smiled. "We did good today, Kendra. Screw Griffin and his fancy Washington D.C. lab. Want to stop and have dinner on the way to get my bike?"

"Why not?" Jessie might be a loner, but she was fun, and she always made Kendra feel a sense of zinging excitement and boundless determination. "You're right, we did good. Do you want to do burgers or Mexican?"

11:05 P.M.

"It took you long enough to phone me," Kendra said when she picked up Lynch's call. "I do hope you didn't have trouble getting out of LA? Jessie and I had a discussion about you always getting what you want and I'd hate if you had even a slight blow to your ego."

"I didn't. I've just been busy since I got here. How did your meeting with Alan Fletcher go?"

"Productive." She swiftly told him about Gensyn and their talk with Farnsworth. "Definitely a connection with Brock. But I'm not sure where it's going. Or why it had anything to do with me or that wedding."

"I'll see what I can discover from this end. I think I might get lucky. That's why I was so long in calling you. I was doing some research. It took me up north of the city."

"Why? What did you find out?"

"That Facey definitely looks like a man on the run. I canvassed the rental car agencies and found out he had rented a Jeep Cherokee after he arrived in Portland. And that he probably had a reason for coming here. He knows this area and thought it might be safer for him. I found out that Facey's stepfather owned a dilapidated cabin in the woods about ten miles north of Portland where Facey spent time as a teenager. I was there two hours ago and there were fresh treads in the driveway."

"But no Ryan Facey?"

"No Facey." He paused. "But he already had company. The place was being staked out by a couple of Brock's thugs."

"They didn't see you?"

"I'm better than that, Kendra."

"More arrogant, at least." She paused. "Maybe Facey won't come back."

"I think he will. He feels like prey and he's hunting a place to go to ground. He was just checking the cabin out to make sure it was livable."

"Then they might kill him."

"He was Special Forces. He'll be careful. He won't just blunder into that cabin. He won't go near the place until after he's checked it out." He paused. "I just have to be the one to get to him first, so that they won't spook him away entirely."

Her hand tightened on the phone. "You're going back?"

"Information, Kendra. And there's no better source than a man on the run. I've got to stake him out, too."

"By yourself?" Her heart skipped a beat. "That's stupid. Call Griffin and get one of the local FBI agents to go with you. Why do you have to do everything alone?"

"It usually works out better. And how else can I claim to get everything I want, if it's handed to me on a silver platter? There's nothing ego-building about that."

"Very funny."

"Of course, there are some things I'd take regardless of how they're served to me." His voice lowered to intimacy. "Anytime, Kendra."

"Call Griffin." She forced herself to say the word. "Please."

"That's all you had to say. You know I hate the thought of worrying you. I'll see what Griffin thinks about it."

But he hadn't said he wouldn't go there alone. "Don't be stupid. Do you hear me? And call me when you get back from going to that cabin and tell me what you found out from Facey. Promise me."

"What a demanding woman. I promise. Take care." He cut the connection.

She put the phone down and drew a deep breath. Things were moving along quite well. Progress on all fronts. There was no reason to be this anxious. Except that she was not in Portland with Lynch. She had to wait until he contacted her again. It made her feel impatient . . . and helpless.

And frightened . . .

10:35 P.M.
San Diego

Derek leaned against the railing that overlooked the twinkling lights of Coronado Island. It was a chilly night and he'd seen only a few dedicated dog walkers on this part of the Embarcadero. It was almost 11:00 P.M., and he'd have to leave soon. He had responsibilities now.

"Where's the woman?"

Derek spun around. Josh Blake emerged from the shadows. The man wore a Burberry trench coat, long scarf, and designer shoes.

"Hello, Blake. You're looking very spiffy. Did Vivianne give you a clothing allowance when she promoted you to the higher echelon? If so, I think I need to get in on the deal. Perhaps I'll make it an additional bonus to our arrangement."

"Once again, Derek: Where's your latest victim? Is she even still alive?"

"You don't want to concern yourself with that." Derek smiled. "You found me, didn't you?"

"Wasn't hard. I think you let me find you. You're obviously not afraid of us."

"I'm not. Should I be?"

Blake shrugged. "Vivianne Kerstine is an unpredictable woman."

"On the contrary. She's extremely predictable in that we know she'll do anything to protect herself and her company. If anything happens to me, she knows that all the dirty secrets come out. That makes me feel very warm and safe as far as Brock Limited is concerned."

Blake was silent. "Some of us think you're bluffing."

"But then the company behavioral experts reviewed my history and psychological workups and concluded that I'm almost assuredly not bluffing. Did he use the term sociopath or did he go for psychopath? Were you at that meeting, Blake? Or was that before she decided to promote you? Did you all shit your pants just a little bit when your expert announced his findings?"

Blake shook his head. "You're enjoying this."

"No. This isn't what I wanted at all. My own endeavors usually go much more smoothly."

"Trust me," Blake said through set teeth. "It's not what we want either. No one is happy about expending resources to clean up your mess."

"I never asked for that. I'm fully capable of tidying up after myself. Most of the time I find it stimulating. Except when you step in and ruin things for me."

"No one gives a damn about you. It's all about the company. If you get caught, it all comes back to us."

"The company is the only reason why I almost got caught. You got careless with that paralegal. You let Corkle take care of her, didn't you? I've never liked his work. He's always a little sloppy. You should have done it yourself."

"It wasn't my call. Vivianne decided to give him the job."

"Oh, that's right, that was before she decided to demote him and give you his position in the company. Maybe next time you should consult me. I seem to be running things around here."

"You son of a bitch."

"Learn from her mistake. She should have given the job to someone more talented. I'm a prime asset and should be given tender loving care. You're the ones who have a problem. Just don't bungle it again."

"No one should have even had to go after that paralegal, dammit. And we're still not finished cleaning up after you. I've got two of my best guys in Oregon trying to tie up a nasty loose end as we speak."

"Oregon? Interesting."

"It's not interesting. It's trouble. You have to stop this. The police and the FBI are onto you. They know about your sick game even if they don't know who you are. They're watching every member of that wedding party. It was over as soon as they had that damned video. They even brought in that Kendra Michaels woman."

"Again, not my fault. Though I admit I'm finding Michaels' interference in my project an annoyance. Things might go more smoothly without her." He smiled mockingly. "And I resent you referring to my work as a sick game. You never called it sick when you ordered me to make all those kills, before you realized that I wasn't just your errand boy. You told me how talented and skilled I was. It's all in the viewpoint."

"It doesn't matter whose fault it is. It's over. Find something else to do to amuse yourself. Doesn't the company provide you with enough of an outlet without you going outside?"

"What can I say, Blake? I'm an artist. You never really understood that, did you? Until it was too late. I'll just have to make adjustments in this situation to keep the game interesting."

"I came here to tell you to give it up. We can all still come out of this all right if you stop right now."

Derek pulled up his jacket collar. "It's getting a little chilly. Time I went inside."

"Did you even hear me? What should I tell Vivianne?"

"You should tell Vivianne that I appreciate her interest in obtaining those nasty records I appropriated, but that I didn't appreciate her sending that clumsy Corkle stumbling around in my business. Poor guy, no doubt he was trying desperately to get back in her good graces."

Blake stiffened. "What are you saying?"

"That Corkle got in my way." Derek chuckled. "So I decided to demote him, too." He walked past Blake and headed toward the parking lot. "You'll find him in the trees over there. Do dispose of him properly, as a good employee should."

1:40 A.M.
Portland, Oregon

Duty call done. He had kept his promise to Kendra.

Lynch hung up after talking to Griffin and moved a little closer to the cabin. He didn't know what the hell he was going to do with that agent Griffin was dispatching to him from Portland, but you never knew when an extra man might prove useful. Provided he made it up here from Portland before the action started.

Lynch knelt in the clump of trees, casting an eye around for the two Brock agents. Unless they'd drastically changed position, they were at least a third of a mile west of his current position.

He pulled a small quadcopter drone from his inside jacket pocket and unfolded its black plastic struts. It was one of the quietest personal drones in existence, further modified by a friend to keep the sound of its motor and propellers to an absolute minimum. It was small enough to avoid detection once it was over a hundred feet or so, and the humid air would also prevent the sound from carrying.

Using his phone as the controller, he launched the drone and took it straight up to three hundred feet, well out of eyeshot and earshot to anyone who might be looking for it.

Lynch squinted at his phone screen for the drone's 4K view of the surrounding area. He saw the cabin, the gravel road, and, after a few moments, the two men staking out the place. And those men were moving around and doing something very interesting and lethal . . .

But still no sign of Facey.

And neither of the Brock men appeared to have spotted the drone. Perfect. He could keep it aloft for forty minutes before bringing it back for a battery swap.

Three batteries later, Lynch had a fairly good idea of the agents' patterns. They took turns making a broad sweep of the perimeter every twelve minutes, each making identical parabolic patterns. Brock's intensive training had obviously been drilled into each of them. If there was a drawback to their training, it was its predictability, even if it meant—

Wait a second.

Lynch moved the screen closer and studied it. A red Jeep had entered the frame and parked in a clump of brush about two miles from the cabin. A lone figure climbed out and hugged the tree line.

Facey!

He moved stealthily through the brush, obviously comfortable in the area. He knew there was some danger here for him, but that caution might not be enough.

Lynch did a quick calculation: If Facey continued his present pace of a hundred yards every two minutes, then he would cross right through the line of sight of one of the men during his timed sweep.

This party would be over before it began.

Lynch sprinted into the woods and made his way down a shallow stream. He didn't have much time. Even if he did manage to avoid the Brock agents, Facey himself probably wouldn't welcome him with anything more than a few rounds from the automatic he was wearing on his belt.

This was going to be tricky.

Lynch didn't break stride as he checked the drone's camera again. One of the men had just left for his sweep and Facey was approaching a small clearing.

He'd mostly likely circle around the southernmost edge, but that would only buy him a few minutes until the Brock guy would have him dead in his sights.

Lynch put on an extra burst of speed. He crouched low through the clearing, avoiding the cover of trees that would have bought him some protection.

He didn't have the luxury of time right now.

He looked at his phone again. The drone camera was dead. Shit, there had probably been interference from that clump of trees.

He was flying blind.

Concentrate. He'd played this three-dimensional chess his entire life. He could do it now.

Figure out where Facey was headed and get there first.

Lynch ran another fifty yards and pressed himself against a tree. He raised the handle of his gun.

Surely Facey was almost there.

Unless Facey had spotted him and was lining up a shot at that very moment.

Don't move, Lynch thought. Trust your first instinct.

Rustling brush. Footsteps.

It was Facey. Inches away.

Three . . . Two . . . One!

Lynch brought down his gun and struck Facey on the back of his head.

The man was out before he hit the ground.

EIGHT MINUTES LATER, Facey stirred. Lynch had dragged him back into a gully and secured his hands and feet with military-grade zip ties.

"Facey, I'm a friend," Lynch whispered. "Got that?"

Facey instinctively tried to squirm free.

"Stop it," Lynch whispered. He held up his phone and flashed a drone photo he'd taken of Brock's two men near the cabin. "That's what's waiting for you down there. You know them?"

Facey froze. He obviously recognized the men.

"That's what I thought," Lynch said.

"Who in the hell are you?" Facey whispered.

"My name's Adam Lynch. I'm helping investigate the murder of Elena Meyer."

Another flash of recognition.

Lynch smiled. "Remind me to play poker with you sometime."

"They'll kill us both," Facey said. "You don't know who you're dealing with."

"Brock's all-stars, I'd guess. But if they were so great, I wouldn't know they were looking for you. At least you know how to keep it on the down-low. Of course, there was the young man at Excelsior Car Rental who gave me the make, model, and color of your car."

"Son of a bitch."

"I need some answers. Now."

Facey held up his arm and leg restraints. "Cut these off me first."

"First we talk."

"Come on, man. If they find us, I'm a sitting duck."

"Then you'd better talk fast."

"Shit."

Lynch glanced around. "Why don't we start with why Brock Limited wanted Elena Meyer dead?"

He was silent.

"I don't want you dead," Lynch said impatiently. "You might be more valuable to me alive. But I need answers and I'm not going to waste time convincing you. I'll just walk away and let your Brock all-stars eventually find you."

Facey was still silent.

"Your choice." Lynch got to his feet. "See you."

"Wait," Facey said. He hesitated, moistening his lips. "You'll protect me?"

"If you give me enough information to make it worth my while."

"That's not much assurance."

"It's all you'll get from me. You're not going to get anything from those guys staking you out."

Facey didn't speak for a moment. "What the hell. Why not? I've been expecting to be a dead man since I was pulled into this." He shrugged. "Okay. This isn't about Elena Meyer at all. It's about one of Brock's guys who's been working out of the Middle East for the past ten years. He just came stateside a few months ago. His code name is Derek."

"What's his real name?"

"I don't know."

Lynch gazed at him skeptically.

"I don't," Facey insisted. "I doubt even those guys out there know. It's above my pay grade."

"So what's his story?"

"Derek is a guy they use for jobs no one else wants to do."

"Dangerous jobs?"

"Naw, lots of operatives get off on that. They use him for the sicko stuff. Things that would chill your shit. Trouble is, you get a guy like that on your payroll, sometimes you can't control him. He has certain proclivities that have nothing to do with the job. There was a series of killings in London a few years back that he was rumored to have committed. He may have been the Docklands Strangler, who killed members of an amateur soccer team."

"You're bullshitting me," Lynch said.

"I'm just going by what I hear. I heard he was also behind a half-dozen murders in Damascus of members of a medical school graduating class. He liked the pattern killings, but random enough that they couldn't be linked back to him. And he was smart, real smart, and slick, damn slick. Yeah, he was a sick puppy, but so good at what he did for Brock, they didn't care. And by the time they did care, it was too late. He had too much on them. He's been using his spare time to gather information about all the dirty tricks that were going on with Brock. His handlers had just assumed he was some crazy psychopath who could be used and thrown away. That's what he'd wanted them to think. Until he sent the evidence he'd gathered to Vivianne and the other bigwigs at Brock. He told them he wanted freedom, steady cash, and protection if he required it. He also stressed the fact that if he somehow disappeared, he'd made arrangements to expose everything that he'd sent them."

"This is fairly big stuff," Lynch said slowly. "I can't believe it would be common-knowledge conversation around the company water cooler."

"It's not. And there's no way I should have found out about it. I was small stuff at Brock, hardly a blip on their radar. I didn't know anything about this Derek until a week ago. And I guarantee you, most people there still don't know it."

"How did you find out?"

Facey swallowed hard. "It was Elena Meyer. She was in San Diego with her law firm working on a case."

"For Brock," Lynch said. "We heard about that. We were led to believe it was fairly routine."

"It was. It was a nothing case. But in sorting through the company documents, Elena found something she shouldn't have. It was due to a mistake in the computer access permissions. She ended up seeing a good part of the company's Derek file. It was enough to throw her for a loop."

"I can imagine."

"But Brock was also trying to keep tabs on Derek's latest little side projects and this file contained some information they'd recently dug up." He paused. "The wedding video."

Lynch was trying to absorb it all. "So this is where that wedding video came from?"

"Yes. If there was some connection between Derek and those people at the wedding, I don't know what it is. And Elena sure as hell didn't know. But given his past, she was afraid that they might be his next target, like the medical class in Damascus and the amateur soccer team in London."

"So how did you get in on this?"

"I worked for Brock in San Diego. During Elena's trips out here, she and I became . . . involved."

"You were lovers."

"She was different. Clean and kind of sweet. I . . . liked her."

"And she liked you enough to tell you all this?"

"Not right away. Not at all during her time out here. Looking back at it, I think maybe she didn't trust me. She didn't trust anyone. Who could blame her? She knew Brock had tentacles in every level of government. She didn't know what to do. But she did know that I was very low on the Brock organizational totem pole just as she was, and I guess that made her feel safer about trusting me. She called me, and I flew out to Connecticut on a red-eye. She told me everything and I advised her to drop it, for her own safety. It scared the hell out of me that she'd stumbled on it. Sometimes you have to close your eyes if you want to survive." His lips twisted with regret. "That wasn't what she wanted to hear. I think she was disappointed in me. I know I let her down. She started talking about going to Kendra Michaels with the story."

"Why Kendra?"

"Her name was in the news. She was leading that dream team of serial-killer investigators at the time and Elena was impressed by her. More than she was of me, I guess. If I hadn't been afraid, I might have protected her. . . . I should have. Before I left her, I'd hoped I'd talked her into staying out of it and forgetting she'd ever seen the Derek file. But I guess Elena was too good a person for that." Facey shook his head. "When I got back to San Diego, two of Brock's directors called me in and asked if Elena had talked to me about anything in particular when I was in Connecticut. I said no, but I admitted to the affair. But that's when I realized they were onto her and she was being watched. Before I could warn her, I found out she was back in San Diego and had been killed. And then I spotted a couple guys watching my place and I realized I could be next. I recognized them; they were Brock men. It was easy enough to figure they were ordered to cover for this Derek to make sure the company's own asses stayed covered. That meant I was—"

Lynch held up a warning hand to silence him. He cocked his head and checked his watch, which he'd placed into stopwatch mode. "Quiet for the next minute or so."

"Why?" Facey whispered.

Lynch raised a finger to his lips.

After a few moments, there was a rustling sound just a few yards away.

Footsteps.

Facey's eyes widened and he motioned for Lynch to cut his restraints.

Lynch shook his head and crouched to look through the thick brush.

A bearded man stood just twenty feet away. Had he heard them?

After a moment, he continued walking.

Once Lynch was sure the man was out of earshot, he turned back. "We need to move. Did Elena still have any of the documents she saw in her possession?"

"No. She couldn't copy anything without leaving a trail to her. Brock didn't even allow cell phones in the records room."

"But she had the wedding video."

"It was on YouTube, so she was able to download a copy later."

Lynch nodded and checked his phone. "Just so you know, I've been recording you. I'm sending this audio file to Special Agent in Charge Michael Griffin at the FBI."

"Why not just tell him yourself?"

Lynch looked at him grimly. "Really?"

"In case we don't make it back." Facey answered his own question. "My car is on the other side of the cabin. If we're careful, we might be able to make it past them."

"That might work." Lynch thought about it. "Yeah, that's the way we'll go." He cut the zip tie around Facey's ankles. "The timing will be tricky, but we can do it." He turned in the direction of the cabin. "Stay close. Do what I tell you. Let's go!"

CHAPTER 11

SEVERAL MINUTES LATER they'd reached the edge of the woods overlooking the cabin.

Lynch pointed to a stretch of flattened brush. "Freshly trampled," he whispered. "Stay sharp."

Pow! A branch exploded next to Facey's head.

Lynch and Facey ducked behind a tree as bark flew from a barrage of bullets.

Lynch cocked his head toward a shallow gully behind the row of trees. "Follow me."

He led Facey down to the gully and ran alongside the cabin.

Blam-blam-blam-blam!

A wall of bullets blocked their path.

Lynch and Facey ducked behind a large rock.

"What now?" Facey asked.

Lynch pulled out his phone.

Blam-blam!

Shredded bark rained down on them from the trees above.

"I think it's too late to call in the cavalry," Facey said sarcastically.

Lynch stared intently at the phone screen. "Maybe not. We just need a distraction."

"From who?"

Lynch slid his thumbs across the screen. "Get ready to run around to the back porch of the cabin."

"When?"

"When those guys start shooting."

"Seriously?"

"They won't be shooting at us."

At that moment there was movement on the other side of the clearing. Branches snapped and the brush rustled.

Blam-blam-blam-blam-blam!

The shooters took the bait, shredding the branches with their gunfire.

"Now!" Lynch said. He and Facey sprinted toward the cabin and threw themselves on the back porch.

Blam-blam-blam-blam!

Still distracted by the movement on the other side of the clearing, the shooters continued their assault on the trees. They fired until splintered branches fell away to reveal the source of the movement.

Lynch's drone.

It sputtered crazily until it crashed in the middle of the clearing.

"Too bad," Lynch said regretfully, as he and Facey watched from their vantage point on the back porch. "I was kind of fond of that thing."

He turned away and started trotting down the porch.

"The trees . . ." Facey murmured.

Lynch looked over his shoulder. Facey was no longer behind him but was climbing off the porch and obviously going to try to run toward the woods.

Lynch swore beneath his breath. "I told you to stay close." Lynch launched a tackle and brought Facey down.

"Why did you do that?" Facey gasped. "I could have made it."

"Not likely. I'm trying to keep you alive, dammit." He jerked him to his feet. "You kept your word and I—" Another bullet struck the porch next to him. "They're moving closer. Shit, they're getting impatient. I thought we'd have a little more time." He grabbed Facey's arm and dragged him after him.

Another series of bullets sprayed the porch in front of them. "We have to keep away from the trees for the next couple minutes. They can see us. From where they are, they'd have a clear shot."

"I might have made it," Facey muttered. But he obeyed Lynch and was staying on the porch for the time being. "And they're not firing any more right now. Maybe we could try—"

Lynch went still. He put out a hand to silence Facey. "No, they're not firing anymore. Why not?"

Then he realized what that answer had to be.

"Jump! Hit the ground!"

He dove off the porch.

But it was too late! He felt the first heat even before the blast.

The cabin's explosion lit up the night sky!

3:40 A.M.

San Diego

Lynch should have called her by now.

Hell, he should have called her long before this, Kendra thought as she turned over in bed. Lynch might think that this kind of surveillance was totally commonplace, but he knew she didn't. And he hadn't thought this stakeout would take this long.

And he kept his promises.

Dammit!

She sat up in bed and reached for her phone.

The light illuminated the screen as she punched in Lynch's number.

It went direct to voice mail.

She drew a shaky breath. Okay, he might have it on

vibrate while he was on stakeout. It didn't have to mean anything particularly dire. But it didn't mean that everything was fine either.

And he had made her another promise.

She quickly punched in Griffin's home number.

He answered in three rings and did not sound pleased. "Between you and Lynch, I might manage to get an hour's sleep tonight. I don't know why I ever gave you my home number. I must be a masochist. What's wrong now, Kendra?"

"You tell me. Lynch did call you tonight? He told you about Facey?"

"You know he did. He said that he'd promised you he'd request an agent be sent up to those woods in the back of beyond. Do you think I'm at your beck and call?"

"So you didn't do it?"

"I did it," he said testily. "Brian Nolan, local field office. He reported back to me when he made contact with Lynch. I don't know why I even bothered. Lynch is probably just pissed off at Brock for wrecking his damn car."

"You don't believe that."

"Only partially. I don't like the idea of Brock being involved in this case. They complicate things. Now can I get back to sleep?"

"Not yet. I haven't heard from Lynch. Have you?"

"No. But when does Lynch contact me except when

he wants something? That's not his M.O. He disappears sometimes for weeks on those missions he does overseas for the Justice Department and then surfaces to collect all the money and accolades." He paused and then said reluctantly, "But Nolan will have to call me if Lynch doesn't. I'll phone you as soon as I hear from either one of them. But don't expect it anytime soon. I've seen Lynch like this before and he gets absorbed when he's on the hunt."

"I do expect it," she said curtly. "He promised me."

"Like I said, I'll call you." He cut the connection.

She sat there and gazed down at the phone.

One more time.

She punched in Lynch's number.

Straight to voice mail.

She put the phone back on her night table.

Go to sleep.

No one could take care of himself better than Lynch. He'd probably found out something from Facey that had led him in another direction. He'd call her when he could.

Close your eyes.

Go to sleep.

"YOU LOOK LIKE HELL," Jessie said when she got in Kendra's car the next morning. "Mega circles. No sleep?"

"I got a little." Kendra backed out of her parking spot

and headed for the exit. "Did you find out anything from your friends at the base?"

"Just a lot of fuming and ugliness," Jessie said. "And the feeling that Brock was trying to expand all over the damn planet." Her lips tightened. "That can't happen. They're too powerful now. What did you hear from Lynch?"

"Nothing. Except that he thinks that Facey is on the run and that he can tap him for information." She drove onto the street and turned left. "And Lynch was supposed to call me back last night and didn't do it."

"Hence the mega circles. You can't contact him?"

"Griffin says it's no big deal. He said he'd call me when he heard from him. That he's a bloody superstar and runs his own show."

"He's probably right," Jessie said quietly. "From what I've seen of Lynch, you don't have to worry about him being able to take care of himself."

"I know that's true. It's just that I can't stop—" She broke off. She had to quit talking about this. "Where are we supposed to be going? Where does Ivan Campbell live anyway?"

"234 Sunset Way. It's a condo near the airport. I called him on the way here and told him we were coming." She smiled. "I used your connection with the FBI to make it happen. He didn't want to talk to anyone. He seems to be pretty broken up."

"Why shouldn't he?" Kendra asked as she turned toward the airport. "He's probably just waiting for word that his wife is dead. This must seem to be a nightmare to him."

"Yeah, I hear you. But maybe we'll get lucky. Or maybe that butcher will change his pattern and hold her until we have a chance to find him."

"You're full of optimism today."

"I think maybe you need a little of that commodity today." She looked at the notes on her phone. "Ivan Campbell married Barbara Labkan three years ago. They seem to be the perfect couple, probably because they were seldom together. He travels a lot with his job for a pharmaceutical company and she worked with her sister starting up a business. She was described as warm and outgoing, and he as very quiet, but polite and likeable."

Kendra was remembering Barbara Campbell's speech at the reception. "She seemed to be very fond of the bride. I only have a vague memory of her husband."

"See? The perfect marriage, she soaked up all the attention. I imagine that he was grateful to let her shine. Introverts usually take comfort from not having to compete. They tend to fall apart when they lose their alpha partner."

"Maybe. Sometimes it doesn't work that way."

But when Ivan Campbell let them into his condo, Kendra had an idea that Jessie had been right. Thin, dark-haired, moderately good looking, yet his expression was so tense and tortured that he looked like a holocaust survivor.

"You still haven't heard anything?" were the first words he spoke after they'd introduced themselves. His voice was sharp, angry. "How can that be? All the technology. All your resources and experts and you still can't find one woman?"

"I'm sorry," Kendra said gently. "I know Special Agent Griffin is doing everything he can to locate your wife. We're sparing no effort. We're just here to make certain we're not missing even one step." She handed him her tablet with the wedding video. "I wonder if you'd just look at this wedding video and see if there's anything that strikes a note with you. Perhaps something not as it should be?"

He stared at the video as if it was a snake ready to bite him. "I don't want to see that damn wedding video. It just makes me remember how beautiful and funny Barbara could be. Why do you even think it's connected?"

"One of the first victims sent it to Kendra," Jessie said. "It's what drew us into this case, sir. It might have taken much longer and many more victims if Kendra hadn't become involved. So you can see that it's important that we make sure that we don't miss anything it might tell us."

"It was sent to *you*." Campbell whirled angrily on

Kendra. “Then why didn’t you catch what it meant? Why didn’t you stop all this before it began? Why didn’t you stop it before he took Barbara?”

“I wish I could have known what it meant,” Kendra said quietly. “It wasn’t clear at the time.”

“Why not?” he said sarcastically. “You’re obviously so clever. Why couldn’t you save Barbara?”

“Easy,” Jessie said. “She’s doing everything she can to help your wife. But you need to help, too. Will you look at the video for us?”

“What else can I do?” He gestured in frustration toward Kendra. “Since she’s already made blunders that might have gotten my Barbara murdered.” He turned on the video.

Jessie gave Kendra a faint shrug and they both were silent, waiting, while Campbell finished watching the video.

“Nothing,” Campbell said sharply as he handed the tablet back to Kendra. “Was I supposed to recognize someone? Pick some bastard out of that crowd so that you wouldn’t have to do your job and catch that murderer? I’m afraid not. Now get out of here and find my wife.”

Jessie took a step forward. “I told you not to—”

“We’ll go.” Kendra put her hand on Jessie’s arm. “Just one more question. Everything on that video is exactly as you remembered it that night?”

"I told you. Nothing is different." He opened the door. "But if there is, you should have noticed what it was. I'm beginning to think all of this is your fault. Get *out.*"

"We're going." Kendra had to quickly pull Jessie into the hall before the door slammed behind them. "Let it go, Jessie. He's in pain. He has to have someone to blame."

"Not you," Jessie said grimly. "I'll show him pain."

"I was convenient. I was the first one to get a clue in this case." She added wearily, "And maybe I might have been to blame for not putting all this together. Who knows?"

"I do," Jessie said as she stepped into the elevator. "You're not psychic, Kendra, and you shouldn't let that jackass make you—"

"Just a minute." Kendra's phone was buzzing and she glanced down at the ID. "*Yes.* It's Griffin, Jessie. Go ahead and wait for me in the car. I'll be right down. I've got to take this. I left him a message to call me back."

Jessie nodded as she pressed the down button. "It's about time he got around to it. You've been on pins and needles all morning. I hate bureaucrats."

"Griffin isn't usually one. Though he can be a complete asshole." She picked up the call, "What have you heard, Griffin?"

"It's not Griffin," Metcalf said. "I'm calling for him. He asked me to get hold of you. He's on the other line."

"Since when have you been his errand boy?" Kendra asked. "I thought you were climbing the FBI ladder pretty steadily, Metcalf. You shouldn't let him use you like this."

"I didn't mind," he said quickly. "I could see that it was important. He'll be right with you, Kendra." He put her on hold.

She found herself tensing. He hadn't sounded like himself. And she couldn't remember when he hadn't taken a few minutes to just shoot the breeze with her when he had the opportunity.

She had to wait for almost four minutes until Griffin came on the line. "Hello, Kendra." His voice was brusque. "Sorry to keep you waiting. I just needed to double-check something before I spoke to you."

"Double-check what?" Kendra asked. "Why are you calling me, Griffin?" She paused. "Have you heard anything from Lynch?"

"Nothing definitive." He was silent. Then he said roughly, "I'm lying. And you don't deserve it. It's about as definitive as it gets without a final ME report. I'm sorry, Kendra."

She couldn't breathe. What was he saying? She must have misunderstood. "What are you sorry about? I only asked you to check on Lynch. I was worried because I hadn't heard from him. What the hell are you sorry about, Griffin?" He wasn't answering and she was beginning to panic. "Talk to me."

"I'm sorry," he said again. "This is the last news I

wanted to give you. That's why I had to double check." He paused. "No mistake. He's dead, Kendra."

She jerked back as the words struck her. The hall was spinning. She was dizzy and sick. "That's crazy. No, he isn't. Not Lynch. Don't tell me it's not a mistake."

"I wish I could."

She swallowed. It took her a minute to get the words out. "You're telling me Lynch is really dead, Griffin?"

"I'm telling you that two hours ago a body was found at that cabin that answered to his general description as far as we could determine. There was also another body that was probably Ryan Facey." He added, "Though the remains were difficult to identify since the place was blown to smithereens and so were Lynch and the second victim. That was why I was on the other line. I was checking to see if they'd managed to get enough DNA from Lynch for a match."

DNA. It was always about DNA, she thought dully. "And did they?"

"Yes. Preliminary match of 98.7 percent. As I said, they'll know more after the ME gets through with—"

"I don't believe it," she said flatly. "It's a mistake. Men like Lynch don't just—" She stopped. "It has to be a mistake. We don't even know if he actually went back to that cabin. He was just going to stake out the area."

"He was in those woods outside that cabin when he called me to get me to send that agent." Griffin's voice was gentle for him. "He called me from there, Kendra.

He had photos of those Brock goons and wanted me to run checks on them. He was in a hurry because he wanted to get out of there in case he'd been followed." He added, "He was joking about the fact that he'd promised you that he wouldn't let Brock kill him. He said he'd hate like hell to have to rely on me."

That did sound like Lynch. "But you're saying they did kill him?" Kendra said hoarsely. She was still too dazed to take it in. "Not Lynch, Griffin," she said desperately. "He was too smart."

"Everyone dies, Kendra. It's just a matter of time. Yes, he was smart, but he didn't walk on water." He cleared his throat. "I'm sorry, Kendra. I realize you were close. Look, as soon as I get the final, you'll be the first to know. But I wouldn't be honest if I didn't tell you that the results are almost certain to be identical."

"You're that sure?" Tell me no. Give me hope. Just a little hope, dammit.

"I'm that sure. I wish I could say I wasn't." Another silence. "Is there anything I can do for you?"

"No," she whispered numbly. What could Griffin do in a world where an extraordinary man like Lynch could be blown away in a heartbeat. What could anyone do? "Goodbye, Griffin."

She pressed the disconnect.

Pain.

She stood there, leaning against the wall, while the waves of pain and loss swept over her. Darkness. It was like being dragged down into a whirlpool where there was no light, no sound. She had never been afraid of darkness, it was familiar, it could be a friend, but this was different. Because Lynch was lost in that darkness and she would never be able to find him again. But she had to find him, because he was alone, and no one was there for him.

No!

She pushed herself away from the wall and stumbled toward the elevator. She couldn't remember taking the elevator to the lobby. But then she was out in the parking lot and heading for her car.

Jessie looked up from her phone as Kendra came toward her. "That Griffin must have been chatty. I was going to come back and—" She broke off and straightened in her seat. "What the hell is wrong?"

Everything. No light. Lost. Alone. "Lynch," she said unsteadily. She opened the driver's side door. "Griffin said Lynch was killed last night." She got into the car and just sat there. She should be doing something. Turning on the engine . . . "An explosion. He said the DNA was 98.7 percent positive."

"No way." Jessie murmured, her gaze on Kendra's face. "Not Lynch."

"Griffin says everybody dies." Kendra was trying to keep her voice from breaking. "But I have to be sure. So I'm going back to my apartment and grab a bag and then I'm going to Portland. I'm going to stay there with

Lynch until I know for certain that all of those FBI statistics aren't bullshit."

"But you don't think they are."

"Griffin doesn't usually make mistakes like that. I've never known him to do it." She swallowed. "He double-checked. And he thinks he's right. Hell, he was being nice to me."

"Imagine that," Jessie said dryly. "Just because you're pale as a ghost and you look as if you're going to shatter into a million pieces when you take your next breath."

"I won't shatter. But I'm having a little trouble keeping myself pulled together. I can't seem to think." She reached out to start the car. "I'll be better when I get on the road and start doing something."

"No, you won't," Jessie said flatly. "Not on this road and not in this car." She opened her car door and got out. "Change seats. I'll drive you home. I want us both to make it through this day without ending up in an ambulance."

"I'm fine, Jessie."

"No, you're numb. And you're trying to stay numb until the pain stops." Jessie was opening Kendra's door and holding out her hand. "But neither of us knows how long that will be. I have an idea that you could break at any moment."

"I won't break."

"Yes, you will." She was holding Kendra's gaze. "You're strong, but whatever was between you and

Lynch was powerful as hell. It's going to hit you and blow you apart. I don't want to be collateral damage." She added gruffly, "And I don't want to have to pick you up and put you back together again. Let me get you back to your condo. Okay?"

She wasn't going to give up, Kendra knew. Jessie never gave up, Kendra thought wearily. "Okay." She let Jessie pull her out of the car. "I know you're just being kind, but I'm really all right. I'll accept the lift home, but then you can leave me."

"Can I?" Jessie started the car. "Get in. We'll talk about it when we get there. In case you haven't noticed, you're starting to shake. That numbness might be on its way out."

She *was* shaking, Kendra realized. She was suddenly cold. Cold as death.

Death.

Everybody dies, Kendra.

"Get in," Jessie repeated. "Now, Kendra."

The next moment she was in the car and Jessie was backing out of the parking space.

Jessie was silent for the first five minutes of the trip. Then she said, "Okay, we're going to Portland. What are we going to do there?"

"I told you, I have to make sure," she said. "And I don't want him to be alone. He should have someone with him. He always seemed to be so alone, Jessie."

Then her words struck home. "We? You're not going with me, Jessie."

"Yes, I am. Why not?"

"Because I don't want you." She closed her eyes. "I don't want you worrying about me or taking care of me. I can do this by myself." Her eyes opened. She added unevenly, "Lynch was my very good friend and I want to do this alone."

"Very good friend? He might have been that to you, too. But he was a hell of a lot more. Anyone could see it."

Could they? Half the time Kendra hadn't known what she was feeling toward him. Yet everyone else could see it? "I still want to do this alone. I don't need you."

"Look, you don't know what you're going to find in Portland. If Lynch was murdered, then what's to keep you from being a target? You should have someone with you."

"Griffin will have agents up there investigating."

"They're not me," Jessie said flatly. "Lynch trusted me to take care of you."

I like you to be surrounded by friends and people who care about you. It makes me feel safer about leaving you.

Oh shit, her eyes were stinging. "But no one took care of him, did they?" she said shakily. "Not ever. He always took care of himself. And those bastards found a way to kill him because there was no one there for him.

But they're not going to get away with it. You'll stay here and keep working on finding out who did this. I'll do the same thing in Portland . . . after I find out what happened there."

But Griffin had said he already knew. Ninety-eight point-seven percent. *Everyone dies, Kendra.*

Jessie was silent. "I don't like it."

"Too bad. It's the way it has to be." She wished Jessie would stop arguing. Her shaking wasn't getting any better and she was praying for the numbness to return. She could tell the pain was waiting, hovering. "I'll be fine. I'll keep in contact."

"How comforting." Jessie was pulling up in front of the condo. "Not good enough." She sat there for an instant and then turned to face Kendra. "Here's how it's going to work. I know I'm not going to be able to talk you out of this, but I've got to make certain you're as safe as I can make you. But you've got to cooperate." She met her eyes. "Listen, you're almost in shock and it wouldn't take much to send you over the edge. I'm going to park your car down in your parking spot, but you're not going to drive it to the airport. You'll take a cab. I'm going to call Griffin and tell him to have an agent meet your plane and chauffeur you around in Portland. You're going to call me when you get there and then once a day and let me know what's happening. Do you agree?"

"All this isn't necessary. I'm not in shock. I'm just very, very sad."

"Yeah, sure. I've seen al-Qaeda torture victims who were in better shape. Give me your word or I'll be on that plane to Portland with you."

It would be easier just to give in and handle this later. "I give you my word." She opened her car door. "Thank you, Jessie. I know you mean well."

"I'm not finished. Remember, Olivia will be here for you if you decide to stay here and you need someone besides me." Her lips tightened. "Because I'm going on record telling you this idea of you going to Portland sucks."

"I know Olivia is always there for me." Now Kendra only wanted to escape. Jessie's eyes were too sharp and she felt as if she could see right through her to the pain that was beginning to stab again. She was feeling very vulnerable as she almost ran toward the front entrance. "And I have to go to Portland."

"Then you might consider letting go before you get on that plane," Jessie said quietly. "It's going to happen soon and you're not going to be able to stop it. You're usually one very cool customer. The last thing you're going to want is to lose control of yourself thirty thousand feet up."

"Right. Anything you say." Then Kendra was inside the building. She stood there, breathing hard, trying to regain composure. One very cool customer? Not cool. Cold.

She was cold again. Ice cold. What was wrong with her? Get moving. Get on the elevator. Get upstairs to her condo and grab a bag and then get to the airport. She'd be fine once she was on the move. Jessie was wrong. She could hold on as long as she had to. She had to get to Portland. She had to get to Lynch.

She was unlocking the condo door. Only a few more steps and she'd be inside and allow herself a few minutes before she started packing.

Because she was feeling very strange. Was this what Jessie had meant about letting go? Because she had no choice in what was happening to her. The ice inside her seemed to be splintering. Not melting, but stabbing her with sharp, cruel jabs of feeling . . . of memory.

I feel . . . valued, Kendra.

She could feel the tears running down her cheeks as she pushed open the door. Get inside. Hide away for a little while. She'd be all right once she regained control. She had to be strong. Because she had to get to him . . .

"Kendra?"

She froze, her gaze flying across the room.

Lynch was coming out of the kitchen with a glass of wine in his hand. He was frowning, his gaze on her face. "What the hell is wrong with you?" Then the wine glass was on the bar counter and he was across the room. His fingers were reaching out to touch the tears on her cheek. "*Talk* to me."

She couldn't talk. She could only look at him. She could only *feel* him.

Alive?

Alive! He was *alive*. This was no hallucination. His touch on her cheek was just as she remembered. Warm and caressing . . . and Lynch.

"Shut up." She buried her face in his chest. "Just shut up and hold me."

He stiffened. Then he relaxed and his arms slid around her. "Delighted." His cheek was pressed against her temple. "But I think we're going to have to discuss this soon. I'm worried about you."

"Why?" The ice was just beginning to melt, but she didn't want to let him go. She couldn't do it. She didn't know if she'd ever want to let him go. "I'm not the one who's dead, dammit."

He went rigid again. "Okay, that's a remark that requires explanation." He pushed her back to look into her face. "And that might deserve my being very pissed off when I get that explanation. You thought I was dead?"

She nodded jerkily. "What was I supposed to think? You were in that explosion. They *killed* you." She knew how crazy that sounded, but she didn't care. She didn't want to ask or answer questions right now. All she wanted to do was hold him and feel the strength and the *life* of him.

He was swearing softly beneath his breath. "Griffin was supposed to tell you. Didn't he call you?"

"He called me. He said that you were dead. Ninety-eight point-seven percent probability that it was you." She buried her head back on his chest. "I don't care about any of that. Shut up right now, Lynch. I'm not in very good shape. I need a little time."

"I can see that." His arms tightened around her. "And it's making me homicidal. Okay, you'll have your time." He was moving her toward the couch across the room. "But you don't mind if I spend that time plotting pain and mayhem?" He pulled her down on the couch and cuddled her close. "And you're still crying, dammit . . ."

"No, I'm not. There would be no reason . . ."

"There's not been anything reasonable happening since you walked into this condo today." He was gently stroking her hair back from her face with a featherlight touch. "I thought I'd cook up some lasagna and we'd have wine and talk and plan our next move. I didn't think that I'd end up aching like this. You've got to stop, okay?"

"Always thinking about yourself . . ."

"Self-preservation. And my plan was much better. Besides, you'll be angry later that I saw you like this and you'll punish me for it."

"No, I won't."

"Yeah, you can't punish me any more than you're doing right now." He cuddled her closer. "But you might not realize that and give it a try."

"I don't want to hurt you." She didn't want anything in the world to hurt him. He was *alive* and the scent of him and his warmth . . . "But I will, if you don't shut up for just five minutes."

He chuckled. "Now I know you're better. Five minutes." He pressed his lips to her temple. "I promise."

And he always kept his promises to her. That was why she had been so upset when she had not heard from him. Don't think about it. Take this time. Just hold onto him and heal . . .

Seven minutes later she straightened against him and then pushed him away. "You did that very well." She took a deep breath and then swallowed to ease the tightness of her throat. "I realize what a hardship it always is for you to not dominate every scene and conversation. Silence is not your forte." She reached up to touch her cheek. It was still wet with tears. She got to her feet. "I've obviously got a few repairs to make." She headed for the bathroom. "Why don't you get me that glass of wine? And then we'll talk and I'll let you gloat over the fact that I behaved like such an idiot."

"That's not fair, Kendra."

She looked over her shoulder. He had gotten to his feet and was gazing at her with those electric-blue eyes and those movie star good looks and neither of those things made a bit of difference in who he really was. What mattered was the gentleness with which he had held her and the empathy she had felt surrounding her during those moments. "No, it wasn't fair."

She went into the bathroom and closed the door.

She looked in the mirror over the vanity. Repairs, indeed. Red, swollen eyes, and her cheeks and nose were little better. She ran cold water and washed her face, ran a brush through her hair and left it at that. It would have to do. She still felt shaken, open and terribly vulnerable, but she looked decent enough.

Lynch was turning away from the bar when she came out of the bathroom. He handed her a glass of merlot. "Feel better?"

She nodded. "Yes." She took a sip of wine and noticed he didn't have a glass. "You're not drinking?"

"I'm very carefully balanced at the moment. I thought I'd pass on anything that might shift me either way." He nudged her back toward the couch. "Are you ready to listen to me now?"

She plopped down on the couch. He hadn't seemed to notice that she was still not entirely normal. That meant she was doing okay. Don't blow it. "Oh, yes, I insist on it. Start with Facey. I'm still too shaky to delve into your death scene. I'll have to work up to it."

She listened quietly to everything he'd learned from Ryan Facey. "You did well. At least we have a grasp on what's been happening." She shivered. "And it's worse than I dreamed. Either a serial killer or Brock's team of military gangsters seemed bad enough. But now we know it's both."

"But the key word is know," Lynch said. "What we know, we can fight."

"I appreciate that word 'know' very much." She took another sip of her wine. "Because it's a concept that none of you wanted to share with me last night." She concentrated and managed to keep her voice steady. "I'm still not good, but I think I'm ready to hear why Griffin was talking about you blowing up."

He shrugged. "We were in a kind of a bad spot and I was looking for a way to get Facey and me away from Brock's people and that cabin. I'd noticed from my drone surveillance earlier that those two Brock goons had taken out insurance at getting Facey by planting explosives in the cabin. Since we had to get to Facey's car on the other side of the cabin, I thought that I'd attract enough gunfire to make them impatient enough so that I could shape the situation to my advantage."

"Advantage?" She stared at him in disbelief. "You have to be an idiot, Lynch. By all means, tell me what advantage that could possibly give you?"

"They were planting a lot of C-4. It was going to be a fairly big explosion. I thought it would be safer to let Brock think that both Facey and I were permanently out of the picture. Facey is giving us all the information he has about Brock. We needed to keep him safe and make certain Brock wouldn't get nervous and start hiding evidence. And having me dead would make them feel even safer and let me work behind the scenes until it was time to move. So I . . . arranged it. No problem. The cabin ended up completely destroyed."

"And how close did you come to being completely destroyed?" she asked carefully.

"Not that close." He met her eyes. "Okay, I did lose my leather jacket."

"Only a jacket. As you said, no problem. And Facey?"

"He was fine. Though he was a little pissed off I hadn't told him what I'd planned. Everything turned out all right. The cabin was such a disaster Brock's men thought they'd done their job and took off. Griffin's agent, Brian Nolan, showed up and took care of all the details about getting us out of there. I called Griffin to stage the bogus medical proof. That went off very well."

"Yes, it did." She drained the rest of her wine in two swallows. "I noticed."

"But I also told him to call you and tell you about what we were doing. I was supposed to meet you back here. I told him I'd go through the building next door and then up to the roof that connects so I wouldn't be seen. I don't know what went wrong." His lips tightened grimly. "But I'm going to find out."

"I'm sure you will." She got to her feet, went over to the bar, and poured herself another glass of wine. She was holding herself together with all her strength. All she could see before her was that destroyed leather jacket he'd told her about. So casual. *No problem*. "But it will still be a little late, won't it?" She leaned back against the wall and sipped the wine. "That little mistake had ramifications. I'd probably better call Jessie and tell her not to get on Griffin's case. She was worried about me and she was planning to make Griffin assign agents in Portland to hold my hand when I arrived there."

"You were going to Portland?"

"Did you think I'd stay here?" She took another drink of wine. "They'd told me someone had killed you. I had to be certain." She lifted her glass to her lips. "And even if it was true, I couldn't stand the thought of you being alone there. It bothered me. You know how weird I can be."

"I know how you can be," he said softly. "And weird doesn't come into it. Thank you, Kendra."

"You're welcome." She finished the glass of wine and set the glass on the bar. "It was a learning experience. I suppose I'm lucky, I've never had to go through anything like that before. I didn't hold up too well. I'll be better next time around." Then she suddenly lifted her gaze to meet his. "No, I won't," she said fiercely. "Because you're not going to let this happen again. You broke your promise. You said you wouldn't let them hurt you."

"I didn't. It was just a mistake that—"

"A mistake that *hurt* me and made me feel things that I didn't want to feel." She was coming across the room toward him. "Terrible regret. Pain. All kinds of other crazy mixed-up emotions." She stopped before him. "And I'm still feeling them. I look at you and I can't shut them down." Her eyes were blazing up at him. "You do it, Lynch."

"What are you asking?" His eyes were narrowed on her face. "I know you're upset. I know you believe I'm somehow to blame. Maybe I am. Just tell me how to make it right."

She reached up and unbuttoned her shirt. "No one needs to tell you anything, Lynch." She stripped off her bra. "I'm sure you're an expert. It's simple." She pressed her naked breasts against him as she started to unbutton his shirt. "Just do what we've both been wanting to do."

"I'm not sure—" A ripple undulated through his body as she lifted his undershirt and pressed her nipples against his bare flesh. "This isn't a good idea."

"Then why have you been telling me it was good all this time?" She ran her tongue in the hollow of his shoulder. So warm. She could feel his heartbeat. So alive . . . "You've convinced me."

"Wait." His hands grasped her bare shoulders. "Not the right time. Not fair to you." He was breathing hard. "Man, that was hard to say. But it's true. I'm trying to tell you that—"

"I know what you're trying to tell me. Now stop arguing when I'm trying to fuck you." She had taken a step back and was tearing off the rest of her clothes. "The next thing you'll say is that I might be drunk because I had two whole glasses of wine. That won't float either, Lynch."

"I can see it won't." He was smiling recklessly as he jerked his undershirt over his head and threw it aside. In the next moment he was naked and reaching for her. "This is probably a mistake, but it's too late now. I'll have to repair it later . . ."

He lifted her and sank deep!

She cried out, her nails biting into his shoulders. Her legs curled around his hips.

She buried her face in his shoulders as she took him and took him and took him.

Then they were on the floor and he was over her.

Crazy . . .

Deep.

Hot.

Fast.

So fast.

Her head was moving from side to side as the intensity grew and grew . . .

How long . . .

It went on and on.

Deeper.

Faster.

Full. So full.

Heat

Heat.

Heat.

Heat!

CHAPTER 12

"OKAY?"

She looked up at Lynch, her breath still coming in gasps from the last time they had come together.

"Fine."

"Yes, you were." His head dipped and his tongue traced her nipple. "Extraordinary."

Extraordinary. Yes, that was what the last few hours had been. Erotic, mind-blowing, and totally extraordinary.

"Again?" he murmured.

She wanted to say yes. She couldn't get enough of him. But that might be because she'd thought she'd lost him entirely. Not exactly a healthy reaction, but nothing she'd done today had been anything resembling her usual pragmatic behavior. Even now she felt totally open, completely vulnerable, yet ready for anything he asked.

He was blowing teasingly on her nipple. “Kendra?”

She didn’t answer. The vulnerability was suddenly there before her, frightening her. She forced herself to roll over on the carpet and then get to her knees.

“I take it that’s a no.” He was resting his head on his hand as he watched her get to her feet. “Second thoughts? I was afraid they’d be popping up. We’ll discuss it later. I need to call that son of a bitch, Griffin, anyway. Do you want to put that frozen lasagna in the oven?” He smiled mischievously. “I’ve worked up an appetite.”

She had also and that appetite was for more than the lasagna. She headed for the kitchen. “I’ll put it in the oven, but you’ll have to watch it. It takes forty-five minutes and I’m going to shower.”

“It’s a deal.” He got to his feet. “I’ll grab a quick shower now so I’ll be ready for kitchen duty.” He headed for the guest bath. “You notice I’m giving you your space. That doesn’t mean we’re not going to discuss it after lasagna.”

Lord, he was fantastic naked, she thought as she watched him disappear into the bathroom. Masculine and sexy and totally Greek-god gorgeous. Which didn’t help either her bewilderment or her wariness. Well, it wasn’t as if there was any great urgency. He was giving her space. *Giving* her? she thought impatiently. She would take whatever time and space she needed in any situation. And what was she doing looking after him like some wistful groupie? She strode into the kitchen and opened the freezer door.

"THERE'S NO MORE delicious scent on earth than fresh-baked garlic bread," Lynch said as he put the bread on a plate. "Though you come pretty close. I like that lemon shampoo you use." He didn't wait for an answer as he put her salad in front of her. "It probably has some exotic, complicated name, but don't tell me about it. I'm just a simple man who embraces the basics."

"Bullshit." She dropped down in her chair. "I noticed that there's nothing basic about you. You're all for experiment and going that extra step." She picked up her fork and started to eat. "For instance, you mentioned lasagna and wine and you turned out a gourmet salad and garlic bread to go with it. This salad is terrific, by the way."

"I was bored." He sat down opposite her. "You took a long time in that shower. Not that I didn't expect it." He started to eat his salad. "And I had to work off being so pissed off at Griffin that I wouldn't go on the hunt. It was very close."

"He had an excuse for those lies?"

"He thought he did. He could have gone another way." His lips tightened. "He didn't have to hurt you. It turned out that he'd tapped an informant he had with Brock and probed for information about how much they knew about me . . . and you. He wanted to make sure that my death was entirely plausible to them. Of course you were prominently mentioned. Brock had already started monitoring your calls when I called you that first night from Portland."

"What?" She felt suddenly violated. She tried to remember that conversation. "They were listening?"

"Yes. And Griffin seized on the opportunity he saw and ran with it. Since you didn't know anything about the explosion, your reaction would give just the authentic touch he needed to prove that they'd managed to dispose of me."

She swore beneath her breath. "That cold son of a bitch."

"No one would expect anything else of him," he said harshly. "When it comes down to who he is, you accept he's all FBI. He had a job to do and he did it in the most efficient way possible. I should have been on the lookout for it. I thought he'd do what I told him to do. I didn't know about his damn informant."

She was looking blindly down at her salad remembering that moment of incredible pain and shock. "Was he pleased?" she asked jerkily. "What was my critique?"

He reached over and covered her hand with his own. "He said you were perfect. He couldn't have asked for anything better. That's when I almost lost it." His hand tightened. "I'll find a way to punish him, Kendra. I can't do it right now, but I'll study and find a way."

"Why?" She put her fork down. "His technique was a little crude, but it accomplished what you needed. I was perfect." She pushed back her chair. "But I seem to have lost my appetite. I'm a little sick to my stomach. I think I'll lie down for a while."

He caught up with her before she reached the bedroom. He pulled her into his arms and was rocking her. "You were *perfect,*" he said fiercely. "You were perfect, and giving, and everything you should be. I didn't deserve that I should have been able to hurt you like that, but I'm grateful that you thought that I was."

"Let me go, Lynch."

"No, because if I do, you're going to hide away and I'll have to work twice as hard to bring you back. I can see it coming." He kissed her forehead and then slipped his arm around her waist and was leading her toward her bed. "You're going to lie down and I'm going to hold you until you forget how vulnerable you felt when Griffin decided to savage you. Because that wasn't really about what we are together." He was pulling her down and holding her close. "And then I'll go and warm up our dinner and we'll talk about how we're going to torture Griffin. Is that a plan?"

"It's appealing." But he was wrong, that vulnerability she had felt when she had thought she had lost him had everything to do with what they were together. "But he was right, you know. It's an opportunity. *I'm* an opportunity."

"Shh, I'm trying to keep you from thinking about that. I knew it was going to occur to you." He drew her closer. "Stick to our plan. I'd much rather torture Griffin . . ."

"YOU DIDN'T MENTION sex when you set out your master plan." She put her arms in the terry robe he was holding for her. "Was that supposed to be a surprise?"

"No, it was an opportunity. That was the only opportunity I was interested in pursuing." He tied the belt of her robe before turning away and starting to dress. "How could I resist when I knew how difficult you were going to be when you recovered?" He smiled as he took her hand and pulled her toward the door. "But it gets better and better, doesn't it? Now come and have a cup of coffee while I heat up dinner. Then you can tell me about all the things you were storing up to hit me with while you took that shower earlier." He settled her in her chair and went to the cabinet and put coffee in the automatic coffeemaker. Then he cleared the table and put the bread in the warmer. "Go ahead, I'm listening."

"Why are you waiting on me? You're acting as if I'm wounded or something. Why are you doing all this?"

"I'm not doing much." He put the lasagna back in the oven. "Not when you compare it to flying away to sit by my dead body just to hold my hand."

"That's not funny, Lynch."

"I know it isn't. That's why it touched me and made

me feel a lot of weird stuff I'd never felt before." He poured her coffee and then one for himself. "So just take what's offered and be gracious about it." He brought the coffee to the table and set her cup before her. "Now go ahead." He sat down across from her. "Get it out so that you'll feel better."

"You think you know me so well," she said impatiently. "It's very annoying."

"I know. But you have to consider I've made a study of you. It didn't come easy." He took a sip of his coffee. "Do you want me to start? Let's see, you're backing away with all due speed. You enjoyed the hell out of the sex, but it's scaring you. Because you're afraid that it's going to bring me closer to you." He looked into her eyes. "And you don't want to ever feel as you did when Griffin opened his big yap and told you that whopper. You might not have even realized that you'd feel that terrible if I bit it." He added softly, "Oh, but you did and I like it very, very much, Kendra. Not your pain, but everything else connected to it."

"Well, I don't," she said curtly. "I liked it just fine when we were just . . . friends. I don't want this . . . other."

"But you've already got it. Tied up in red ribbons." He tilted his head. "You could tell me to go to hell. But I probably wouldn't go and you'd miss me if I did. You might even worry about me if you couldn't be there to take care of me. You were really upset about Portland."

He took another drink of coffee. "And it would also demonstrate to you that you weren't strong enough to handle me. That would hurt your pride. Wouldn't it be better to just learn how we can get through this together?"

Not if it meant repeating those hideous moments that had almost devastated her today. "Until the time someone really does kill you? Until you actually do get blown up because you're trying to manipulate every situation to suit yourself? With your track record, it could happen anytime. You seem to go looking for it on every assignment you take. And if that's your choice, I have no right to even question it. But I've made my own choice, Lynch." Her hand was shaking and she had to put her cup down. "I can't deny I feel . . . something for you. It's a little late for that. But I won't go through this again. And I can't let it get any deeper." She moistened her lips. "I'll be your friend, I'll help you and keep you safe, but I won't let myself in for that kind of punishment. It was a wake-up call."

He shook his head. "It's not going to work, Kendra," he said gently.

"It's the only thing that will work."

He was silent. Then he shrugged. "I thought that was where this was going. I knew Griffin had probably squashed any slow and gradual approach with his damn shock tactics. It's a definite setback, but not irreversible. I'll take what I can get, and I'll play your game." He smiled. "We actually took several steps forward. We found out what we have sexually and it's very, very hot. Even if we try to forget it, that's not going to happen. There will be a moment, an hour, a day . . ." He got to his feet and went to the oven and pulled out the lasagna. "Get used to the idea that we won't be able to stop it."

But he was agreeing to acknowledge that she meant what she'd said and wasn't walking away from her. Somehow the thought of him doing that was causing her to panic. She didn't know if it was relief or disappointment that was making her feel this strange letdown. "Maybe that won't be a factor." She smiled with an effort. "You might get bored with me and decide to wander off. I'm not exactly a femme fatale. You always have lots of women revolving in your orbit."

"I won't get bored." He was dishing out the lasagna onto their plates. "No, we're going to have to work this out on our own. So start accepting the challenge." He sat down again. "Now to problem two on the agenda. I could see how quickly you snatched at Griffin's using you to help fool Brock. You want to twist it and for us to use you to stage a trap?"

"It seems the logical thing to do." Her lips twisted. "After all, I'm perfect. Heartbroken, willing to do anything for revenge or to complete your mission. I'm even distantly involved in the wedding party killings. All we'd have to do is create a plan."

"I don't like this concept at all. It's scaring me." He

was studying her expression. "But I'm not going to be able to change your mind, am I?"

"They were *listening* to me. I feel dirty when I think about it. And they tried to kill you." Her lips tightened. "I want to see just how perfect I can be."

He didn't speak for a moment. "Okay. But only as a last resort. There may be another way to avoid it. I told you we wanted to use Facey. When I was talking to Griffin tonight, he was practically salivating. He wants to use the information we got from Facey about Brock right away instead of waiting." He grimaced. "So much for all the trouble we went through to make everyone think we were dead. I argued with him, but now I may have to go along. Griffin's planning a raid on the main Brock Limited headquarters that would include an in-depth search and bringing in Vivianne Kerstine and her merry band. We're hoping to find any records pertaining to Derek as well as anything else incriminating."

"*Yes.*" She leaned eagerly forward. "When?"

"Later today. Probably this afternoon." His lips twisted. "And you're looking a little too happy. I was afraid of that. This is an FBI raid. You shouldn't be anywhere near it. If you like, you can be present when we bring them in for questioning."

"Yes, I will. And Griffin can assign an agent to drive me to those headquarters and I'll watch them being taken into custody." She gestured impatiently. "Don't worry, I'm not going to bust into that place with guns blazing. That would be stupid. I just want to see them taken down and shown that they don't own the entire world."

"I like my way better."

"You always like your way better." She started to eat. "But I want to squeeze every bit of satisfaction I can from those bastards. I'm going to eat this dinner that's now really breakfast. While I'm doing that, I want you to call Metcalf and tell him to get me a burner phone so that those assholes won't hear me unless I want them to hear me. Then I'm going to shower and dress and head for the FBI office and make my demands known to Griffin." She smiled. "And I'm going to enjoy every minute of it."

"I DON'T LIKE THIS IDEA." Griffin scowled as Kendra climbed into the van beside the special agent he'd assigned her. "This is FBI business and civilians should not be involved."

"I'm merely an observer and I have no intention of being involved." She slammed the door. "And what about Lynch? I saw him get into that van over there."

"Lynch is different," Griffin said. "You know that, Kendra."

"Yes, he's a dead man walking." Kendra leaned out the window and said between her teeth, "What a surprise. I wonder if you realize just how angry I am with you, Griffin."

He shrugged. "Yeah, Lynch spelled it out for me. But I thought it was the right thing to do. Once I knew how important Facey was going to be, I had to make certain that both their deaths appeared authentic. I'll make it up to you, Kendra."

"Oh, will you?" He was incredible, she thought. Lynch was right, nothing was important but his damn job. "I'd be interested to see how." She started to roll up her window. "I'm going, Griffin."

"Whatever." He turned away. "But don't get yourself killed. It would be very bad press."

Was he trying to joke? She thought he might be.

Incredible.

LYNCH RAN ALONGSIDE Griffin as the two-dozen FBI agents ran across Juniper Street to the Brock Limited's office building. Lynch nodded to a pair of agents with assault rifles. "You really think those are necessary?"

"If I did, we'd all have them. But I know it's a language Brock understands."

"Agreed."

The group moved through the building lobby and commandeered four elevators to the fourteenth floor. They burst into the Brock Limited lobby to the surprise and consternation of a pair of receptionists seated at a long granite counter.

Griffin held up a badge and warrant as agents rushed

past him to the offices. "FBI. I need to address everyone on this floor. Now!"

With trembling hands, one of the assistants picked up her phone and punched a three-digit code.

Griffin took the phone and spoke into it. His amplified voice echoed down the hallway. "This is the FBI, operating under the force of a Federal warrant. Everyone must immediately stand and step away from their offices. I repeat, everyone must immediately stand and step away from their offices. This is the FBI."

Vivianne Kerstine strode into the reception area, glaring at them. The Brock CEO was as strikingly attractive as Lynch had seen in photographs, but her expression was ugly.

"What the hell is going on?" she asked.

Griffin handed her the warrant. "Records and data seizure."

Her already chilly demeanor grew downright icy. "Why?"

"It's in the warrant. We suspect this office is in possession of material vital to a murder investigation."

"Ridiculous."

Brock employees spilled from their offices as FBI agents moved in. A second wave of FBI agents emerged from the elevator behind them with flattened cardboard boxes, packing tape, and hand trucks.

"What are you taking?" she asked.

"All computers, data, and paper records."

"This is a multinational corporation. We need these things to function."

Griffin nodded. "The sooner we find what we need, the sooner you'll get them back. Some of them will even be examined here on the premises. You and your management can help by joining us for a discussion at our office. We have vans waiting downstairs."

She looked at him incredulously. "You're taking us in?"

"It's in your best interest to talk to us," Griffin said.

Vivianne whirled and strode back down the hallway. Griffin nodded to Metcalf, who quickly followed her.

Along with the dozens of curious Brock employees who appeared in the lobby, Josh Blake rounded the corner. He froze as he caught sight of Lynch. "Shit."

Lynch smiled. "Hi, Josh. Why, I thought you'd be at the training center again."

"No. I . . . no."

Josh awkwardly turned away.

"Why, he looks like he's seen a dead man," Griffin murmured.

Lynch nodded. "Exactly what I thought. But if Vivianne Kerstine was surprised to see me, she didn't show it."

"Doesn't mean anything," Griffin said. "She's smooth."

His mobile phone beeped in his pocket. He pulled it

out and looked at the Caller ID screen. "That didn't take long."

Lynch looked at the name. "Senator James Morant."

Griffin nodded. "Head of the Senate Armed Services Committee. Brock has friends in high places."

"It won't be the last call you get."

Griffin put away his phone. "All in good time."

Vivianne Kerstine came back into the lobby closely followed by Metcalf. "I'm ready to go. Let's get this nonsense over with." She headed for the elevator. "But if you've notified the press about this indignity, you might be in for a reprimand. I won't let my reputation be sullied."

"We wouldn't think of doing that." Griffin smiled. "Unless we found proof that it was 'warranted' I'll see you back at the office, Ms. Kerstine. Metcalf will escort you."

Lynch entered the elevator at the last minute and moved to the back of the car. Vivianne Kerstine ignored him as if he wasn't there. For that matter, Metcalf was getting the same treatment, he noticed.

She strode ahead of them as they exited the elevator and crossed the lobby to the sidewalk. Metcalf had to hurry to catch up with her. "This way, Ms. Kerstine."

But she stopped as she reached the street. She was gazing at Kendra, who was standing outside her van watching the Brock employees stream out of the building.

She didn't hesitate but strode straight up to Kendra. "You're Kendra Michaels, aren't you?"

Lynch stiffened and took a step toward Kerstine.

But Kendra was staring directly into her eyes. "Yes, I am. Ms. Kerstine. Do you have something to say to me?"

She stared at her for a long moment. "You've made a mistake."

She turned and let Metcalf lead her away.

Kendra gazed after her. Then she shook her head as if to clear it and turned to Lynch. "Are you coming back to the office with me?"

"I was thinking about it." He turned back to the building. "But I believe I'll go back upstairs and help with the search. It might be a good idea to have all hands on deck to find a way to eliminate that lady."

FBI Regional Office

Kendra's hands clenched on the arms of her chair in the lobby as Metcalf shrugged, shook his head at her, and then disappeared back into the interrogation room.

This had been the fourth time in as many hours that ritual had been repeated. It was driving her crazy that Griffin had decided she was not to be allowed in there while the questioning was going on. She almost wished she'd stayed back at the Brock building with Lynch.

Her phone rang and she jumped at answering it. "Lynch?"

"I'm afraid not," Trey Suber said apologetically. "I understand there are all kinds of interesting things going on with you and the bureau today and I didn't want to disturb you. But I've found something I regard as interesting as well and I wonder if you could come and talk with me for a few minutes?"

She gave a glance at the closed door of the interrogation room. At least someone believed she could be of help, she thought in frustration. If anything broke, Metcalf would call her anyway. She jumped to her feet. "I'll be right there. Where are you?"

"Fifth floor conference room."

Three minutes later Kendra walked into the fifth-floor conference room, which was now entirely covered with freestanding billboards plastered with gory murder-scene photos. Trey Suber was seated at the end of the long table, hunched over his laptop.

"I thought you'd take over this room," Kendra said as she glanced at the posters.

Trey stood and gestured around them. "This is pretty much where I live these days. And the possible connection with the Damascus and London serial killings has suddenly opened up our investigation quite a bit."

Kendra blanched at the sight of a particularly gruesome London killing. "You didn't waste time tracking those photos down, Suber."

"Oh, I already had them all in my laptop."

Kendra smiled. "Of course you did."

"I knew the details of every one of those crime scenes, but there's nothing so distinctive about them that they made me connect the Damascus, London, and San Diego scenes to each other." Suber walked across the room, motioning toward the boards like an enthusiastic college professor. "Now that I can directly compare, I can see that the killer employed a frontal strangulation in the Damascus and San Diego killings accompanied by a knee against the chest. In London, it was left-to-right swipe across the throat with a nine-inch serrated blade. So of course, no one noticed any connections with that one." He shook his head regretfully. "Though I wish I had. There has to be more connections here."

"If anyone can find them, you can."

Suber studied the boards. "I just wanted to make certain you knew how obsessed this killer is with patterns in each series. Perhaps more than any murderer I've ever seen. It's all about the pattern with him. He kills just long enough for law enforcement to recognize the pattern, then he stops. The medical school class in Damascus, the soccer team in London, and the wedding party here. The wedding party connection was recognized here sooner than it would have been, thanks to the video that was found on Elena Meyer's body."

"You think he'll stop here?" Kendra asked.

"Hard to say. He's obviously extremely disciplined,

so that's a possibility. But he may just look at it as a challenge and try to move forward anyway." Trey shook his head. "I just don't know him well enough yet." He stepped back from the boards, trying to take them in all at once. "But I can't help but think . . ."

"What?"

Trey took off his eyeglasses and wiped them on the tail of his untucked shirt. "A killer this pattern-obsessed would link each series of killings somehow. It may be here right in front of our eyes, but he doesn't want us to see it yet. In his grand plan, there might be a common element that would be evident only after a half-dozen cities over a couple decades."

Her eyes widened. "A couple decades?"

"Oh, yeah. Trust me. He's just getting started," Suber said soberly. "We have to find this guy. Fast."

"We're trying, Suber. That's the unanimous decision." She turned and headed for the door. "But that pattern you're talking about is getting more complicated all the time. Now I have to get back and see if Griffin has managed to find an answer."

METCALF WAS JUST COMING out of the interrogation room again when Kendra arrived back at the lobby.

"Anything?" Kendra asked. "Is she talking at all?"

"Not a word," Metcalf said. "Neither is Josh Blake. And we're not going to be able to keep her from lawyering up for much longer. She's had a crew of expensive lawyers waiting downstairs since we pulled her in. Hell, we've had her and Blake in that room for over five hours and she's threatening a suit for false imprisonment." He added grimly, "She'd win. Lynch called from Brock headquarters and said that so far they haven't found a shred of evidence that would link her to anything illegal and certainly nothing about Derek. There have to be records, but she has to have them stashed so deep it would take a Geiger counter to unearth them."

"They probably are," Kendra said, frustrated. "They learned their lesson when Elena Meyer blundered across that file on Derek. They must have scrambled to make certain nothing like that would ever happen again."

"We had a chance," Metcalf said. "We'll just have to find another way to go. Maybe this will discourage Brock from dealing with Derek."

"When he also has copies of the evidence that they hid so industriously? Not likely." She shook her head. "It might just make them more eager to please the bastard." She remembered that moment when Vivianne Kerstine had given her that fierce glare before she had been taken away. "Because she definitely didn't like having her dignity ruffled when she was hauled off so unceremoniously."

"Yeah, I noticed she was looking daggers at you as we passed. I couldn't decide why you were taking the heat."

She shrugged. "Because I'm a woman. She's probably

been fighting the male world all her life and winning. She wouldn't think they were worthy adversaries anymore. But she'd accept that I might cause her trouble."

"If that's true, then she might feel that she should get rid of a possible threat," Metcalf said quietly. "Maybe Lynch was right about keeping you in the background. Her dossier is pretty impressive and she— Uh-oh." His gaze was on the elevator doors that had just opened. "Here come the legal eagles. Griffin must have decided to give up on Kerstine and her crew."

Kendra watched the herd of sleek, expensively dressed men and women hurrying toward the interrogation room. "Shouldn't you go back in there and help referee?"

"Maybe," Metcalf said. "But there's not much use. The minute those lawyers get in there, their 'innocent' clients are going to be released and will be streaming back through here and be allowed to go back to Brock headquarters, smirking all the way." He paused. "And I wanted to take a minute to talk to you and apologize for—"

"I'm not ready to listen to your apologies right now," Kendra said curtly. "Let's just keep doing what we have to do to find Derek and keep him from killing Barbara Campbell."

"I just wanted to—"

"Here they come," she interrupted as the doors of the interrogation room opened and Vivianne Kerstine strode out, followed by her battery of lawyers. "As you predicted."

Vivianne must have heard her voice because she stopped and turned to the chairs where they were sitting. She lifted her chin. "I told you that you'd made a mistake." She almost spat the words out. "I worked very hard to get where I am, Dr. Michaels. You should have thought twice before you tried to shred my reputation. There are always consequences."

"That sounded like a threat. I believe the only mistake we made was not getting to your files soon enough. We'll know better next time." She cocked her head. "And what do you think my mistake was?"

Vivianne smiled sweetly. "Why the persecution of a perfectly innocent woman, of course. What else could I have meant?" She turned and sailed toward the elevator with her entourage.

"She's very sharp," Kendra said as she watched the elevator doors close. "And she's very angry. Where the hell are those records? Where would she think they'd be safe?"

"We'll try doing a search of other Brock locations in the area, but I can't see her letting anything vital be taken too far away from her jurisdiction."

"Unless she had to find—"

The text on her phone was buzzing. She didn't recognize the number and she tried to turn it off.

The text wouldn't turn off. It kept on buzzing.

What the hell?

She pressed the access.

Hello Kendra,

You've had a busy day haven't you? You're proving to be very annoying. And my wedding arrangements have been going so splendidly up to now.

Kendra dropped the phone.

"What is it," Metcalf asked, startled.

"I'm not sure." She moistened her lips. "I . . . think it might be Derek." She forced herself to pick up the phone again and continue reading.

But you're forcing me to curtail some of the finer details and characters since you arrived on the scene. Not that I object to you causing problems for my friends, it rather amused me. But now they're going to be nervous and that might cause me time and effort to correct. So I've decided that I won't be able to let them take care of you. Unfortunately, I'm not sure they're competent enough. I'll have to do it myself. That's not good news for you. You should really never have had the arrogance to accept this assignment that would pit you against me. But I do believe you should be given a lesson that only I can teach.

She showed the text to Metcalf. "What do you think? It's him?"

He nodded. "I think so. Answer him." He was hurriedly taking out his phone. "It's a long shot, but maybe it can be traced."

Her hands were shaking as she typed.

Derek?

Who else?

Shock. She took a deep breath.

Murderer. You can't get away with this. You think you're so clever. But you might as well return Barbara Campbell to us. Because I'll never stop. I'll be there behind you until you make a mistake and then I'll take you down.

His answer came quickly.

I don't like threats. But I'll forgive you this time. And I am very clever. Because I wouldn't have been fooled by all that flim-flam you all used to make my friends believe Facey and Lynch were dead. Though I understand you were very convincing. Is there some real feeling there, Kendra? I admit I'm disappointed. I don't really believe in all that man-woman garbage. It's too limited. There are so many more relationships that can offer me so much more. I was hoping for something more challenging.

She glanced at Metcalf, but he was still talking frantically on his phone.

Challenging? I don't know what you mean?

Derek's answer didn't come for more than two minutes.

Of course you don't. And you're trying desperately to keep me on the phone to trace this text. You won't succeed, so why shouldn't I accommodate you? I do get so bored, Kendra. Anyone with a superior intellect does. Don't you find that? Not that you're near to my capacity, but you're close enough to be teachable. Challenging? My philosophy? The most exquisite thing on earth is power. The ultimate power can only be gained by inflicting the ultimate amount of pain. Because that's what all human beings fear most.

She typed quickly and with perfect truth.

That's totally sick.

Another pause.

You're disappointing me again. I've let you into my world and all I get is scorn. That's all right. As I said, you're teachable. And there are so many other ways I can show you I'm right about the power and the pain. How does it feel to be the target, Kendra? If you were as smart as they think you are, you'd have already made that connection about me. But don't worry, I've already started the process to show you the error of your ways. I look forward to completing it.

The text ended.

She whirled on Metcalf. "Did you get the trace?"

"I don't think so. They're still trying. It was blocked." He took a deep breath. "*Shit,*" Metcalf said. "I think we stirred up a hornet's nest."

Kendra thought that, too. Her heart was pounding as she looked down at her phone. "But at least he responded. He gave us information." And he'd given them an insight into how he thought that was chilling. Well, what had she expected? He was a psychopath and they were usually about pain. "I need to talk to Lynch. Where is he?"

"On his way back from Brock headquarters, he should be here anytime." Metcalf was frowning. "Can't I help?"

"Not this time." She took out the burner phone Lynch had given her and pressed his number.

He answered immediately. "Pay dirt?"

"Derek texted me on my personal phone. It was weird. It wouldn't go off until I accepted the text. I'm giving my phone to Metcalf for analysis to see if they can tell anything more about how he did it. And make sure Derek or Brock can't trace me through it." She paused. "But he said . . . things that might help. I think we need to talk about it. Can I meet you somewhere?"

"I'm almost there. Go down to the tech department and meet me. There's a private office next door we can use. You'll be able to remember the text?"

"I'm grabbing a copy. But I assure you there would be no problem," she said dryly. "I'll definitely be able to remember every word of that text."

CHAPTER 13

"SHIT, THE THREAT COULDN'T be more clear," Lynch said tightly. "We've got what you wanted. He's going to go after you."

"But how?" Kendra asked. "I think he's dangling the answer in front of me, just to show me how stupid I am compared to his superior, brilliant intellect." She was mentally going over the text, line by line. "He's obviously all about pain, Lynch. Facey said he was one sick puppy. Yet Liz Gelson's torture wasn't extreme. Probably just enough to show her how powerful he was." She was working her way through it. "It had to be something else."

"No, it doesn't," Lynch said quietly. "There are all kinds of pain in this world. He told you that. I'm beginning to think that our Derek has much more sophisticated tastes."

"He said that he wouldn't have chosen to kill you." She said slowly, "He didn't believe in that man-woman garbage." She added tentatively, "Because the pain factor wouldn't have been intense enough for him? He definitely sounds like he doesn't believe that destroying a couple relationship was worth his time." She had another thought. "Or because it would possibly have such a limited scope that he'd feel cheated? He did use the word limited."

"Go on." Lynch said. "It's coming to you, isn't it?"

"Maybe. I don't know." But she thought that perhaps she was seeing a glimmer. "But he said that he'd just gotten started with that wedding party. It annoyed him that he was feeling hobbled by us. He was planning on creating much more chaos. How? He'd already killed the bride and presumably the maid of honor was to be next. Why did he choose them? Why did he think they were worth his attention? The bride was supposedly at the peak of her romantic happiness, but that obviously wouldn't have had an effect on Derek. The maid of honor had been married for a couple years and was just an ordinary woman starting a new business." She suddenly snapped her fingers as a thought came to her. "But they both had large families, large groups of friends and business acquaintances. The wedding party itself was very large. Five bridesmaids and groomsmen and then parents and . . ." She broke off. "We don't how many people would be affected if they also died. To kill them all would affect a sizeable group of people. That could be what he wanted, to cause as much pain as possible to the victims' circle as a whole. It might not have had anything to do with the victims' husbands other than to furnish Derek an occasion and an opportunity. Derek would have considered them 'garbage' compared to the sheer mass of other people in their lives." She looked up to meet Lynch's eyes. "And you told me about those two groups of people Derek killed that were his pride and joy. The deaths in that soccer team and those medical students must have had a tremendous effect on their family, friends, and fans. Derek must have gotten a big thrill out of those kills."

"And so went looking for an equally satisfying kill here," Lynch said. "If he was planning on going down the list of all the people in the wedding party, it might have turned out to be a new first for him."

She shivered. "I can see how he'd be irritated that I'd gotten in his way."

"Irritated? That's a mild word," Lynch said roughly. "And we just added fuel to the fire. I think he's now in punishment mode. We've got to catch him and do it quick."

"That's what I've been saying. But this is a start."

"Screw it. We gave him an invitation and he just accepted. How long do you think it will be before he makes a move? He already said he was in the process."

"Then it's done, isn't it?" She smiled with an effort. "We've just got to make certain that he doesn't get any further with the process."

"Yeah, but that's not going to be simple to do if he's as smart as Facey said. Unless you'll just let us surround you with agents until we can catch Derek."

"With Brock protecting him? How long would that take?" She shook her head. "We're close. We're getting closer all the time. We can do this."

He muttered a curse and got to his feet. "Then I'm going up and telling Griffin you're going to have twenty-four-hour surveillance from now on."

"That might scare Derek off."

"Tough. I don't think so. He'll probably think of it as a challenge. And I'm staying with you in the condo."

She shrugged. "Do you think I'd argue? This is my life, Lynch."

"Tell me about it." He headed for the door. "And I'll also check with Metcalf and see if he's making progress on that text. I'll bring your phone down here to Hi-Tech and we can go over it with a fine-tooth comb." His lips twisted. "It might be a long night."

She watched the door close behind him before she looked back down at the text message. His anger and tension were both understandable and upsetting, but no more than the words jumping out at her from that paper. Was there anything else she should have noticed?

Other than that Derek was even more crazy and diabolic than she had thought. That he was going for the maximum amount of pain, spreading it like a giant fan among the loved ones of the victims and nothing was going to stop him.

No, until *they* stopped him, she corrected quickly. They *had* to stop him.

LYNCH WAS RIGHT ABOUT it being a long night. They didn't leave the FBI office until after midnight.

"Metcalf was pretty pissed off." Lynch glanced at Kendra as she made the turn on the street of her condo. "He expected us to be able to pull an IP address out of the stratosphere and it wasn't happening. We did everything we could, Kendra. The people who crafted that text for Derek were experts."

"Brock Limited," she said bitterly. "And they are experts, as we all know." She shook her head. "And no one knows that better than Metcalf and Griffin. He's not really blaming anyone, he's just frustrated."

"And wanted to make it up to you for helping Griffin lie to you. He's feeling guilty."

"He should feel guilty." She glanced at him. "Are you saying he shouldn't?"

"No, I'm just feeling so guilty myself that I guess I'm feeling sorry for the guy."

"It will take a while before I get that far along. Maybe next year."

"Ouch. That's pretty harsh."

"So was what they did to me." She looked him in the eye. "Any argument?"

He shook his head. "No way. I've done my duty. I'll toss them both under the bus if it will keep me in your good books."

"Very wise." She grinned as she started to approach the entrance to the condo garage. "It's always better to be—"

"Don't drive down to the garage," Lynch said. "Pull over to the curb."

"Why?" she asked, startled. Her gaze followed his to the front entrance as she pulled over. "What's that policeman doing at the front door?" Then she grimaced. "You must have put a lot of pressure on Griffin to get him to assign my surveillance this quickly, Lynch. You said twenty-four hours but this is—"

"That cop is San Diego PD." Lynch got out of the car and started to stride toward the vestibule. "Griffin would have assigned an agent. Stay here. I'll be right back." But his phone was ringing and he checked his ID. "Griffin." He answered. He listened for a moment. "Holy shit. Yeah, she hasn't gone in yet. I'll take care of it." He pressed the disconnect. "We have a problem."

She went cold. "What the hell are you talking about?"

"Forty minutes ago the janitor of your building

discovered the body of a woman in the stairwell. She was dead. He called the police, and they just notified Griffin."

"In the stairwell?" She tensed. "What was the woman's description? Could it have been Barbara Campbell?"

"We don't know yet. Griffin's going to call me back to give me the rest of the details in a minute."

"If it is her, Derek could have done it as a warning to me. He asked how I liked being the target. I have to *know,* Lynch." She jumped out of the car. "Let's get in there."

"We will. Calm down." He took her arm and was pulling her toward the entrance. "They don't even have a complete crew here yet. There's only that cop on duty and a few detectives and a medic in the stairwell."

It took a few minutes of Lynch's persuasion, but then they were allowed into the building. She heard the sirens and saw the flashing lights of the squad cars and coroner's van pull up outside as Lynch punched the button of the elevator. "And I can't calm down," she said shakily as they got into the elevator. "Not if that woman turns out to be Barbara Campbell. And not if it's my fault she's dead. I'm scared to death that he killed her today because he was angry and wanted to warn me."

"You're only guessing. Stop it. Wait until we get the facts." His phone rang again and she watched his face as he listened to Griffin. "Okay, I'll tell her. I'll call you back." He held Kendra's eyes as he punched the button to put the elevator in motion. "It's Barbara Campbell. Preliminary examination by the detectives puts her time of death to be at least twelve hours ago. That means she was already dead when you were texting with Derek." He paused. "He evidently already had his plan in place."

She shuddered. "To put her corpse on my doorstep?"

He didn't answer.

She suddenly inhaled sharply, her gaze flying to his face. "*My* doorstep, Lynch?" Then she saw the answer on his face. "*No!*"

"Not the stairwell where your condo is located," he said gently. "One floor down."

"Olivia?" she asked hoarsely. "Olivia's condo?" She felt as if she'd been kicked in the stomach. "That can't be the truth, dammit. Tell me that it's not true, Lynch."

He shook his head. "I can't do that, Kendra. And Griffin said that she was the only one who didn't answer her door when the police were trying to question the tenants. The super unlocked her door and took a look around. She wasn't there."

Of course she wasn't, Kendra thought numbly. Deliver a dead body. Take a living person. That was Derek's MO. Why had she thought his action would be aimed at her just because he'd told her she was the target? Maybe because she hadn't been able to bear that Olivia or anyone else she loved would be.

"I want to go see for myself." The elevator door

opened and she pushed her way through the crowd that was gathered around the stairwell. Why hadn't she realized the button Lynch had pressed was not for her floor? Because he hadn't wanted her to know before he could ease her into it, she realized.

"Of course, you do." Lynch followed her down the corridor to Olivia's condo. "Should I get the super?"

"I have a key to her condo." Her hand was shaking as she unlocked the door. "But if the super didn't have one of Olivia's keys the alarm should have gone off." Her voice was feverish. "She has very good security. It will only give me two minutes to disarm after I go inside." She pushed open the door.

The keypad was dark. It had been disarmed.

"Dammit." Her hands clenched into fists at her sides. She could feel the panic rising. "*Really* good security. I saw to it myself a couple years ago, remember? I wanted to make certain she'd be safe because she was blind and alone. But Brock would have been able to do it, wouldn't they? They'd have been able to give that son of a bitch, Derek, anything he wanted. Just like that text message."

"Good chance," he said. "Kendra . . ." He took an impulsive step toward her.

"No!" She backed away from him. "Don't touch me. I can't have anyone touch me or I'll—" She stopped. "I'm okay, Lynch. Can't you see? I'm okay."

He nodded, his gaze intent on her face. "Yes, I can see that, Kendra," he said quietly. He shifted his glance to the alarm. "I'll have the security system checked out and see if we can get any idea about who disabled it."

"You do that." She nodded vigorously. "Have someone go over the entire condo and see what they can find. I need to know where they took her." She swallowed. "I have to know, Lynch. Before she ends up like that poor woman in the stairwell." She crossed her arms across her chest to keep them from shaking. "That can't happen. Do you hear me? We have to find her and bring her home."

"I hear you," he said gently. "I'll see to it. And I'll call Griffin and tell him to get his entire crew out here, too. We're going to do everything we can, Kendra." He paused. "I need to go talk to the detectives in the stairwell about what they might know. Do you want me to take you up to your condo?"

"No, why should I want you to do that? I have to stay here and make sure that none of us misses anything. And I want to search myself."

"Right." He gave her one more glance and then went out into the hall, and she heard him talking on his phone. He was worried about her, she knew. She was aware that she wasn't behaving normally, but she couldn't help it. She couldn't think of anything but Olivia and how to keep that murderer from hurting her. She felt so helpless . . .

But she couldn't stand here and do nothing. She had to search for some kind of clue as she'd told Lynch she'd do. Perhaps Olivia had managed to leave her a message. Olivia was so clever, and she'd know that Kendra would be looking for her.

Start in the bathroom . . .

No messages in any room in the condo, she realized desperately twenty minutes later. After searching every inch, she had found nothing. Olivia's condo was its usual clean, organized space. It was as if she'd just walked out the front door.

But if she'd walked out that door, it had been because she was forced. And Olivia would have fought. She'd never give in without a battle. All her life she'd been—

She heard a beep across the room.

She recognized that sound. It was the signal for an incoming fax from the machine on the desk across the room.

She froze, staring at the red light and then listening as the machine started to chatter.

A fax at almost one in the morning?

She slowly crossed the room and stared down at the machine.

Hello, Kendra,

I can't tell you how delighted I am at this moment. I can almost feel your pain. This is the first lesson I'm teaching you. Now pay attention, this is very important to you . . .

* * *

"KENDRA?"

Kendra forced herself to look up from the fax she'd been staring numbly at for the last fifteen minutes.

Lynch was standing in the doorway, gazing worriedly at her. "Okay? Griffin and Metcalf have just arrived and they're talking to the detectives and ME. I want to bring the forensics team in here to—"

"Bring them in," she interrupted him. "I don't think Derek would mind them going over the place. I'm sure he'd be happy that they'd appreciate what a good job he'd done in staging this. He'd regard it as another teaching experience." She got to her feet. "It appears that I might be going to get a good many of those." She took the fax out of the machine and headed for the door. "But I don't want Griffin to see this first lesson Derek sent me. Because I don't know what I'm going to do about it."

"Derek?" His gaze was on the sheet in her hand. "He sent you a fax? Why didn't you call me?"

"You might say I was in shock." That was an understatement. "And I wasn't certain that I'd want you to see it either."

"What?"

"Don't be insulted. I decided I had to tell you. I trust you and I couldn't be alone in this." She looked back at him from the door. "I'm going up to my condo. Do what you have to do with Griffin and Metcalf, but don't bring them to me. Not if you want to read what Derek sent me." She went out the door and straight to the elevator.

A few minutes later she was unlocking the door of her condo and going inside. She leaned back against the door and closed her eyes. She had to be stronger than this. There had to be something she could do, but right now she could only fight off the nausea and the fear.

Move. Think.

She went to the bathroom and got a glass of water and drained it. It didn't help.

But Lynch was using his key to unlock the door and she immediately felt a rush of adrenaline when he walked into the condo. "You were quick."

"What did you expect? Let me see that fax."

She handed him the fax and stood beside him as he read it. "You'll see that he's in great form. He wasn't lying about his pain-power philosophy. She quoted softly, "Hello Kendra, I can't tell you how delighted I am at this moment. I can almost feel your pain. This is the first lesson I'm teaching you . . ." She shook her head. "But after that I kind of lost it when he went into details."

But the words were right there before her again and she steeled herself not to flinch from them.

I generally don't set myself against a single individual. Their pain tends to bore me now that I've experienced what I can feel from more complex and massive waves of emotion. But I've decided you're an exception that I can't ignore. I wish to feel your pain and I realized when I looked up your dossier that it would be simple enough to do. Your dear friend Olivia is the key. Make her suffer and you will suffer, too. So much that you'll run to her side and try to stop her pain. Then I will have both of you. Isn't that clever?

But the question was what would you consider a terrible enough torment to drive you to risk your own life? Not any of the ordinary means. Then it came to me. She's blind, Kendra. Just as you were. Now what other senses could I take away from her that would drive her almost insane? Just temporarily of course . . . until I choose differently.

I can practically see you leaping for the door to come to her aid. It's very amusing. But I'm not going to let you do that yet. I want the pleasure of having both of you go through that hell for a long time. Maybe I'll permit you to come together sometime tomorrow or the next day or the day after. You'll never know when. All you'll know is how she's suffering while I make you wait. If you bring the FBI or Lynch into this then it will not happen at all. If you're obedient, you'll receive a text and be told to go to a location of my choice. Then you'll be brought to me . . . and Olivia. I can't wait to bring the two of you together . . .

Lynch dropped the fax on the floor. "That son of a bitch."

"Yes." She looked down at the sheet of paper on the floor. "And he meant every word. He's already making her suffer, Lynch." Her lips tightened. "And he won't let me stop it. He just wants me to think about it and imagine how much it's hurting her." She moistened her lips. "And he has to be a devil to realize what that would do to Olivia. When you're blind, you're totally in the dark, but if you can hear, it saves you. If you can speak, it helps you. Touch can make you feel as if you're not isolated. If he's taking all that from her, it could make her panic . . . and go a little crazy. Heaven knows what else he's doing to her." She swallowed. "I want to *kill* him, Lynch."

"I know. Stand in line." He went to the bar and poured himself a whiskey and a glass of wine for her. "We'll get there. We've just got to find out how to get around the roadblocks. You're not going to bring in Griffin or the FBI?"

"I don't trust him. If he thought he could get Derek, he'd probably consider Olivia collateral damage." She took the glass of wine from him. "Besides, Brock might be keeping tabs on what's happening at Olivia's *and* with the investigation. They seem to be everywhere."

"We might need Griffin at some point." He held up his hand as she started to protest. "Only as an emergency backup if necessary. However, the first thing we need is to double the surveillance on you. I agree with everything you've said. But since I'm also on Derek's *verboten* list, I suppose I also can't be seen near you by Brock." He grimaced. "I thought I was done with being incognito when I showed up at their home office today. I'll make a show of leaving here tonight and going to my house. But I'll call as soon as I get home and we'll get on with it."

"On with what? I'm feeling very blank at the moment."

"You're not blank." He dropped down on the couch and pulled her down beside him. "I was worried about you when we first found out about Olivia, but that was only shock. You're thinking, you're analyzing, you're being Kendra." He sipped his whiskey. "Kendra going through a hell of a lot of pain."

"Don't say that." She lifted her glass to her lips. "It's what he wanted. I don't want to give Derek anything he wants."

"Then we won't." He paused. "I was afraid that you were going to insist on going to Derek when he snapped his fingers. He seems to think you'd do it. He must have done some in-depth research on your and Olivia's relationship."

"Would I be tempted? Of course I would. But I know what would happen. He'd kill her, kill me, and get a real thrill on doing it in the most painful way possible." Her hand tightened on the stem of her glass. "And he'd win and then go on to the next victim. I can't let that happen. The only way to save Olivia is to find that monster and destroy him like a rabid animal."

"Oh, I like the way you're thinking. And Derek doesn't know you at all." He smiled. "You might have tossed Griffin out in the cold when Derek told you to do it. But you thumbed your nose at him when you decided to keep me around to help."

"Of course I did. That was the intelligent thing to do. You're brilliant at this kind of game. And I can always trust you. Why wouldn't I want you?"

"No reason at all," he said. "I was just complimenting your rationality. Because I'll always be the person you should call when you need someone." He finished his whiskey and put the glass on the coffee table. "Now drink your wine and try to relax. There's nothing we can do now but try to think and go over possible options."

"We should *do* something."

"And we will, but I've always found that putting pressure on yourself never gets you to the finish line. Just let it go and let it come to you. I'll go down and talk to Griffin and get him to do all the probing we want him to do and then I'll take my very obvious leave."

She finished her wine. She didn't want him to leave, but he was making sense. And she must not cling, she was already asking too much of him. "It might be better if we only knew his damn pattern. Suber said that he was almost controlled by it."

"Which means he's as much caught in what he's done as we are. He's set it up and now he has to complete it. He's not going to run." Lynch said slowly, "We just have to figure out how to trap the son of a bitch."

"And how are we supposed to do that?" She suddenly clutched the front of his shirt. "You're the one they hire to cause entire countries to go down the tube. You must be able to think of a way to get Olivia away from him." She knew she was being unfair. Her hands dropped away from him. "I'm sorry. I know it's my responsibility. Forget I said that. I'm just scared."

"I won't forget it. Because it will remind me to do everything I can to bring her home." He drew her close. "Hey, you said you trusted me. I promise I'll find a way." He cradled her face in his two hands. "Just give me a little time. Nothing has been more important to me." He brushed his lips on the tip of her nose. "Except that you get a little sleep. What I don't promise is that it won't be rough for all of us."

"Sleep? All I can think about is Olivia."

"Then think about her." He pulled her over to cuddle against him. "But think good thoughts. Think about getting her away from that asshole. Think about all the good times and what you are together. You've been friends since you were children. I've seen bits and pieces but there's so much more, isn't there?"

So much more . . .

It was like a kaleidoscope flashing before her. The

two of them sitting together on the cliffs above Woodward Academy, hearing the waves crash on the rocks below. Olivia, teasing her because she wouldn't take enough chances. Olivia, holding her hand and telling her how happy she was that Kendra could see even when they both knew that Olivia might never regain her own vision. Olivia, panic-stricken at the hospital, running down the corridor beside Kendra's gurney.

"Too many to even count," she said huskily. "But do you know what I'm remembering right now? When I was first getting to know Olivia at school, she was so different from me. Braver, funnier . . . But she was so generous, Lynch. I'd been born blind, but she had lost her sight in an accident. You'd think she'd be bitter, but she wasn't. She hated that I didn't have the memories that she had of the world around me. She'd spend hours trying to describe what was out there, what I should be able to see. She'd take my hand and have me feel textures and then try to compare it to what I should be seeing. She got so frustrated . . ." She smiled. "But then for a few months after my operation, she'd come and visit me and have me tell her exactly what I was seeing. She'd laugh and say, "See? I told you so. Am I good or what?"

"She was very, very good." Lynch was stroking the hair at her temple. "And that's why we're going to take her back. No question." He kissed her forehead and then sat up and got off the couch. "Just lie there and think good thoughts. I'll call you when I get to my place and we'll try to firm up a plan." He was heading for the door. "I mean it, Kendra. We're not going to let anything happen to her." His lips turned up in the faintest smile. "How could it? Are we good or what?"

The door closed softly behind him.

She lay there for a moment, letting his soothing words and the memories of Olivia stay and comfort her.

Then she sat up and swung her legs to the floor.

Think good thoughts? The only good thoughts she could have would be how to gut that son of a bitch, Derek. She didn't have the slightest doubt that Lynch's mind and efforts even now were busy trying to put all the pieces together. But he should have known better than to think she could do anything else.

He probably did. He might just be trying to give her that brief healing moment to make her strong enough to go on.

But that moment was over.

She got her computer and started typing.

Start at the beginning. It was time to make notes of every single thing she knew or had heard about Derek. Every little fact, every hint of feelings or instincts she'd had about him.

Accept everything.

Ignore nothing.

We're going to nail you, bastard.

10:40 A.M.

"Are you still working?" Lynch asked when she picked up the phone.

"Barely." Kendra rubbed her eyes and straightened on the couch. "Right now it's all a blur to me."

"That's the time that you should get a nap. I should have known that I shouldn't leave you. You've been at it all night."

"No, that's the time I should follow your advice and just let all the information I've stuffed into my brain come together. There's no way I could exert any pressure on myself in my present condition." She took a drink of her cold coffee. "I'll just go back to the beginning again and let it flow. Did Griffin find out anything?"

"Only that there were no fingerprints found in Olivia's apartment and probably not a trace of DNA. Strictly a professional job."

"But we already knew that it was Brock."

"Yes, it all goes back to Brock. I've been doing a lot of thinking about Vivianne Kerstine's crew. I was going to head over to your place, but I'll be there a little later. I'm at the FBI checking to see if we missed a scrap of evidence in the stuff we took from their offices."

"Then do what you have to do. But it's not going to do any good if someone doesn't stop Derek from killing Olivia." She added wearily, "We've got to find him. Let me get back to work, Lynch."

"Right. Like you said, go back to the beginning. I'll call you later." He cut the connection.

The beginning . . .

She put on the wedding video that she'd already played innumerable times. She practically had the damn thing memorized. Okay. Relax. Don't go after it. Let it come to her.

The speeches. The laughter. The music.

Now that bit of whispered dialogue that Olivia had called to Kendra's attention that night in her apartment.

No pressure. She closed her eyes. Let it come to her.

The harsh urgency of the first whisper. "We should get the hell out of here."

Then that silky, amused reply. "Why? When it's all here."

What was all here?

And the tones were so different . . .

She put it on repeat and kept her eyes closed. She let every nuance flow over her.

You're the one who first noticed it, Olivia. Help me.

No, she had to help herself. As she'd told Olivia, she'd trained her hearing to crystal clarity after her operation. That skill must still be there to call upon. Concentrate. Shut everything else out. Catch the rhythms and tempos.

What were they talking about? That whisper was so soft it was almost unidentifiable, but the more she played the tape the more she thought she caught . . . something.

Something familiar.

What?

Which thread of speech?

Lynch had said don't force it. Let it come to her . . .

Why? When it's all—

And then it *did* come to her!

"Oh my God!"

She sat up straight, her eyes flying open.

She reached for her phone and punched in Lynch's number. "Stay at the FBI Office," she said. "I'm getting dressed and I'll be right there." She pressed the disconnect and flew across the room toward her bedroom.

CHAPTER 14

FBI Regional Office

METCALF MET HER IN THE lobby when she came in from the parking lot.

"Did you get it?" she asked as she stepped into the elevator. "Tell me you got it."

He nodded as he handed her the disk. "It wasn't easy. There was nothing at the wedding. I had to dig long and hard. You owe me."

"Yes, I do. We might be even now." She got off the elevator at the tech lab and saw Lynch coming toward her. She held up the wedding video. "You were right. No pressure. But that was only part of it. Metcalf got me the rest of the equation."

"I'm sure that he was happy to do so," Lynch said. "But you could have asked me, Kendra."

"It was simpler this way. He had all the contacts." She

followed Metcalf into the sound booth at the end of the hall. "And he said that it wasn't easy." She put the wedding video into the machine and then popped the disk Metcalf had just given her into the same machine. "Go ahead, Metcalf. Run the comparison. See if you get a match."

"What are we doing, Kendra?" Lynch asked.

"It's those damn whispers. I swore to Olivia that I hadn't heard either of those voices from anyone at the party that night. I told her they must be guests. They were almost totally unidentifiable and were so soft that I missed them on the first runs. But Olivia didn't and called my attention to them. One was rougher than the other and the content was . . . interesting. Not what you'd expect to hear at a wedding." She quoted. "The first. A. 'We need to get the hell out of here.' And the second. B. 'Why? When it's all here.'"

She looked at him. "Today I think I did recognize just a thread of familiarity with the speech pattern of one of those voices. But I had to get a comparison before I could be sure." She nodded at Metcalf. "Will you run it?"

He pressed the keyboard, and the monitor displayed two audio waveforms. Comparison data scrolled down the screen, then came to an abrupt stop. "Done," Metcalf said as he pulled the report from the machine. He glanced at it and smiled. "A match. Like I said, you owe me, Kendra."

"Not until you tell me which one was the match," she said dryly. "A or B?"

"B," Metcalf said. "Not the rough one."

Lynch looked between them. "What kind of game is this?"

"Not a game," Kendra said. "A test. I didn't even tell Metcalf what I was after. I didn't want him influencing the results when he took these audio samples to his colleagues. In the research 'game' it's what we call a 'double-blind' test." She turned to Lynch. "Told you I was a scientist."

"I never doubted you," Lynch said. "So now am I allowed to ask to whom we're comparing this guy?"

Metcalf nodded. "The second disk was a quarterly sales presentation given by Ivan Campbell. Who I had to call last night and inform that his wife's body had been found." He glanced at Kendra. "What are you doing? I don't see any connection here."

"I didn't either. It's still fuzzy. I think he was making sure that I didn't see any connection. Ivan Campbell knew that his voice was on that video. But he also knew that whisper was almost unidentifiable. When I came to interview him, he tried to make his voice totally unlike that whisper except perhaps on a machine like this. When I showed up at his door, he seemed to be in a towering rage at me and the FBI. His voice was harsh, rough, and sharp. Nothing like that whisper, which was soft, smooth, and almost mocking."

"But not in the least incriminating," Metcalf said gently.

"Do you think I don't know that?" Kendra said. "And on the surface I could even go along with him almost attacking me that day at his condo. I felt sorry for him." She paused. "Until last night when I thought about what Jessie had said about him always being soft-spoken and quiet. He didn't give any speeches at that wedding reception and I hardly remember seeing him with his wife, Barbara. She was totally involved with the wedding party. I didn't make the connection with those people whispering in the background. And I was chalking all that ugliness and harshness up to his grief that day at his condo." She added, "But I would probably have gone back later and thought it was a little peculiar . . . except that I got that call from Griffin just then." She looked at Lynch. "And you might say I was distracted."

"And Campbell escaped that razor-sharp brain of yours," Lynch said. His gaze was narrowed on her face. "Are you telling me that you think Campbell is Derek?"

"I'm telling you that he could be." Her hands were clenched on the wedding video. "I'm saying that day Campbell went against everything people thought about his character and was almost violent toward me. He was enjoying hurling insults at me." She grimaced. "And particularly my stupidity in handling this case."

"He'd lost his wife," Metcalf said.

"I thought about that." She ignored Metcalf and said

to Lynch, "But if he's Derek, then he'd think nothing about killing his wife himself. Remember, he said he didn't believe in that man-woman garbage. She would only have been a convenient addition to his grand scenario." She went on quickly, her mind leaping from point to point. "And then when you go back to that whispered conversation, it begins to make sense. That first speaker must have been one of Brock's men who'd been assigned to try to persuade Derek to back away from those wedding killings. Kerstine must have thought it was the height of madness to take a chance like that. And Derek's reply was completely in keeping, too. 'Why? When it's all here.' He was telling him that the situation was completely to his liking and he was going to go for it. In short, go to hell."

"Possibly," Metcalf said. "But it's not exactly—"

"Thanks for your help, Metcalf," Lynch said as he got to his feet. "Why don't you do Kendra another favor and go tell Griffin what we've been discussing. Get his input and perhaps suggestions. Then we can talk later."

Metcalf looked at Kendra. "What do you think?"

"I think that's a very good idea. I'm too tired to talk to Griffin right now."

He shrugged. "Whatever you say." He turned and left the sound booth.

She turned immediately to Lynch. "Do you believe me?"

"I always believe you." He took her elbow and led her

toward the door. "But Griffin can be a doubting Thomas on occasion and he's training Metcalf to walk in his footsteps. I think we need to distance ourselves for a while."

"And we're going to go see Ivan Campbell?"

"Yes, that's exactly where we're going." He held the door open for her. "We need to talk to that poor, half-crazed widower about his deplorable manners in attacking you."

234 Sunset Way

Lynch rang the doorbell of the Campbell condo.

No answer.

He tried again.

No answer.

He pounded on the door and shouted. "FBI, Mr. Campbell."

"He's not here." A plump, white-haired woman stuck her head out of the door of the condo down the hall. "I saw him in the parking lot as he was leaving yesterday. He said being in the condo reminded him too much of his wife and he had to get a hotel room for a few days. I wish you folks would just leave him alone. The poor man has enough to worry about." She slammed the door.

"Poor man," Lynch repeated. "Evidently he managed to inspire sympathy in his neighbors."

"But Metcalf didn't mention he'd decided to move," Kendra said. "Yesterday Campbell's wife was still only missing, you'd think that he'd want to stay where it would be easy for the FBI to get in touch with him."

"His neighbor would say that the poor man must have been distracted." He was bent over the lock. "Maybe we'd better take a look around to make sure he didn't leave anything important behind." The lock clicked and he pushed the door open. "We have to be kind to those in need." He nudged her inside and closed the door. He looked around the living room. "But I don't believe he took more than the bare necessities with him."

Kendra nodded as her gaze wandered over the living room. It looked exactly as she remembered it from that brief visit. "I could be wrong," she said. "Maybe if we check the hotels, we'll find him registered at one of them. I could be on the wrong track."

"Then we'll humbly apologize." He looked at her. "But I can see that your every instinct is telling you that you're not wrong. Correct?"

She nodded.

"Then I'll trust you and back you all the way." He turned away. "I'll check out the bedrooms. You go through that desk over there."

She went to the desk and went carefully through the four drawers. Pencils, pens, stationery, pharmaceutical order forms literature . . .

"He left a closet full of clothes," Lynch said as he

came out of the bedroom. "He was definitely traveling light." He headed for the kitchen. "Let's see if he tucked anything into the refrigerator."

"I'll check the powder room." She moved toward the door across the living room. "Though I can't see him—"

She inhaled sharply.

She stood there, staring at the mirror over the vanity. She couldn't look away from it.

"Kendra." Lynch was standing behind her.

But she couldn't take her eyes away from that sheet of paper fastened to that mirror.

"He . . . left . . . me a message."

Lynch moved closer behind her, his hands cradling her shoulders. "I see that he did."

The bold print was jumping out at her.

Hello Kendra,

Congratulations!

But lesson one is that I always win.

She drew a shaky breath. "I'm surprised he didn't sign the damn thing."

"I'm not; there's no real evidence that Campbell is anything but the creature he created to hide his Brock activities. That message could mean anything. I'm surprised that he risked going that far."

She whirled to face him. "But you *know* Campbell is

Derek. It's clear he left here because he expected it to eventually all come together for me."

"Shh. *I* know, but he wanted to create confusion and uncertainty that would allow him more time to complete his plans. It might take a bit of work and persuasion to get Griffin on board."

She knew that was true just from that hint of doubt she'd noticed in Metcalf. "Then we'd better get started at convincing him," she said harshly. "Because we can't wait for Derek to show his true colors while he has Olivia. We don't have any idea where he's keeping her."

Lynch nodded. "He has to have a place here in San Diego where he kept Elizabeth Gelson and Barbara Campbell before the murders. It would have to be close enough for him to transport the bodies when he wanted to put them on display." He looked around. "And this condo was obviously not used for anything but window dressing." He added quietly, "But I'd judge the charade is over now. He'll want to establish a new identity and location to continue his passion. He could be planning on heading anywhere in the world courtesy of Brock Limited."

"You're saying he might take Olivia out of the country?" She immediately shook her head. "Of course he wouldn't do that. Olivia is a dead woman as far as he's concerned. He's just got to finish what he started. And teach me how superior he is along the way."

Lynch nodded. "But that will take time considering

that gigantic ego he appears to possess. We've just got to make sure that it's enough time."

"It *will* be enough time," she said fiercely. "Because we're not going to let anyone spin their wheels. We're going to do everything we have to do. We're going to use everyone we have to use." She reached for her phone. "We're going to *find* her, Lynch."

"WHY DIDN'T YOU TELL ME about Olivia right away?" Jessie's lips were tight. "Did you think I wouldn't care, dammit? She's my friend, too." She whirled on Kendra. "You're the one who brought us together a couple years ago because she's blind and you thought there would be times when I could protect her. Well, why the hell didn't you let me do it?"

"I didn't realize she'd be the target," Kendra said. "I thought it would be me." Of course, Jessie would be upset, she thought. The relationship between Jessie and Olivia had started out as tentative and sometimes adversarial, but it had developed into strong friendship. "You're right, I should have told you what was happening. My only excuse is that we were frantically busy trying to figure out what was happening ourselves." She looked her in the eye. "And I was going a little crazy with worry about her."

"I'll attest to that," Lynch said quietly. "Back off, Jessie."

"Okay. Sorry." Jessie nodded jerkily. "I can see it. But

we're on the same page now. You said that this Derek creep took it on the lam when he thought you had a chance of identifying him as Ivan Campbell. Then what do we do to get Olivia back?"

"You'll be happy about this," Lynch said. "We go after Brock."

"Hallelujah. How?"

"We know Brock is protecting Derek. According to Facey, they're terrified that he'll reveal everything about his work for them if he's brought down. To protect him *and* themselves they'd need to know what he's doing." He paused. "They need contact with him."

"Has Griffin tapped their phones?" Kendra asked.

Lynch nodded. "He's already on it. But they're too smart to leave a digital footprint. I'm betting some of the Brock people are having a face-to-face contact. Facey said that only a limited number of people even knew about the Derek problem. Actual contact would be something Kerstine would only trust to her top people."

Kendra said slowly, "You mean like Josh Blake?"

Lynch nodded. "I would start with him. He appears to be on Kerstine's favorite list at the moment. Blake was extremely surprised to see me in their offices yesterday morning. He didn't give a second glance to two dozen FBI agents, hustling past him, but he looked at me like I'd risen from the dead. He knew about what happened in Oregon and that means he would likely be in Kerstine's confidence about Derek." Lynch smiled at Jessie. "Now I wonder how we could make sure of that?"

She nodded. "I can track his car."

"He might be expecting a tail," Kendra said. "Especially after what happened yesterday."

"Come on," Jessie said. "It's what I do. Page four of the 'How to be a Private Investigator' textbook. I'll put a tracker on his car."

"Remember the company you're dealing with," Lynch said. "They're paranoid under the best of circumstances."

Jessie smiled and shook her head. "Have a little faith. I'm fully aware his car may have a motion-activated squawker that will go off if I get within six feet of it. And that he may also get some kind of notification if my tracker starts broadcasting at one of the ninety most common frequencies. Trust me. I've got this."

"I do trust you," Kendra said. "But be careful."

"Don't worry, I'm not going to let those Brock bastards come out ahead on this one." Jessie grabbed her leather jacket from the back of a chair. "I'd better get going if I'm going to make it to the Brock building before Josh Blake does. Keep your phones close. This could get real very fast."

The next moment Kendra and Lynch were watching her tear out of the parking lot on her motorcycle.

"We have a good chance of being right about this,

don't we?" Kendra murmured desperately as Jessie disappeared around the corner. "It could be Blake who could lead us to Derek?"

"We could be right." He put his hand on her shoulder. "No promises. But as I said, I'm betting on him."

"Then I guess all we can do is go down to the FBI office and try to persuade Griffin that we're right about Ivan Campbell. We can see if we can pick up any other information while we're waiting to hear from—"

Her text notification was buzzing.

She looked down at her phone. This time she recognized the phone number.

And she knew it would not stop buzzing until she took the call.

Lynch was swearing beneath his breath. "Derek."

She nodded jerkily. "Let's see what he has to say."

She pressed the access.

Hello, Kendra

Did you have a good night? I'm afraid your friend, Olivia, had a terrible one. We'll see what tomorrow brings . . .

The text cut off.

She closed her eyes as the pain bit into her. "Just enough to stab deep and then flit away." Her eyes opened and she added dully, "And to let me know this is going to go on and on. A refresher lesson."

Lynch was suddenly holding her close. "We'll *get* him, Kendra."

"I know." But would Olivia be able to bear what he was doing to her until that happened? It's what he wanted Kendra to think. She couldn't let Derek play her like this. She pushed Lynch away and straightened. She smiled with an effort. "And maybe it will be today. Maybe he won't be able to send me another one of those damn messages tomorrow." She turned and headed for her car. "Let's go to see Griffin and then wait for Jessie's call."

JESSIE EASED BACK ON HER motorcycle's throttle. She could see Josh Blake's green Lamborghini from over a quarter mile away on Carmel Valley Road and she needed to make sure she wasn't spotted. She looked at the small screen clipped to her bike's handlebars. Even with the bright sun washing out the picture, she could see that her tracker was doing its job. She had placed it on the exit ramp of his building garage, then watched and waited from across the street. When Blake's car rolled over it, she'd remotely activated a powerful electromagnet that adhered it to the undercarriage.

So far, it was working like a charm. She'd been following him for hours, tracking his movements to two downtown office buildings and a bay view restaurant. Each time it was necessary to drop visual contact, she could still quickly zero in on his location with her tracking device.

She looked ahead. Where was he going now? If he was travelling far up the coast, he'd already be on the I-5. She passed the Del Mar Racetrack, then Solana Beach, and Carlsbad. Finally he veered off on Oceanside Boulevard and she allowed even more distance between them as they moved through less populated streets.

For the last mile of their journey, she relied entirely on the tracker until he finally came to a stop in the upscale neighborhood of Loma Alta.

She put on an extra burst of speed to position herself on a nearby hillside she hoped would offer a view of Blake's position. She cut her engine and silently rolled to the edge of the elevation. She looked down.

There, in the courtyard of an enormous, Spanish-styled mansion, was Blake's Lamborghini. He was apparently already inside the house.

But was it the house where Olivia was being held?

Are you here, Derek?

She looked up and down the street for the white van that had been that sicko's stock in trade. No sign of it.

She pulled out her phone and checked the bookmarked page she'd searched for Ivan Campbell's vehicle. According to DMV records, he drove a late-model white BMW M6 Gran Coupe. No sign of that either.

At least on the street. A six-car garage fronted the estate's east side, with two small windows visible from where she stood. She pulled out a pair of binoculars and focused on the windows. They were tinted. Damn.

She slid a pair of CPL filters over the binocular lenses and tried again. Much better. She could make out a workbench, a pair of Jet Skis . . .

And a white BMW M6 Coupe.

Jessie lowered the binoculars and smiled with fierce satisfaction. "*I got you.*"

"WILL HE GO FOR IT?" Kendra asked as Lynch strode out of Griffin's office. "Maybe we should go without them. It's already been forty-five minutes. What if Derek is there like Jessie says and he leaves before Griffin gets around to giving his OK?"

"Easy," Lynch said. "We'll do whatever has to be done. Jessie is still out there keeping an eye on what's going on at the property. She's not going to let him scoot away. But Griffin said to give him ten minutes to do some checking, and it's worth a delay to have the power of the FBI behind any attack."

"But we spent half the morning trying to convince him that Ivan Campbell is Derek. He's skeptical as hell. You think he's going to okay a possible attack on some lush million-dollar estate because we tell him Derek is holed up there? You told me he's all FBI."

"And so I am." Griffin came out of the office. "And

I'm paid to be skeptical." He glanced at Lynch. "I checked out that Loma Alta address with our data miners and the ownership is buried very deep. Could just be some corporation avoiding taxes. Or could be Brock who purchased a possible hideout in case they needed it for an emergency."

"Substitute Derek for emergency," Kendra said.

"And there's no real proof that Campbell is Derek," Griffin said. "All very flimsy."

"We could lose him if you don't stop questioning the fact that Derek's out there just waiting for us," Kendra said desperately. "And Olivia could be dead. Is it yes, or no?"

He looked at her. "I'm getting around to it. Of course it's yes. Didn't I tell you that I'd make it up to you for that small necessary prevarication? I just had to make sure you were aware how generous I'm being."

"And how much trust you have in Kendra." Lynch added, "And how good it's going to look to the director when you bring Derek in."

"That's all true, also," Griffin said. "But don't you think we should stop chatting and get this show started?" He glanced at Kendra as he headed back to his office. "Stay out of the line of fire. I don't want you to mess this up for me."

"Take it." Lynch grabbed her arm and dragged her out of the office. "You've got what you wanted. We'll be out of here before you know it."

* * *

"YOU LIED," KENDRA SAID. "It's been almost thirty minutes." She glanced around at the army of FBI agents still assembling their gear outside the FBI office building. The fleet of vans, which had been pressed into service that morning, were now being loaded for a far different operation. Kendra turned toward Lynch. "Jessie called and wants to know where we are."

"But Jessie will appreciate the equipment once we get there." Lynch checked his automatic and tugged at his shoulder holster. "It'll just be a couple more minutes."

"You said that before."

"I mean it this time." He stepped over to a pile of black flak jackets, picked one up, and dropped it over Kendra's head. He stepped behind her and pulled the Velcro fasteners.

"I'm surprised you're even bothering with this," Kendra grumbled. "You heard Griffin. He won't even let me near the place."

"Yes and I also know there's a good chance your best friend is inside that house. That means there's no way in hell you're spending your afternoon in a van parked a discreet, safe distance away from it. Am I right?"

"Damned straight."

"I'll do whatever I can to help keep you safe." He reached down, opened his pack, and took out a 9mm pistol in a leather holster. "No arguments. I know you don't like guns. This time you take it."

"No arguments." She stood still as he fastened the belt around her waist.

"And at least let the team make their sweep before you go charging in there."

"Of course." She gazed around the parking lot. "Look at them. Why would I interfere? They're experts. They'll know exactly what they're doing."

Griffin, outfitted in his own flak jacket, happened to hear Kendra as he walked by. He stopped. "Did I just hear you suggest we're actually a competent organization?"

"Naturally, you had to hear me admit that." She looked him in the eye. "You're the only one I have a problem with, Griffin. Your people are the best. I've never thought any different. They've always come through when it mattered."

"Then you should appreciate me as well." He smiled. "As Lynch told you, this is who I am. And because of that, I just might manage to get your friend Olivia back."

Then Griffin stepped to the center of the group and clapped his hands. "Let's move! See you at the rendezvous point."

CHAPTER 15

IT TOOK LESS THAN twenty minutes to reach Jessie on the hillside overlooking the mansion, but to Kendra it felt like hours. The vehicles and most of the team stood back far enough so that they would avoid detection by the house's occupants. Kendra, Lynch, Jessie, and Griffin were met by the mustached SDPD SWAT team commander, Sergeant Davenport. Kendra had met him on two prior investigations and found him to be both smart and experienced.

"Any luck with infrared imaging?" Griffin asked him.

Davenport shook his head. "Hell, no. It looks like he's lined the house with thermal Mylar material. He'd really have to know what he's doing, though."

"He does," Lynch said. "He's a highly-trained operative and he has at least one other in there with him. Whatever you do, don't underestimate those men."

He shrugged. "Don't worry. That's always a good way to get killed."

"There may be a female hostage inside," Griffin said. "She could be in one of the thermal-shielded areas."

"You're not getting it," Davenport said. "The whole place has been thermally protected." He showed them his tablet screen. "All except the garage, changing rooms near the pool, and what looks like a half bath near the front of the main floor. Those are the only areas we can safely rule out."

Kendra studied the house's exterior from their hill-top perch. It was an enormous two-story Spanish mansion that enveloped a massive U-shaped courtyard that opened out to a swimming pool and two cabanas. The courtyard was lined with thick stone columns and centered by a long reflecting pool. Balconies overlooked the courtyard on the three closed sides, cascading with lush, colorful vegetation.

Davenport nodded down toward the house. "My men are already down there, scoping the place out."

Griffin squinted. "I don't even see them."

"Huh. Then I guess they're good at their jobs." Davenport tapped his earpiece. "Once they take their positions, this will be your show, Griffin. We're here to provide support for whatever you need."

"Thanks, Davenport."

As Griffin huddled with his team, Kendra turned toward Jessie. "Good job."

Jessie shrugged. "Would have been a better job if I'd been able to pull Olivia out of there myself. The less people, the cleaner the extraction."

"Providing we knew where Olivia was located. You did enough. Thank you."

Jessie shook her head uneasily. "Something about this doesn't feel right."

"What do you mean?"

"If Brock is so concerned about protecting this guy and the dirty secrets he has on them, they wouldn't have just one guy here. They could have a whole platoon. Where are they?"

Kendra glanced around at the surrounding hillsides, then back to the house. "You think they're in there."

She nodded. "It's why I didn't even try to go in myself."

Boom!

An explosion rocked the far side of the house.

"What the hell?" Davenport raised his binoculars and tapped his headset once again. After a moment he turned to Griffin. "One of my guys hit a tripwire."

A man's horrible, gut-wrenching screams came from the other side of the house.

"Shit," Davenport said, still listening to his headset. "He's still alive, but it's bad."

Gunfire from automatic weapons echoed in the courtyard.

Griffin waved to his team. "We're going in. Stay away from the courtyard windows. We'll circle from the outside perimeter."

Jessie muttered a curse as she pulled a small black knapsack from her motorcycle and ran to join the FBI team.

Griffin called after her. "What in the hell do you think you're doing?"

"Trying to save that poor guy before he bleeds to death." She nodded toward the screams still wafting from the house. "I was trained as an army medic. If the shock doesn't get him, the loss of blood will. That man needs help *now.*"

"I can't be responsible for your safety."

Jessie slung the backpack over her shoulder. "Did I ask you?"

"You'll need a flak jacket."

She lifted the lapel of her jacket and showed him the Kevlar lining. "Brought my own." She took off running down the hillside.

More gunfire rained from the house below.

Lynch turned to Kendra. "Stay here?"

"No way." Her eyes were fixed on the front entrance of the mansion. She was catching glimpses of the men firing those shots and she thought that she'd just seen Josh Blake for a tenth of a second.

"Okay. Then at least bring up the rear. Can you do that?"

"For now," she said absently. Blake was no longer in view. She had to get closer . . .

"I'll take what I can get." Lynch whirled and joined the FBI team moving down the hillside as more shots were exchanged around the house.

Kendra followed as they made their way across the hill to a residential street two blocks over and began to close in.

Bam!

Shots.

Brock militia were now streaming out of the house into the courtyard.

Where was Blake?

"Down." Lynch jerked Kendra behind one of the huge columns.

Then he was on his knees crawling toward the cabana that was taking heavy fire.

There were more explosions and gunfire, but it looked to Kendra as if Griffin and Davenport far outnumbered the Brock militia. It appeared the attack was going well.

But out of the corner of Kendra's eye she saw something that was not going so well. Josh Blake.

He'd been with his men in the courtyard, but he was no longer there. She caught a glimpse of him as he reentered the mansion and disappeared.

No! Not only was Derek probably somewhere inside,

Blake would know where Olivia was being kept in that mansion. There was no chance she could let him find his way out of this rabbit hole without telling her where she could find Olivia.

She was on her feet and dodging around and behind the ornate Spanish columns lining the courtyard until she reached the arched entrance. She glanced over her shoulder and saw that Lynch was trading gunfire with a shooter at a second-story window. There was no way he'd be able to leave the courtyard now. Then she was inside the mansion, running down a long hall with a multitude of carved mahogany doors leading off it. It looked like the grand hall of a Spanish castle with statues and armor and two rows of columns marching down either side of the hall. There were tall leaded-glass windows bordering the upper second story on both sides, shining down on the dark wood and tile floor below.

But where was he? Through which one of those damn doorways had Blake slipped?

Careful. Blake was a professional. He probably was anticipating pursuit. Be alert. Watch for any slight movement of those closed doors.

And there it was! Two doors behind her there was a narrow beam of light at the bottom of one of the doors.

She dove for the floor, lifting her gun as Blake came through the door shooting. She aimed for his hand holding his gun as she rolled to one side. Blake screamed as the bullet plowed through the bone in his forearm. He cursed as his gun dropped from his hand. But he was diving for the weapon as Kendra stuck the barrel of her own gun in his stomach. "Don't *move,*" she said. "I'm very angry right now, Blake. And I'm very frightened for my friend, Olivia. It wouldn't take much to make me pull this trigger." Her eyes were blazing at him. "The only thing that's on your side is that I think you probably know where she is and can take me to her."

"You stupid whore." He was clutching his arm. "I'm bleeding like a stuck pig. I hope Derek cuts your throat." He pulled back his lips in a feral smile. "Or does the same thing he did to that blind bitch."

Her gaze narrowed on his face. "Olivia? Where is she?"

He nodded at a door at the far end of the hall. "Behind door number one. You want her? Go get her."

"I will." She nudged him with the gun. "But you're coming with me. You've been lying to Lynch and me since the day I met you. This is too important for me to take a chance."

"Even if you find her, you'll probably not be able to save her," he said maliciously as he stumbled ahead of her down the hall. "That asshole, Derek, is too good and he really wants you to see that he's beaten you. He spent a lot of time on your Olivia. If I hadn't had to bow and scrape so much to him, I might have admired his technique. Except he wouldn't let me rape her. He said the effect he wanted was for her to feel nothing. I admit I would have preferred him not to have been such a purist."

"Where's Derek now?"

He was silent.

"Where's Derek now?" she repeated. "Answer me or I'll put another bullet in you."

He still didn't reply.

She jabbed the gun against his ribcage.

His eyes widened as he looked at her. "You'd do it, you bitch."

"Try me," she said.

"I haven't seen him for hours. When he saw we were under attack, he probably went on the run. He's always got a way out. A boat, a helicopter, a tunnel . . . I was going to try to find him and hitch a ride when things got hot out there in the courtyard." His smile was twisted. "But I had to perform my final duty for him or I knew I wouldn't stand a chance of having him take me along."

"Duty?"

"He said that if anything went wrong, if there was a chance that his little plan for you wasn't going to be successful, I was to *make* it successful." He said softly, "I was on my way to cut your Olivia's throat. If I'd only had a few more minutes . . ."

She knew he was trying to shock and panic her and he was succeeding. Don't let him see it. "He must have considered you were just one of Vivianne's errand boys if he set you to do his cleanup work. And you thought you were so important."

"I *am* important," he said through set teeth. "Do you know how hard I've worked to pull myself up out of the ranks and get Vivianne to accept me as one of her team of directors? This should never have happened. Before Derek decided he had to take that blind woman, I was only supposed to supply him with my men to guard this place. But then he told Vivianne he wanted one of her executives to be on site to make certain there wouldn't be any slipups about any orders he might give those guards. She gave in to him. I thought she just wanted someone here to try to locate those docs he's holding over her." He gave her a vicious look. "But it was probably your fault. She was pissed off that you were there when we were dragged into the FBI. She got her nose seriously out of joint. She was ready to give into him on anything that would hurt you." He had reached the door at the end of the hall and was throwing it open. "He told her that this would do the trick." His eyes were fixed spitefully on Kendra's face. "Here she is, Kendra. How much does it hurt?"

At first, Kendra didn't know what she was seeing.

Olivia was lying on a cot across the room. She was pinned to the mattress by four stakes piercing a sheet covering her from her chest to her feet. Her eyes were closed in her pale, still face.

"What have you done to her?" Kendra whispered. "Is she still alive?"

"She's alive. And it was Derek, not me, who did it," Blake said. "I only assisted when he required it. Actually, I found this method of persuasion rather innovative. He told me he calls it 'The Butterfly.'"

Her gaze was fixed in agony on Olivia's still face. "You're sure she's still alive?"

"Oh, yes. You might say she's just had a rough couple days. She's pinned in that sheet he calls her cocoon and she can't move. And he rubbed some kind of chemical on her body wherever the cloth touched that would completely numb her. He did the same with that tape on her mouth. He left only the tiniest opening at the corner of her mouth so she could breathe, but nothing that would interfere. The whole point was that she wasn't to feel anything."

Sense of touch gone. Kendra had known it was what he'd threatened, but the reality was hideous. She swallowed. "What else?"

"He put special sound-proof plugs in her ears to prevent hearing. He did the same with her nostrils to keep her from being able to smell." He whispered, "When he was through, she was like a wild animal caught in a cage. Only she couldn't even struggle to get free. I'd never seen such panic. It went on and on until she finally fell unconscious."

"And you did *nothing*," she said harshly. "You're almost as bad as he is."

"You got in his way, so in the end this is your fault, too." His gaze was narrowed on her face. "And I see he *did* hurt you. Good." He tilted his head and said mockingly, "Do you know, my arm doesn't hurt nearly as much now, Kendra."

"I wish I'd blown your head off." She was suddenly burning with rage. "It still seems a very good idea if I didn't have to get to Olivia. I can't—"

Blake sprang forward and his uninjured arm lashed out and struck her face. He lunged for her gun.

Fight! She wasn't helpless. Remember what Lynch had taught her . . . She staggered back, grasping desperately at the pistol as she whirled back and punched him with all her strength in his stomach. He gasped as he lost his breath. She gave him a karate chop to the throat that sent him to his knees.

That seemed to have done it. But she was breathing hard as she turned back to Olivia's cot. "I don't have time for you. I need to take care of my friend. If you give me any more trouble, I'll kill you." Then she ignored him as she ran across the room to Olivia's cot. The closer she got the more frightened and angry she became. Her hands were unsteady as she yanked the sheet off Olivia. "You're *not* a damn pinned butterfly," she said fiercely. "Do you hear me? They can't do this to you, Olivia." She tore the tape off her lips. "Open your eyes and tell me—"

"She can't hear you." Blake had recovered enough to begin lurching toward the cot. "You stupid bitch, I told you that. And you won't be able to—" He stopped, staring at the gun Kendra was training on him. Then he said with disgust, "Screw it. I'm through with this. I'm not Derek's slave. I've done enough of his dirty work for one day. I'm getting out of here." He turned, strode out of the room and slammed the door.

She scarcely heard him. Her gaze was fastened on Olivia's face. Why hadn't she opened her eyes?

Her ears . . .

Kendra's hands were shaking as she carefully removed the ear plugs. "Olivia?"

Nothing.

She extracted the nose plugs.

Nothing.

"Stop this, Olivia," she said unsteadily. "You're scaring me. You know I was never as brave as you."

Then Olivia's chest moved as she took a deep breath.

"Good." Kendra was drawing a relieved breath herself. "Now open your eyes."

Olivia's lids slowly opened to reveal those huge brown eyes. "What's that . . . supposed to prove?" she said hoarsely. "You're not making . . . sense. You know I can't see."

"I'm making perfect sense." Kendra's arms slid around Olivia and she was hugging her with all her strength. "It means he didn't do anything else bad to you. It means you're okay."

"Not so . . . okay. I can't feel you yet. I'm still numb all over." Olivia closed her eyes again. "And you're here and he got what he wanted. You shouldn't have come, Kendra. I prayed you wouldn't come."

"Of course I came. It's my fault you're here." She lifted her head. "And don't we always hang out together?"

"Not this time. You should have let me go it alone." Her lips were trembling. "It was bad . . . what he did to me. I've never felt anything that bad before. I wanted to scream, but I couldn't do it. And I couldn't stop shaking and yet it was like being . . . dead. But I knew it would be worse if you came. I can't watch him do that to you."

"Don't think about it," Kendra said quickly. "He's just a coward who thinks all that killing and pain make him powerful when it only proves how weak he really is. We'll deal with him together. The way we do everything else." She smiled. "And we've got a head start. Can't you hear all that racket in the courtyard? Lynch and Griffin's men are probably wrapping up Brock's scum as we speak."

"You're not alone?" Olivia closed her eyes. "Thank God."

"Don't act so relieved. It's not as if I wasn't very efficient in dealing with that asshole, Josh Blake. Lynch would have been proud of me. Or maybe not. I was aiming for his gun hand and I hit his forearm instead."

Olivia's eyes flicked open. "Derek?"

"We haven't located him yet." She could see Olivia start to tremble and said quickly, "Blake seemed to think he might be on the run."

"I don't think so." Her voice was scarcely above a whisper. "He wouldn't run away. Not until he got what he wanted. He's like a monster who just keeps coming, devouring everyone around him, until there's nothing left. We have to find him."

"And we will." She was shivering herself as she realized what Olivia must have gone through with that monster during these last days. "But I think we'll just get you out of here for the time being. Let's go to the courtyard and see if we can find Jessie." She straightened and took off her denim jacket. "But since I got rid of your 'cocoon,' I think I'd better give you something to cover you up before you catch cold." She slipped Olivia into the jacket and buttoned it. "Very stylish. You always look better in clothes than I do." She frowned. "But you're still shaking."

"I can't seem to stop . . . it just comes."

And there was no telling how long it would continue to come or what kind of mental and emotional damage she might have suffered. Kendra's arms swiftly enfolded Olivia again and she held her close. She could feel the ripples of violent tremors still going through Olivia's body. She whispered, "Then we'll just find a way to chase it away, won't we? Come on, let me help you get to your feet."

It took a few minutes to get Olivia to her feet and then to walk her haltingly to the door. "Wait just a minute." She carefully opened the door and looked down the hall.

Nothing.

She still heard the sounds of conflict from the courtyard, but the hall still appeared dim and empty. "It's okay." She took Olivia's arm and was going to lead her toward the courtyard. "I think we'll be—"

Blood.

Kendra stopped short as she saw a thin river of blood running from behind one of the north columns halfway down the hall to pool in front of her.

Olivia felt her hesitation. "What is it?" she whispered.

"I don't know. Blood. Something's not right." Her gaze was searching the columns on either side of the hall. "There could be someone . . . there." Her hand tightened on Olivia's arm. "I have to go and see, Olivia."

"No!"

"It's going to be okay," she said quickly. "It's not as if I don't have a gun. I'll be fine." She couldn't take her eyes off that pool of blood. "But just in case, it might be a good idea to be prepared. If you hear anything, if I call, if there's a shot, anything . . . you need to get to the courtyard so that someone can see you and bring help."

"I don't think this is a good idea, Kendra."

Neither did Kendra, but it was better than standing there and waiting for someone to glide toward them from behind those rows of columns and pick them off.

And she was beginning to worry about that blood. She knew that Lynch would have followed her as soon as he'd broken free of that brouhaha outside in the courtyard. "Stop complaining," Kendra whispered. "It's the best plan that I can pull together on short notice. Stay here until I come back for you. If you think there's trouble, then start running. Remember how I usually give you directions as we run on our morning jogs? This time you'll have to keep everything in mind yourself until you reach that courtyard. When you leave this bedroom, you go right eight feet to reach the south columns. Use them for cover and start running. This hallway is about forty-two yards, then you'll turn left and go another ten yards until you reach the door to the courtyard. Five steps down. There's another column to your right if you think you need it for cover. Got it?"

"Of course I've got it. It's still a bad idea."

Kendra gave her hand a squeeze. "Don't wait because you think you're right and I'm wrong." Then she was leaving the bedroom and dodging in and out of the north columns as she made her way down the cavernous hall.

Toward the blood.

Let it not be Lynch's blood.

Listen.

No sounds.

Even the sounds from the courtyard seemed to have faded away.

The pool of blood was right ahead of her.

She slowed, drawing closer to the column from where the blood appeared to be streaming.

Let it not be Lynch.

And let there not be anyone there waiting.

Her hand tightened on her gun as she dodged behind the last column.

No Derek.

But there was a body crumpled on the floor.

And then she saw the source of the blood.

Another relief. Not Lynch.

Josh Blake's eyes were wide open and staring straight up at the cavernous ceiling.

His throat had been sliced open and the blood was pouring from the wound.

"Surprised? Blake certainly wasn't," Derek said from behind her. "I'd told him what to expect."

She whirled to face him. He was standing only yards away from her and yet she hadn't heard him! She instinctively dropped to the floor and got off a shot as she dove behind the column.

But he was no longer there. He'd ducked into the

doorway behind him. "Blake told me that you had a gun and managed to wound him. But you're not dealing with him now," he said as he moved out of the doorway. He was smiling as he showed her that he was holding a black remote detonator in his hand. "And that gun won't really do you any good unless you want to play chicken. Do you think I wouldn't be ready for this kind of standoff? When I took over the property from Vivianne, I made sure that the grounds were suitably prepared for any assault." His thumb caressed the button. "If you shoot me, I'll still be able to press the button that will blow up everyone in that courtyard. Including perhaps that Adam Lynch you appear to be so fond of. So why don't you put the gun down and we'll go back to my original plan."

"You mean the one where you put me through the same hell you did Olivia? I don't regard that as an option." She paused. "And Blake must have told you that I'd freed Olivia and you no longer have any way to force me to do that." She hoped she was telling the truth. She'd gotten off that shot and Olivia should have taken it as a signal to get out of the mansion. But if she was now in the courtyard, she would be in just as much danger from the explosives as Griffin's men . . . and Lynch. "Give it up, Derek."

"Why should I?" he asked mockingly. "I know you so well now. I know how soft you are about those students of yours. I know how you feel about your friend Olivia. How terrible you felt about that woman who died when she sent you on my trail. And what I know, I can use. You were smart enough to do everything you could to avoid that final sacrifice for Olivia. You even thought that you'd beaten me, didn't you? Yet I managed to destroy who your friend really was during this time."

"No, you didn't," Kendra said fiercely. "She's stronger than that, you son of a bitch."

"No, she's not." He was meeting her eyes. "She's soft, like you. And do you know the proof of how soft you are? Because you're not going to let me blow up those people in the courtyard if you can possibly help it. You're going to go with me and try to force me or persuade me not to press this button." He smiled. "And because I'm so much better at this than you are, it will be no time at all until I'll be able to have you exactly where I want you." He lowered his voice to a mocking whisper. "In your very own cocoon, dear Kendra." He held out his hand to her. "Don't you want to come with me? Just take my hand and I'll lead you down to that tunnel in the basement and we'll be out of here in seconds. You have to consider the advantages. They'll all be safe. It's so many lives. And what a worthwhile thing to do. How can you not take the challenge?"

"You still don't get it, do you? It's done. No more killing." But she couldn't take her eyes from that remote. As long as he had that detonator she was helpless to stop him. In this light the dull shine of the remote seemed to have taken a sleek power of its own.

In this light?

She went rigid. Sunlight streamed in through the leaded windows over twenty-five feet above the foyer. But one of the shafts of light was different, Kendra was noticing. The light was pure. Unfiltered. Why?

Then she saw the broken glass on the floor. One of the high windows had been broken in from the outside.

Could it be . . . ?

Don't question. Obey your instinct.

She stepped a little to her left, forcing Derek to turn his back to the shattered pane.

Now distract him.

"It's over, Derek. The world knows you're Ivan Campbell."

He smiled. "So Ivan Campbell disappears. That world you're talking about is so forgetful. I have identities set up all over the planet. The possibilities are endless. There's an Arctic research base that could represent an intriguing problem."

Kendra remembered Trey Suber's warning.

He's just getting started.

Kendra heard the faintest sound overhead. Had Derek heard it?

No.

"But first I have unfinished business here, Kendra."

His hand was still extended toward her. "Put down the gun and I'll put away this remote. I'll spare those people in the courtyard that you've put in my path. Trust me."

Trust him? The hell she would.

Because the next instant a shadow was descending from the platform above!

Lynch!

He hit Derek with a flying tackle, his hand striking the man's hand holding the remote against the hard tile floor.

The remote skidded across the foyer.

Derek pulled Lynch over with him and struck his torso with both elbows. Then he jumped to his feet, but Lynch was on him a heartbeat later.

Kendra was trying to take aim, but she couldn't get the shot, she realized desperately. Lynch and Derek were bobbing and weaving, throwing punches and blocking each other's blows. She couldn't shoot. Not yet. Not when Lynch was being pushed and pulled across her potential line of fire.

And Derek was doing it on purpose, she realized. Damn, the bastard was cool. As he struggled, he was purposely using Lynch to block her aim.

The men collided with a tall sculpture—a suit of armor—which fell on them and brought them back to the floor.

Derek recovered more quickly than Lynch. Still lying on the floor, he grabbed an ornamental axe that had fallen from the display and swung it toward Lynch.

Lynch rolled away. A miss.

He swung again. This time Lynch wrestled it from his hand and sent the axe flying.

Derek spun around, stretching, extending his left hand across the foyer floor.

Toward the remote.

And she still didn't have the damn shot!

His forefinger touched the edge of the remote. He almost had it in his hand.

His fingers reached for the trigger mechanism . . .

No!

"Not happening, bastard," Lynch muttered. The next instant he jumped to his knees behind Derek. He grabbed each side of Derek's head and gave it a sharp twist.

Craaaack!

Kendra had never heard such a sickening sound and she hoped never to again.

Derek collapsed to the floor as if Lynch had just yanked his power cord.

There was no breathing.

No twitching.

Nothing to indicate that he had been alive only seconds before.

Lynch was breathing hard as he got to his feet. "Are you all right, Kendra?"

She was still in shock, but she managed to nod.

Lynch's gaze shifted to Derek's perfectly still body. "He's not. I guess you got your demonstration."

"I guess I did. Dead . . ." Kendra couldn't take her eyes from Derek's limp body. It had happened so quickly that she was still dazed. So much ugliness. So much evil. All the monstrous things he'd done through the years . . .

"Okay?" Lynch was beside her, helping her to her feet. "Did he do any damage?"

"Of course he did," she said unevenly. "Well, not to me, but to Olivia. But he was wrong, she's stronger than he thought." She shook her head to clear it. "But did you see her when she ran out of here? Did she reach the courtyard all right?"

"I don't know. I guess I was already inside looking for the bastard." His hand gently brushed the tousled hair away from her face. "And you. Why the hell didn't you stay where you'd be safe?"

"You know the answer. Because I couldn't be sure Olivia would have been safe." Her lips twisted. "And she wouldn't have been. Blake was on his way to cut her throat per Derek's orders." She looked back at Derek's body once more. "You were very efficient in disposing of him. You only did one thing wrong."

"Really?" His brows rose. "I can't wait for you tell me how I failed you."

"There wasn't enough pain. And it was too quick. It should have taken a long, long time."

"That's two things. But I'll keep them both in mind next time."

"There won't be a next time. Not with a monster like Derek. He was unique." She turned and started down the hall toward the courtyard. "I have to go see if Olivia's all right. She has to know that Derek's out of her life."

"Very permanently."

"That head twist made that crystal clear." Her gait quickened as she neared the courtyard door. "But you might have been right. I'm not sure I want you to teach me that move, Lynch."

CHAPTER 16

THE COURTYARD LOOKED like a battle staging area when Kendra and Lynch walked out of the mansion. Prisoners being manacled. FBI agents. SWAT officers. Flashing red lights on the vehicles.

And there was an ambulance pulling into the courtyard. Kendra could see another vehicle approaching on the road in the distance.

"There." Lynch nodded to Olivia, who was walking with Jessie toward the first ambulance. "Olivia seems fine." He turned to stride toward Griffin and Metcalf near one of the vehicles. "I have to give a report on Derek that will make Griffin very happy. I'll see you later."

"Okay," Kendra said absently. She was already hurrying across the courtyard toward the ambulance. She wasn't sure he was right. It was a warm day and yet Jessie was taking a gray wool blanket from an EMT and wrapping it around Olivia.

"Whew," Jessie said as she looked up and saw Kendra. "It's about time you showed up, Kendra. I was going to have to sit on Olivia to keep her from running back in that house. I told her that I knew Lynch was inside, but she thought she'd do a better job."

"I would have," Olivia said unevenly as she turned into Kendra's arms and held her for a long moment. "Because you have such terrible ideas and no one but me will tell you so." She stepped back and asked, "That blood?"

"Josh Blake. Derek cut his throat." She saw Olivia go rigid. "No, don't be scared," she said quickly. "You won't have to worry about Derek again. It turned out that Lynch did do a very good job, after all."

"Dead?" Olivia whispered.

"Yes," she said quietly. "It's over, Olivia."

"No, it's not. But it will be." Her hand clutched Kendra's. "It *has* to be."

"Well, as far as I'm concerned, we're well on our way in that direction." Jessie stepped between them. "But you need to get a clean bill of health, Olivia, so we're going to ship you off to the hospital for a checkup."

Olivia wearily shook her head. "I just want to go home."

"It won't take long," Jessie said brusquely. "And it

will make Kendra feel better." She looked meaningfully at Kendra. "So pamper her and get into the ambulance."

Kendra gazed at Jessie thoughtfully and then said, "That's right, pamper me." She motioned to the EMT. "Get her settled. I'll be riding to the hospital with you." She watched the EMT carefully lift Olivia onto the gurney in the ambulance before she turned toward Jessie. "You're worried and that scares me," she said curtly. "I'm all for having her checked out, but what did you notice?"

"Maybe nothing. No one knows how strong she is more than I do. But she's been shaking, she's suffering severe tension, and she's not quite there." She added grimly, "And I've seen plenty of patients in Afghanistan who started out that way and completely broke down later. I just want to be careful." Her lips tightened. "And I'm as mad as hell with Lynch for not letting me be there when he killed that son of a bitch who did that to her."

Kendra nodded. "I *was* there and I felt that same way. I wanted to kill him myself." She looked back at the mansion. "Derek told me he'd destroyed her. May he burn in hell." Her glance shifted to Jessie. "But he lied. She's too strong. *We're* too strong. We're not going to let anything happen to her." She opened the door of the ambulance and got into it. "Tell Lynch I'll see him at the hospital."

Tri City Medical Center Oceanside
San Diego

"How is she doing?" Lynch took Kendra into his arms when she came out of the ER.

"Not good." She buried her head in his chest. "How do you think she'd be? She tries not to show it, but that son of a bitch nearly tore her apart."

"He didn't do such a bad job on you either," Lynch said, his hand rubbing the back of her neck. "He wanted to find a way to hurt you and he found it, didn't he?"

"Yes," she said hoarsely. "But I don't matter. It's what he did to her that's so terrible. You don't know what it's like to be blind and then to have sound, speech, and all sensation taken away. I could feel her shaking while I was holding her. There's nothing more frightening. And she was holding my hand so hard in the ambulance coming here . . ."

"You do matter." He pushed her gently away and took his handkerchief and dabbed at her wet cheeks. "You matter very much. But all you can see and feel is for Olivia right now. What can I do for you?"

"Nothing." She cleared her throat. "You're right, it's all about Olivia. She's going to talk to the hospital psychiatrist and then they think they're going to let her go home. But I'll go and stay with her in her condo until I'm sure she's okay and herself again." She grimaced.

"Whenever that will be. She was still shaking when I came out here. And when I told her I was going home with her, she didn't argue. That's bad in itself. You know how independent she is. But she didn't say anything. She just held my hand very tightly before she let it go."

"Give her a chance," he said. "She's tough, Kendra."

"Of course she's tough. But I don't want her to have to be tough right now. I want to help her. I want to take care of her. I believe that's what I should be doing right now."

He gently touched her cheek. "If that's what you believe, then it must be right. Go and take care of your friend, Kendra. If I can help, let me know." He let her go and nudged her toward the hospital room. "And I'll bet our Olivia will be bouncing back before you know it."

"I hope so," Kendra murmured. "I hope so . . ."

Six Days Later
San Diego

"Hi, Olivia. I brought sandwiches from the deli across the street." Kendra put the bags she was carrying down on the kitchen bar. She glanced at Jessie, who was sitting on the couch beside Olivia playing chess. "Did you beat her yet? Don't you find this constant chastising humiliating?"

"No. And extremely." Jessie grimaced as she got to

her feet. "But I regard it as a learning experience. I'm sticking with it. I keep telling her it's those braille chess pieces."

"Excuses. Excuses," Olivia said. "How did it go with the kids today, Kendra?"

"Pretty good. No breakthroughs." She glanced at Jessie. "Are you going to stick around for supper? Those sandwiches are delicious and I bought plenty."

"Nope. I have to get going. I need to tie up some loose ends before I start my next job." She looked at her watch. "Time got away from me."

"Loose ends?"

"Yeah, I have to get a couple shots at the health department." She made a face. "Damn, I hate foreign assignments. With my luck I'll end up with some weird exotic bug."

"You've changed your mind about going to Abu Dhabi to babysit your action hero?"

She shrugged. "What the hell? I decided my action hero might actually need me." She headed for the door. "See you later."

"Bye." Kendra was taking the sandwiches out of the sack. "Do you want to make the salad, Olivia? You're never satisfied with the way I do it."

"Because your kitchen skills are barely passable. I'll do it." Olivia smiled gently. "Because it will be a very small salad for a party of one. I'm kicking you out, Kendra. Go away."

"What?" Kendra whirled to face her.

"You heard me," Olivia said. "You're driving me crazy. I can stand only so much hovering. Look, I kind of understand. I know that you're feeling all sorts of guilt feelings and that's a little crazy, too. You risked your life to save me."

"Big deal. If you weren't my friend, you wouldn't have been a target. And I got really scared when I saw you lying on that stupid cot looking like some kind of effigy on a tomb." She smiled. "You just have to put up with me until I get over it."

"No, I don't," Olivia said flatly. "I have to take care of myself. I can't do that with you coddling me and ready to jump in if I show any sign of weakness." She hesitated. "Because I *do* have weakness and I have a right to show it until I beat it." She reached out and grasped Kendra's hand. "And I *will* beat it. But I have to do it alone. You're bad for me right now. I've never felt more vulnerable than when Derek had me penned in that room and took everything away from me that he thought would make my life worth living. You can imagine the panic."

"Yes, I can," Kendra said unevenly. "It nearly killed me just knowing he was doing it."

"I know it did." She paused. "And that's why you won't be able to take half measures about walking out that door and leaving me alone to work this out for myself. You've got to go cold turkey."

Kendra was gazing at her in bewilderment. "For heaven's sake, you're talking as if this is all about me."

"No, only half of it is about you." Olivia smiled faintly. "Because we're like two halves of a whole and we always have been. It's perfectly natural that you would overreact a bit."

"Look, what you went through was a traumatic experience. There's nothing wrong with taking it slowly for a little while."

"I have been taking it slowly. I've let you stay with me for the last six days. I've even let you arrange with Jessie to visit me when you had to be gone so I'd never be alone. I've been pampering myself. Now it's time I got back to being who I am." She shook her head. "I can tell you're frowning and thinking of ways to talk me out of it. It's not going to happen."

"Six days isn't that long."

"You're wrong, I'm beginning to get too comfortable." Her hand tightened on Kendra's. "Because my friend Kendra is here and I like that a lot. I'm closer to you than anyone else in the world and it's too easy. I'm beginning to depend on you. You make me feel safe. Do you realize how dangerous that is?"

"I want you to feel safe."

"And I want to feel that Derek hasn't destroyed who I am. I want to be able to take everything he threw at me and still be myself. I have to be totally independent." She leaned forward. "I got very confused about that when he had me in that damn cocoon. But do you know what I found out? That no matter what senses he took away from me, I was going to be okay, because the mind is a wonderful, splendid thing." She grinned. "And I have a particularly good one. I just have to know that I can always rely on it when nasty things like this show up." She reached into her pocket and pulled out a small case and flipped it open. "But I also have to be sure I never forget it."

Kendra was staring in shock at a set of ear plugs like the ones Derek had put on Olivia. "Where did you get those?"

"Jessie. I told her I needed a pair. She didn't even question, they just appeared the next day. Our Jessie is very clever."

"Yes, she is." She moistened her lips. "But I'm not quite so clever. Why did you want them?"

"So I'll never be afraid of them." She touched the nubs gently. "I used them after I went to bed last night. A little panic and then it was gone. I only wore them for a few hours and then I put them away. But I'll use them every night until I'm so accustomed to them that they're like old friends. I'll lie there and think and dream and gradually all the fear will go away. Doesn't that sound like a good plan?"

Kendra had to clear her throat to ease the tightness. "It sounds like a very brave plan."

"Self-preservation." Olivia said brusquely, "When

this is over, I'll be stronger than ever. Screw you, Derek." Her voice softened. "But it will be easier for me if you're not around to lean on. As I said, I have to be totally independent. So you're going to hug me and then you're going to get out of here. When I've become my usual Wonder Woman persona again, I'll give you a call and you can come back."

"But I don't want to leave you alone."

"Please. I'm not Little Orphan Annie. I'm never alone. I have friends. I have a career. They're all fine. You're the only one I have to kick out."

She wasn't going to be able to talk her out of it, Kendra thought in disbelief. "I'm not the only one who has bad ideas. This one is lousy. I don't want you to kick me out."

"Because you love me. That's your hard luck. You shouldn't have made a friend of me all those years ago at Woodward Academy." She reached out and hugged Kendra. "Hey, it won't be that long. Soon I'll be so independent again that I won't need you around at all. You'll just be entertainment value. You know how superior I am."

"Yes, I do." She hugged Olivia tightly and then forced herself to let her go. "Are you at least going to let Jessie come? She wouldn't get in your way. You said that she didn't even question you."

"I'm tempted, but she probably won't be around for long. She has plans."

Kendra nodded. "Abu Dhabi."

"Maybe. Jessie doesn't lie, but she's dropped a hint or two in the last couple days. If you think about it, you'll probably come up with the same answer I did. You would have probably done it already, if you hadn't been concentrating on me." She waved at the door. "Out."

Kendra hesitated.

"Out," Olivia said again.

"For a little while." Kendra sighed and then headed for the door. "But I'm going to call and text. You're not going to get rid of me."

"Now that would be a nightmare worse than any Derek could concoct for me." Olivia's luminous smile lit her face. "I'm counting on it."

Kendra stood for a moment outside in the hall after the door closed behind her. She felt a little lost and bewildered as she turned away. She had been so intent on making certain Olivia was completely back to normal that it had not occurred to her that she might be one of the problems. Was it true? How could she know? Olivia was so intelligent and knew herself so well that it might very well be true. But it seemed nothing was as Kendra had thought it to be.

Including Jessie?

Those few cryptic sentences that Olivia had uttered before Kendra left had pointed in that direction.

You would have noticed yourself if you hadn't been concentrating on me.

Well, it seemed she wasn't concentrating on Olivia now, she thought wryly.

Start thinking so she wouldn't make any more dumb mistakes as she'd done with Olivia.

Scripps Coastal Medical Center Hillcrest
San Diego

"What are you doing here?" Jessie asked warily as she saw Kendra straighten away from the building as she came out the front entrance. "Something wrong?"

"You tell me," Kendra said. "Did you get your shots?"

"Yes and it hurt like hell." Jessie's gaze was still narrowed on Kendra's face. "I've never taken shots well. My arm usually swells up like a watermelon."

"I'm surprised you don't become accustomed to them. You've traveled all over the world, haven't you?"

"Yes," Jessie said cautiously. Then she shook her head. "I'm blown, right? Okay, stop playing games. Shall we go to your car and talk? I don't think you're in the mood to hop on my bike."

Kendra waved at her Toyota parked down the street. "You're right. After you." She waited until they were settled in her car before she said, "You didn't exactly lie to me, but you came close, didn't you?"

"Not extremely close. I hate lying." She shrugged. "I was trying to walk a balanced line. But you can never please everyone and I thought you might be so busy with Olivia that I might get away with it." She raised her brows. "She kicked you out?"

"You saw it coming?" She made a face. "I didn't. Did she say something to you?"

"Not a word. I just read between the lines. She was ready to be on her own." She paused. "It's going to be inconvenient."

"You mean inconvenient for you. I imagine it will be. Where are you going, Jessie?"

"Where do you think?"

"Afghanistan?"

She nodded. "First. But we might not stay there. It depends on what we find there and how he can manipulate the climate to get what he wants."

"He," Kendra repeated. "Lynch."

"Who else?" Jessie said. "I told you I hated lying. He *is* my favorite action hero." Her lips tightened. "He can get things done that nobody else can. And he's in a mood to do it. He doesn't like how well Brock is managing to cover their asses and get rid of evidence. They're claiming that only a few of their employees were involved with Derek's activities and they were making every attempt to weed them out and capture him. Between bribery and Senate influence, they're beginning to cloud the issue."

Kendra shook her head. "They can't get away with it."

"They might. Derek's evidence against Brock never surfaced after his death. Which means that Blake or maybe someone else in the Brock stable might have discovered where it was hidden and retrieved it." Jessie shrugged. "Lynch has a hunch that Vivianne Kerstine shipped most of the incriminating evidence we were looking for overseas to Afghanistan since she has so much influence there. That might include the Derek blackmail bonanza." She paused. "Put that all together with the fact that Lynch is very pissed off about Brock's part in what you and Olivia went through. He wants to bring them down."

Kendra tried to control her temper. "Yet he didn't say a word to me. I've scarcely seen him in the last six days."

"He's been busy." She grimaced. "And he's probably been avoiding you. I'd imagine he's superb at lying, but he doesn't want to lie to you."

"But he told *you* what he was going to do. He's taking you with him."

"I went to him. I could see where he was headed and I asked him to let me go along. I told him how useful I'd be. I know the military over there and they know they can trust me." She met Kendra's eyes. "I need to do this. I owe it to my guys over there. Like I said, Lynch is the person people bring to the table when they want a regime change. It's time the Brock regime goes down the tubes."

"I can understand how you feel, I'm just mad as hell at Lynch for doing this to me," Kendra said jerkily. "When do you leave?"

"Another two days."

"Lynch?"

"Tonight. He borrowed the jet that his billionaire friend, Giancarlo, keeps at Montgomery Field and he's going over early to make contact with the Justice Department bigwigs in Kabul."

"And not let me know until he was on his way?"

"I don't know." She held up her hands. "That's way above my pay grade."

"But I'm sure you could see where that was heading, too," Kendra said. "But you'd leave it up to him because you're now on the same team."

"As I said, he's going to find it inconvenient. But that's between the two of you. I'm out of it now. I've given you the entire scope and I didn't try to dodge." She opened the car door. "And you're my friend so I won't call Lynch and warn him you're on the warpath. But you're right, I'm on his team or anyone else who goes after Brock. You're on your own, Kendra."

She was gone.

Kendra sat there, her hands clenching the steering wheel. She was feeling a mixture of anger and frustration and sheer terror.

Lynch.

Afghanistan.

Brock Limited.

The combination was deadly.

And Jessie was right.

Kendra was on her own.

Montgomery Field

Lynch was getting out of his rental car at the parking lot and locking it.

"Maybe it's a good thing that you don't have to worry about taking care of that fancy Ferrari right now." Kendra stepped out of the shadows. "You wouldn't have wanted to leave it here."

He stiffened but didn't turn around for an instant. "One can always make arrangements for a Ferrari, Kendra."

"When were you going to call and let me know you'd left? Jessie wasn't sure."

"I was figuring on maybe tomorrow morning when I was over the Atlantic." He turned around and smiled at her. "Because then you couldn't do me physical damage and it would be a done deal. How angry are you?"

"Angry enough." She met his eyes. "And hurt and maybe a little humiliated."

His smile faded. "That won't do at all." He took her arm and pulled her across the tarmac to the plane. "I'll take the anger. But the rest has to go. Come on board and have a drink with me and get it all out of your system."

"You make it sound simple." She didn't look at him as she climbed the steps and boarded the Cessna Citation. She dropped down on one of the white leather couches. "I don't believe it's simple at all, Lynch."

"Not simple." He got her a glass of wine from the bar. "But not complicated enough to cause us any real problems. I told you we'd have to work things out." He sat down opposite her. "I take it everything blew up and you began thinking instead of feeling."

She took a sip of wine. "Which you obviously didn't want to happen. Heaven forbid, I think."

"I wanted whatever was good for you at this particular time," he said softly. "Anything. But I do admit that I took advantage of the situation. I didn't offer you any alternate solution."

"You were planning this from the time I told you I was going to move in with Olivia."

"Before that." His lips tightened. "From the moment that I saw what that maniac and Brock's people were doing to you and Olivia. I couldn't allow them to get away with that, Kendra."

"So you sent me away to take care of my friend and started plotting and planning."

"You sent yourself off to be with Olivia. As I said, I just took advantage."

"But you would have plotted and planned if you'd had to do it."

"Yes."

"Why?" she said fiercely. "Why not just be honest with me?"

"You would have worried, you had enough on your plate with Olivia near a breakdown."

"Olivia evidently handled it better than I did. But I guess you didn't trust me not to fall apart after the way I behaved when I thought you'd been killed." She crashed her wine glass down on the coffee table. "Well, I'm *not* that weak and I wouldn't have fallen apart if I'd been given the chance to do something to keep it from happening. But you closed me out then, just like you're closing me out now. Guilty?"

"Guilty," he said. "I admit I wanted to keep you safe. And it hurt me to see you hurting, so I just did what was easy for me. Does that take the hurt and humiliation away? If it doesn't, then what will? I'll do anything you say. Is that humble enough?"

"No, it's probably just another ploy or manipulation." She got to her feet. "And you *will* do whatever I say. Because it's my turn, Lynch."

"Interesting." His eyes were narrowed on her face. "But I'm thinking that I'm not going to be particularly happy about this, am I?"

"No. Because you're not going to get all your own

way, and that's something that you're not accustomed to." She met his eyes. "Though you might have been trying to avoid it when you pulled this bit of chicanery. You didn't even ask me what my attitude was toward Brock Limited and the possibility of all their sleazeballs slipping out from under the punishment they deserve. You just decided to go take care of it yourself." She took a step toward him, her eyes glittering. "Well, that's another thing that I'm angry about. Because you're not going to leave me out of being there with you to take them down."

"No!" He got to his feet. "Not a good idea."

"A very good idea. I'm sure Jessie had to plead and wheedle and furnish her credentials before you agreed to take her. Well, I'm not going to do any of that business. You're going to take me because I'm smart and I have abilities and I'll do anything I have to do." She paused. "And because we're partners and we should work together. It doesn't matter if you think I shouldn't be anywhere near that country or what's going on there. I'm going to be there with you. Have you got that, Lynch?"

"Oh, I've got that." The muscles of his face were tight, his eyes glittering and intense, and Kendra could almost see the volatility and displeasure behind that expression.

"Stop glaring. I'm not going to get killed. Neither are you. Neither is Jessie. Because we're going to take care of each other. That's how it should be. None of us are going to be alone. You're not leaving me back here to worry about you. And if you worry about me, then stay close enough to me to take care of it on the spot." She turned toward the door. "Now I realize I can't leave tonight. I'll probably have to get shots tomorrow and see that my practice is taken care of after I leave. It will be better if I catch that flight with Jessie in a couple days."

"Wait." He was next to her, his hand on her arm. "I have a few words to say."

She tensed. "You're not going to change my mind, Lynch."

He muttered a curse. "I know that." He turned her around. "I'm still working out how I'm going to handle this. There has to be an advantage or weapon for me somewhere in this. Maybe I'll start like this." He kissed her: long, hard. He whispered, "Listen, I know that country. I know what you'll have to face. This is driving me crazy. Stay here, dammit."

She drew a long, shaky breath. "Sex is good, but it's not all-powerful. You'll have to do better than that."

"Not much better." His mischievous smile was suddenly lighting his face. "You definitely thought that it was worth the effort in spite of being pissed off at me."

"Arrogance, thy name is Lynch." She broke away from him. "Reconcile yourself to the idea that you're stuck with me in Afghanistan until we're on the way to bringing Brock down and there's nothing you can do about it." She started down the steps. "I'll see you in a few days in Kabul."

"That's not the reconciliation I have in mind. But it might be acceptable until I figure something else out." He added softly, "Because you know I can't give in, don't you? It means too much to me. *You* mean too much."

She glanced back over her shoulder and then she couldn't look away. He was standing there, smiling faintly, but there was nothing mocking or mischievous in his smile now. It was full of warmth and tenderness and the intimate knowledge of who and what she was. Who else would ever be able to smile at her quite like that?

She had to make sure that she was there to make certain he was still around to do it, didn't she? That was what this was all about, whether or not she said the words, whether or not he understood.

She smiled back at him. "Take your best shot at it, Lynch." She turned and kept on going down the steps. "This time you'll lose."